"Do you
Her une
hesitated a m   ...oughts before
he answered. '   ...ke you. Why do you ask?"

He could feel the rise and fall of her breasts as she stood so close to him. Her emerald eyes were dark and her lips were pink, inviting him to taste them if he dared.

My God yes, I like you. Inwardly he groaned, but did he dare to confess his desire to her?

"Come with me." He entwined his fingers with hers and led her quickly into the library past the many bookshelves of leather bound volumes. He walked over to an alcove for privacy. Turning around, he pulled her close until she was pressed against him. "I like you far more than I should for the time I've known you, Rebecca."

She swallowed. "You do?"

With his free hand he cupped her cheek, caressing it gently. He rubbed the pad of his rough thumb over her lips. They trembled in response and he lowered his head, nibbling at her mouth with small kisses until she responded in kind. Without warning, he parted her lips with his tongue and captured her mouth, exploring its depths.

Her hand crept up his arm to his neck, holding his head so he couldn't pull away. Her fingers speared through his damp hair, sending shivers down his spine.

His body hardened and he groaned, pulling away before he lost his head completely.

Praise for Leanne Tyler and...

AVA: "Reminiscent of Jane Austen's Emma, this charming tale set in nineteenth century Georgia will have you chuckling at Ava's schemes while longing for her to find her own true love."

~*Carolynn Carey, award-winning romance writer*

"Matchmaking has never been such fun!"

~*Karen Hall, award-winning author*

~*~

VICTORY'S GATE: "Leanne Tyler's award-winning story *VICTORY'S GATE* is a must read. She guides the reader through the Civil War's era so that two people from different centuries can find love."

~*Loretta Rogers, award-winning author of*
ISABELLE AND THE OUTLAW

"A delightful tale of unending love"

~*Jessie Verino*

~*~

IT'S ALWAYS BEEN YOU: "What would you do if your long lost love, presumed dead for twenty years, turned up at your high school reunion? If you're as hooked on the premise as I was, this charming tale won't disappoint!"

~*Jannine Gallant*

"The kind of story we all love to read—a second chance for a happy ending. Author Leanne Tyler tackles the dreaded 'high school reunion' with skill and fun...the perfect read for a lazy afternoon..."

~*Karen Hall, award winning author*

Because of Rebecca

by
Leanne Tyler

American Heroes Series

This is a work of fiction. Names, characters, places, and incidents are either the product of the author's imagination or are used fictitiously, and any resemblance to actual persons living or dead, business establishments, events, or locales, is entirely coincidental.

Because of Rebecca

Cover Art by *Tina Lynn Stout*

The Wild Rose Press, Inc.
PO Box 708
Adams Basin, NY 14410-0708
Visit us at www.thewildrosepress.com

Publishing History
First American Rose Edition, 2013
Print ISBN 978-1-61217-751-9
Digital ISBN 978-1-61217-752-6

American Heroes Series
Published in the United States of America

Dedication

To my critique partners: Debbie, Teresa, and Kerri.

Prologue

Memphis, Tennessee
Christmas 1857

"You must try, dearest." Rebecca wiped her sister's brow with a damp cloth and held her hand as another contraction came.

Mariah's face contorted. "I—I can't."

"Just one more push," Doctor Baldwin ordered from the foot of the bed.

"It's too hard," she screamed and squeezed her sister's hand, bearing down on the bed.

"Now, take a deep breath and push," he instructed.

She screamed with the push and a drawn out silence filled the room. Then Mariah gasped and slumped against the bed, her wool gown, limp and soiled, crushed against her bloodstained thighs.

Finally, the baby's wail broke the silence and brought tears of joy to Rebecca's eyes. The doctor handed him to her to hold while he severed the umbilical cord.

"Let me see him," Mariah urged in a faint voice. She touched her sister's arm and Rebecca turned, holding the baby in the lamplight for her to see.

"A fine boy." Baldwin wiped his brow with his forearm. "You did well."

When the cord was severed Rebecca carried the new life over to the dresser, where a washbowl waited with warm water, and she proceeded to bathe and swaddle him.

"I'll call him Lucas." Mariah's weak voice was barely audible. "Lucas Samuel Davis after Papa. What do you think?" Her voice wobbled as the doctor finished up the delivery.

"I think it's perfect." Returning to the bed, Rebecca sat on the edge and handed Lucas to his mother once the doctor left her side.

She smiled down at her son, and kissed his soft, tiny head. In the next instant, her eyes closed and she winced for a moment.

Rebecca watched her sister's face contort and her eyes cloud as she took in a quick breath. "Are you all right, dearest?"

"I want you to take him," Mariah murmured, making another face as she took a shallow breath. "Raise him as your own. Tell him," she paused, "tell him I loved him dearly."

She pushed the baby back into Rebecca's arms and reached for one of her hands, unable to grip it. "Never let Stuart Delaney near him. Promise me."

Puzzled by her sister's request, she took Mariah's hand in hers and agreed. "I promise, but you can tell Lucas yourself how much you love him. After a little rest you'll feel better. The worst is over."

"No," Mariah whispered, closing her eyes. Her head slumped back against the pillow and her hand slipped out of Rebecca's as she drew a ragged breath.

"Oh God." Rebecca's voice rose in pitch. "Doctor, come quickly. What's happening?"

He rushed from the washbowl to the bedside drying his hands on his trousers in haste. "Go get your aunt."

Rebecca hurried from the room with Lucas safely in her arms. She found her aunt kneeling before her mother's rocking chair in the small parlor near a warm fire. The smell of fresh cut pine draped over the mantel permeated the room.

Josephine, wearing her prayer veil, looked up expectantly, wiping tears from her face.

"The doctor has asked for you," she pleaded. "Please hurry."

Her aunt crossed herself before rising to her feet. She pulled back the blanket and looked at the baby. "He lives, but Mariah dies for the sin committed."

"Don't say that," Rebecca admonished in a hushed whisper. "Whether you believe her or not, she truly thought Delaney had married her that night on the riverboat."

Josephine shook her head. "One day you'll understand." She turned and walked toward the door, but before she reached it the doctor appeared, wiping his bloody hands on a towel.

"I'm sorry, Miss Davis, I did all I could, but she's gone. Your sister hemorrhaged and by the time I got to her it was already too late. I couldn't stop it."

"But—but—" she sucked in her breath until her chest ached.

Josephine crossed herself and kissed her rosary, murmuring a silent prayer.

Lucas wailed. Rebecca bounced him in her arms and began to weep, recalling her sister's last words. She'd found them odd at the time, but now she had to wonder how had Mariah known she was dying? Had she sensed this was the end? Had the pain she felt after the birth been more than she showed?

It wasn't fair. Lucas needed his mother. She needed her sister. She'd already lost her parents, yet she was expected to give up her sister too. For an instant she allowed herself to sink in despair, but Lucas stirred in her arms and she remembered Mariah's last request. She'd promised to take Lucas as her own. She'd agreed without knowing what she was doing, but she didn't regret it. Nothing would prevent her from keeping her promise.

Through tear-filled eyes she stared at Baldwin. Her aunt had sent for him from a county over to keep her sister's delivery silent. From the few visits he'd made to their cottage he'd seemed like a good man. He'd never asked why they didn't call upon the town doctor. Surely, he'd agree to what she proposed to keep her promise to Mariah. She'd pay him handsomely to ensure it.

She walked to the mantel and removed her money purse from the ornate box.

The doctor's baritone voice broke the mournful silence. "I'll notify the Parish of the birth and death records."

Rebecca nodded. Her real problem wouldn't be the doctor, but convincing her aunt.

"What shall we name him?" Josephine looked up from her rosary.

Wiping away her tears with the back of her hand, Rebecca turned and looked her aunt squarely in the eye. "Lucas Samuel Davis. That's what Mariah named him before she…before she…"

"That's a fine name for him," her aunt agreed.

"Mother's full name?" Baldwin sat down at the table.

Swallowing, Rebecca stiffened, prepared for her aunt's reaction. "Rebecca Kathleen Davis."

"Rebecca!" Josephine turned pale and crossed herself.

The doctor looked up, their eyes locking for a brief moment and she saw understanding. He'd obviously heard her sister's last request. He nodded. "Father?"

"Unknown."

"Rebecca, no! You can't take your sister's sins. You'll ruin yourself," her aunt pleaded.

With resolve, Rebecca looked her aunt in the eye again and stated, "It is done. Mariah asked me to take him as my own. If I'm to do this, I *must* become his mother. There'll be no record of Mariah giving birth and no shame to her name. Nor will there be a link between Lucas and his father if the man ever comes looking for Mariah."

Josephine turned away, but Rebecca heard her weeping.

Taking a deep breath, she walked to where the doctor sat and handed him the more-than-generous handful of gold coins for his services. "Can I count on you to keep silent?"

He nodded without examining the gift. "Are you certain you want to do this, Miss Davis? You'll be changing your life forever."

She looked down at the baby in her arms. His tiny hand reached up and grasped the lace on her dress and he yawned, closing his eyes. He was hers and nothing would change that. "Yes."

He repositioned the wire glasses on his nose and cleared his throat. "I need to enter the death record. Her full name?"

"Mariah Kimberlynn Davis."

Chapter One

Jackson, Mississippi
June 1858

"Surely we can do something about this, Mitchell."
Jared Hollingsworth tossed the missive on his
attorney's mahogany desk and paced across the room.
"I won't turn over Oak Hill to this Delaney fellow. I
don't care how many IOUs Rory signs with my name.

"You know as well as I that my cousin was asked
to leave West Point for lack of interest in his
coursework. He had little need to study, since he could
easily forge any high ranking officer's signature to get
himself promoted."

"Knowing and proving are two different things
when it comes to the law, Jared. The boy was good at
his art...or should I say craft." Mitchell Cooper stood
and crossed to the credenza. He poured two fingers of
whiskey from a cut crystal decanter into a pair of
matching glasses, and offered one to him. "It isn't
right," he agreed, "but unless you can persuade Mr.
Delaney to accept monetary compensation for the
markers, he could go to the magistrate and insist
ownership of Oak Hill be forfeited to him."

"I'll be damned if I'll allow that." Jared slammed
his fist down on the desk, rattling the contents and

causing stacks of papers to slide. "I've slaved myself and the few workers I can afford to make Oak Hill what it is today. I don't have the money to pay Delaney what the plantation is worth. I already owe the bank a small fortune to cover the expenses of the last three years."

"Then you *must* find Rory," his attorney stated.

"I haven't seen him since his mother died. No doubt he's used up his inheritance and is off somewhere writing more bad drafts using my name. Isn't there some way to protect Oak Hill?"

Shaking his head, Mitchell sat in his leather chair and read over the letter again. "Delaney says he'll be here within the month with the auctioneer to look over the estate. It may be an idle threat, but you have until then to get Rory back here and face the man. I'll help any way I can. I'll send a few inquiries around to cities known for their gaming clubs and see what we can turn up."

Jared ran a finger around the rim of his glass. "What do you propose I do until then?"

"Pray that we find Rory in time."

"And if we don't?" he countered.

Silence filled the office for a few moments until Mitchell grinned. "Have you thought of remarrying?"

"Remarry? You want me to marry a woman I can't even support?" He scoffed. "Not likely."

"Her dowry could buy you some leverage with Delaney, or at least the bank."

"Listen to you. You're getting married tomorrow so you think everyone should be consumed in marital bliss."

"It's a thought. Besides, Elizabeth has a former Augusta Seminary classmate attending the wedding. I had hoped you'd agree to be her escort. Keep her company during the afternoon festivities."

Chuckling, Jared shook his head. "Too priceless. You've waited *how* long now to drop this little request on me?"

"Only a week. I wanted to make sure you hadn't changed your mind about coming," Mitchell confessed. "Besides, Elizabeth just received word her friend is going to attend. She assures me Rebecca is a very beautiful woman and she comes from a wealthy family."

"At least you didn't say *likeable*." He didn't appreciate the position his attorney put him in, especially since he rarely went to social functions anymore. The last thing he wanted was to be saddled with a chattering female. However, Mitchell was more than his attorney. He was a friend and he rarely made requests. Jared took a breath before speaking. "I'll consider it if you allow me to dance with the bride at the wedding."

Mitchell smiled and came around his desk to shake Jared's hand. "Absolutely. Try not to worry too much about this ordeal with Delaney."

"Easier said than done." He drained the rest of the whiskey from his glass and sat it on the credenza. "I'll see you tomorrow."

Jared left the office and headed to Maple Street to check with the postmaster for any mail. He prayed Rory wasn't dead. If he could get his cousin to return to Oak Hill and show Delaney there were two Mr. Hollingsworths and explain his fool hearted actions, then perhaps the man would reconsider staking a claim on the plantation. Since this fellow wanted to auction it off, he surely cared more about the money than the land.

Jared opened the door to the post office and paused to allow a young woman to exit. As she passed, he smelled lemon verbena and saw the glow of her auburn hair peek from beneath her fashionable bonnet. Enchanted, he hesitated before going inside, choosing instead to watch the sway of her hips as she strolled down the street toward the Bakersfield Hotel. It had been years since he'd noticed a woman.

****

Rebecca watched in the mirror as the mulatto servant repinned her hair for the wedding. She'd left her maid at the hotel to help her aunt with Lucas while she attended the wedding festivities.

"Ah, there you are." Elizabeth entered the guest room, looking flushed. "I thought I'd never get away from Mama to have a word with you."

Rebecca dismissed the servant and turned to her friend. "You look beautiful."

"I think so too." Elizabeth grinned and slowly turned a complete circle showing off the dress. "I'm so nervous. Does it show?"

"Not at all." Rebecca stood and helped her friend carefully sit down on the bed without wrinkling the heavy, beaded wedding dress of imported Italian satin.

"I can't wait until it's your turn to marry. I just know you'll meet someone handsome, and he'll sweep you off your feet."

"Perhaps." Rebecca doubted any man would give her a second look with an infant in tow.

Elizabeth fidgeted, touching a tendril of golden hair near her ear. "How's Lucas doing?"

"Trying to crawl. He'll be walking before I know it. The doctor says he's healthy."

"I wish you could have brought him out for the wedding. I do adore babies. Does he look like Mariah, or is it too soon to tell?"

"I'm not sure who he looks like. He does have my auburn coloring though, so I believe he must take after Papa." Rebecca smiled. "But good heavens, I couldn't have brought him today."

"Why not?" Elizabeth asked. "It's my wedding. Shouldn't I invite who I want?"

"Aunt Josephine would have died at the mere mention of my bringing him here. She made a big enough fuss when I asked for her and Lucas to make the trip from Memphis with me." Rebecca shook her head. "I'm so tired of being trapped out in the country, never seeing anyone. I feel we're constantly in hiding. Josephine keeps us there for fear gossip might start about Lucas and damage her stellar reputation among the parish women. I believe she's told them I'm traveling and she's living at the cottage alone."

Elizabeth rolled her eyes. "I remember you telling me about your prim aunt when we were at seminary. It doesn't sound as if it has been easy on you raising Mariah's child as your own."

"No. She won't let me forget what I gave up by taking Lucas as my own. But I wouldn't change one single day. I love him more than I could ever imagine possible. I'm so glad that scoundrel Delaney never knew he got Mariah with child during their brief farce of a marriage. I don't know what I'd do if he tried to take my boy from me."

"I can't wait to have a child." Elizabeth looked

wistful for a moment. "But not right away. I want to enjoy *my* husband first."

"Don't be enjoying him too much or you'll be starting a family sooner than you think," Rebecca warned.

Her friend blushed and looked away as a knock sounded at the door. The mulatto servant peeked inside.

"Missy, your Mama be lookin' for ya. Says it's bout time and you ain't got your veil on yet. She's a waitin' for ya. Now's hurry up."

"Thank you, Tilda." Elizabeth stood with Rebecca's help. "I love the pale green of your dress. I wish I could wear that color, but it makes me look ill."

She smiled. "It's one of the few colors that work well with my hair. Besides, it's gay and alive. I'm so sick of black bombazine that I've had to wear every day for the last six months."

"I detest black and having to wear it when Grand Mama passed away." Her friend scrunched up her nose for a second but perked up again. "I'd better go or Papa will be walking the floor. He nearly wore a hole in the carpet when Hélène got married because she wasn't ready on time."

"All right. I'll see you after the ceremony."

"Oh, I almost forgot." Elizabeth stopped near the door and turned back around. "Mitchell has arranged for you to have an escort for the afternoon. His name is Jared Hollingsworth. He's a very nice man, though not very active in the social circles. I've never met him so I asked Mama about him, but she couldn't tell me very much either. He owns his own plantation and runs it *without* slave labor."

Rebecca took note of that last tidbit and smiled.

"Mitchell didn't have to go to any trouble on my account."

"Nonsense. You don't know anyone here, and I didn't want you to feel lonely. I want you to have a good time. Besides, I'll be able to enjoy myself knowing you're in good hands."

"If it'll make you feel better."

"Excellent. My older brother, Josiah, will introduce you. He'll be waiting for you downstairs. Wish me luck!"

"The best of it." She hugged her friend, careful not to crush her beaded gown. Then she watched Elizabeth move as swiftly as she could down the hallway.

Stepping back inside the room, she closed the door and quickly pulled the folded note she'd received at the post office the day before from her reticule.

Dear Miss Davis,

Thank you for agreeing to help me in this matter. Our mutual acquaintance has assured me you will be very discreet. I will contact you shortly after your arrival. You will recognize me by the yellow rose bud in my lapel.

Your devoted servant,

Hollingsworth

When Elizabeth said the name, Rebecca had known it sounded familiar. Could her escort for today be the same Mr. Hollingsworth?

Heart fluttering, she refolded the note and tucked it securely back into the hidden pocket she'd made in the lining of her purse. She'd been so frightened taking her first road assignment from the Vigilante Committee, especially now that she had Lucas. The thought of being caught and the consequences of the crime left her weak in the knees. Nevertheless, they'd chosen her for this important job and she vowed to see it through.

She poured a small amount of water from the pitcher into the washbowl and dipped a portion of a hand towel in it. She ran the damp towel over the back of her neck to calm her nerves and closed her eyes. When her pulse settled, she took a deep breath, picked up her elbow length gloves and slowly walked out of the bedroom and down the hallway.

She stopped for a moment at the top of the wide staircase to slip on her gloves and spotted Elizabeth's brother waiting for her at the foot. When she reached the bottom, he offered her his arm with a gentle smile and walked her through the house to the back loggia where the many guests waited on the lawn for the wedding to begin.

Arrangements of fresh flowers decorated the perimeter of the yard. In the center, a dais signified the altar. White chairs positioned in rows around the dais were available for the guests.

Outside, she noticed a very handsome man dressed in black standing alone near the back of the fashionably dressed gathering of men and women. His blond hair was pulled back at the nape in a queue, and he stood military straight with hands clasped behind his back. The string quartet began to play and he turned toward them.

Oh my goodness! He's wearing a yellow rosebud.

Rebecca's mind went numb. She hadn't expected to meet her liaison at her friend's wedding, nor that he'd be *so* handsome. The mere sight of him astounded her.

Josiah motioned to him and the man in question

came toward them.

"Mr. Jared Hollingsworth," Josiah said. "I'd like you to meet Miss Rebecca Davis. Miss Davis, Mr. Hollingsworth."

Rebecca nodded appreciation to the young Mr. Calhoun and curtsied when Mr. Hollingsworth took her gloved hand in his. Tingles of awareness halted her midway, and she forced herself to rise without prolonged hesitation. His blue eyes sparkled as she boldly stared into them, mesmerized by his handsome face.

"It's a pleasure, Miss Davis. Mr. Cooper tells me you attended Augusta Seminary with Miss Calhoun."

"Yes, I did. Did you also attend West Point with Mr. Cooper?" she asked, still unable to look away from his ruggedly handsome face.

"Class of forty-eight." He offered her his arm. "We'd better take our seats. The ceremony should begin soon."

Rebecca placed her hand in the crook of his arm. Her heart pounded as she walked beside him down the aisle to the reserved seats near Elizabeth's family members. She felt honored to be included, and oddly, she felt sensationally alive being by this stranger's side. She couldn't explain what had come over her, but she had never felt more at home.

Awareness of him consumed her thoughts, and she paid little attention to the wedding ceremony. Yet, when Elizabeth and Mr. Cooper sealed their vows with a kiss, she wondered how it would feel to have Mr. Hollingsworth's lips pressed against hers and his strong arms holding her close.

Rattled, she chastised herself for her thoughts. She

was in Jackson on a mission, and Mr. Hollingsworth as fortune would have it, was her cohort. There was no room for daydreaming about him, even if she did find him handsome.

Today was a day of celebration, but tomorrow would be a day of joy for a very lucky young woman. Rebecca knew what role she would play in this mission, but she couldn't help but be curious how Mr. Hollingsworth would go about doing his part. She'd love nothing more than to discuss it with him if the opportunity arose, but it was unlikely. Neither of them could risk being overheard.

****

Jared shifted in his chair beside Miss Davis. She was the first woman with whom he'd spent company since his wife had died in childbirth three years earlier. Charisse was his first love and had been a wonderful woman. Losing her and their son had nearly killed him, but fate had been cruel and left him to bear the burden alone.

Now here he was at Mitchell's wedding playing host to this beautiful young woman whom he couldn't deny he found attractive. As he'd walked her to their seats, he'd overheard murmuring. One guest wanted to know why he was there and another had wanted to know who she was and why she was here with him.

He feared word had already spread through the town about cousin Rory's latest scandal, another black mark against the Hollingsworth name. As if he needed any help spreading scandal. He'd been doing fine all by himself being branded a societal outcast when his father had died, and he'd taken over running Oak Hill. Plantation owners from all around Jackson rebuked him for giving his father's slaves their freedom and hiring those that wished to stay as tenant farmers instead.

Pushing those thoughts aside, Jared stole another glance at Miss Davis. Mitchell hadn't lied when he assured him she was beautiful. He chuckled at his good fortune to escort this stunning woman. Her auburn hair glistened in the afternoon sun like honey dripping off the wax comb, and reminded him of the young woman he'd encountered in passing at the post office the day before.

Could it be her?

His thoughts wandered back to the vision of the young woman walking down the street toward the hotel. He hadn't gotten a good look at her face, but the memory of her slender neck, the shape of her back and trim waist, not to mention the sweet smell of her that somehow still lingered in the air, stirred something deep inside.

Could it be a coincidence that the beauty sitting beside him smelled just as sweet? That her hair shined just as bright? His interest in her perplexed him, especially when he'd initially not welcomed the request to be her escort. He had no doubt there would be competition from the other male guests to be her dance partner at the reception.

"Don't they make a lovely couple?" Miss Davis whispered, breaking his train of thought. She wiped her eyes with a hanky.

"Yes, they are a striking pair." He joined the applause at the end of the ceremony. Standing, he offered his arm to her again and asked, "Shall we go inside for some refreshment?"

She smiled up at him. "That would be most

enjoyable."

Music drifted from the ballroom as they approached the house. He wondered what it would feel like to have Miss Davis in his arms, her body pressed just so against him as they danced. He shook those thoughts away and focused on making small talk.

"How long will you be staying in Jackson, Miss Davis?"

"I'm not sure. Elizabeth has asked me to stay on and help her with a few social functions once she and Mr. Cooper return from their wedding tour."

"So there is nothing pressing that insists you return to—"

"Memphis? No, not really." Her emerald eyes sparkled as they joined the mass of guests waiting in the receiving line to bid well wishes to the newlyweds.

Jared found it strange that the beautiful young woman didn't have suitors lined up waiting to spend time with her. Before he realized, he'd spoken his thoughts. "No suitor eagerly awaiting your return?"

"Mr. Hollingsworth!" Her cheeks pinked with color as they reached Mitchell's parents.

While they waited to congratulate the bride and groom, Miss Davis modestly leaned closer and whispered, "In answer to your question. No. There are no suitors at present. I've just come out of mourning."

He hadn't realized she was a widow. Why had she been introduced to him as a miss? Puzzled by her remark, Jared clasped Mitchell's hand tighter than he intended as they shook hands.

"Are things going that bad?" his friend asked, looking concerned.

"No. Not at all." Jared released his grip before

taking the bride's hand and raising it to his lips for a kiss. "Congratulations to you both. I hope you'll reserve at least one dance with me, Mrs. Cooper."

"Thank you," Elizabeth cooed, reaching for Miss Davis' hand. "Mama, this is my dearest friend from Augusta Seminary, Miss Rebecca Davis."

"It's a pleasure to finally meet you, Mrs. Calhoun. Thank you for allowing me to attend the wedding. It was absolutely beautiful," Miss Davis said. "Mr. Calhoun."

"Miss Davis," Mr. Calhoun responded.

"You must be proud, Mr. and Mrs. Calhoun," Jared greeted.

"Thank you for coming all this way to be with us today," Mrs. Calhoun said coolly without shaking his hand.

"Mama!" the new Mrs. Cooper gasped, giving him an apologetic look and drawing further attention to the slight.

Again Jared heard murmuring behind him and decided to escort Miss Davis away from the line before she questioned the snub. "How about that refreshment now?"

She nodded, but looked confused.

He left her in a small alcove in the ballroom while he fetched punch. When he returned, he found his companion swaying to the music.

"Would you like to dance?" he asked, handing her a glass cup.

"That would be delightful." She drank the punch, discarding the empty cup on a nearby table.

A waltz played and he offered her his hand. Ever aware of the sweet scent of her perfume, Jared pulled her as close to his body as proper. "I didn't realize you were a widow, Mrs. Davis," he said. "Forgive me for not extending my condolences earlier and for not addressing you properly. You should have corrected Mr. Calhoun."

"Thank you. But I prefer to be called Miss Davis. I'm n-" she began, looking up at him. She didn't know how to rectify his misinterpretation of why she'd been in mourning. *Perhaps it will be easier to explain Lucas if I don't correct him.* But no, that wouldn't be right. She must correct him.

"I'm n-" she tried again, but he cut her off.

"I'm a widower myself. Three years now."

"Yo-you are?" Rebecca noticed the sorrow and pain behind his blue eyes. *Is that how one looks when they've lost their true love?*

"Then it is *I* who am sorry for bringing up painful memories, Mr. Hollingsworth." She smiled, dipping and swaying around the room with his lead.

Jared shook his head. "Life goes on. We cannot dwell in the past. I've learned that the hard way. I've lived as a recluse for far too long."

Before she could speak, the dance ended and a young man swept her away before the next reel began. Several dances and partners later, she finally returned to Mr. Hollingsworth's arms.

"Having a good time?" he asked.

"Yes," she replied, relaxing in his gentle hold as they waltzed once more.

Soon the music ended and they made their way to the refreshment table for more punch and a sampling of the wedding cake.

"Hollingsworth, good to see you," a balding

gentleman said, breaking line to refill his cup of punch. "How are things out your way?"

"Well, thank you," Mr. Hollingsworth replied. "And yours?"

"Couldn't be better for this time of the season though we can always use a little rain," the man said, nodding his head in her direction. "I don't believe we've met, miss?"

"Forgive my manners. George Wimple, this is Mrs. I mean Miss Rebecca Davis. She's a close friend of the bride. Miss Davis, this is Mr. Wimple. He owns a plantation near mine."

"It's a pleasure, Mr. Wimple." Rebecca greeted him with a slight curtsy and a smile.

"Same here and I hope you find Jackson to your liking. Couldn't be a better place to live," he said, taking a plate of cake and beginning to munch. "Though, I sometimes wonder if there is a place safe to live. A person's property can be taken so easily. Have you heard what happened over in Macon?"

"No, I can't say that I have," Mr. Hollingsworth said, shifting his weight from one foot to the next. He glanced at her and smiled, though he didn't appear pleased by the conversation.

"One of the slaves disappeared in broad daylight. She was working one minute and the next she was gone." The man snapped his fingers for emphasis to what he said and Rebecca felt her stomach knot.

"Mercy," she murmured, wondering if Mr. Wimple spoke of Ruth's disappearance or another. The Vigilante Committee had several branches and she was only privy to her mission. She hoped this disappearance would not make her task of seeing Ruth safely out of

Mississippi more difficult.

"Exactly, my dear," Mr. Wimple said with a nod. "I hope they find her and find her soon and she is dealt the strictest of punishments. We don't need word spreading amongst the plantations and causing others to attempt running off."

The knot in her stomach tightened a notch or two. "So you think she ran off?"

"Aye, I do." Wimple finished his refreshment and discarded the plate, refilling his cup for one last gulp of punch. He nodded at them both before sauntering away.

"He's a lively chap," Mr. Hollingsworth said, offering her his arm. "Shall we go find the bride and groom?"

"Let's do," she said, allowing him to lead once more as they danced their way over to the newlyweds.

Rebecca admired her friend and her husband as he held her close in his arms. They looked lost in a world of their own, despite their dancing in the middle of a crowded room. They made a striking pair, with her fair coloring and his dark features.

Elizabeth looked their way as they approached.

"Rebecca, can I steal Mr. Hollingsworth away for a dance?" she asked when the music stopped for a moment.

"Of course," Rebecca replied, stepping out of his grasp.

"Allow me." Mr. Cooper offered her his hand in return.

As she danced with the groom, she found herself watching Mr. Hollingsworth instead of paying attention to her partner. She admired Mr. Hollingsworth's profile and then his back, amazed how the cloth of his clothes stretched and relaxed over his solid form as he moved. Realizing she'd been staring at him, she chastised herself and lost her footing, stepping on Mr. Cooper's boot.

"Oh dear! Clumsy me," she exclaimed apologetically. "I'm so sorry."

"Wool gathering will do that," Mr. Cooper replied. Her cheeks burned and he chuckled, dancing them closer to Elizabeth and Mr. Hollingsworth before smoothly changing partners.

"Oh my!" Rebecca gasped with delight, finding herself once again in Mr. Hollingsworth's strong arms.

"Couldn't be without your bride that long, Mitchell?" Mr. Hollingsworth asked.

"Neither would you if you were just married," Mr. Cooper said, giving a wink.

The two men laughed, while Elizabeth glowed.

"By the way, Jared, would you mind seeing Miss Davis back into town? We're going to be pressed for time getting away to catch our train," Mr. Cooper asked.

"It will be my pleasure to see Miss Davis to town."

"Excellent," Elizabeth stated as the music died away. "Rebecca, be a dear and come upstairs with me while I change into my traveling suit?" Then she placed a hand on her husband's shoulder. "Darling, I promise not to be long."

"If you'll excuse us," Rebecca said to the men before following her friend away from the party.

Once they were upstairs, Elizabeth closed her bedroom door and leaned against it. She placed her left hand, now graced with her wedding ring, over her chest. "I think I've died and gone to heaven!"

23

Unable to keep from laughing, Rebecca fell down on the bed, lying on her back and recalled the many evenings they'd spent talking into the wee hours at Augusta. A twinge of sadness pricked at her heart and she realized she missed those carefree days very much.

"Does getting married make you feel that celestial?"

Elizabeth nodded and pushed herself away from the door. "It's so glorious to be in love. To have someone whisper the unthinkable in your ear and promise you'll feel splendor in his arms."

"Elizabeth!" Rebecca exclaimed, sitting up and pushing herself off the bed before she wrinkled her dress. "Come, let me undo your gown or else your husband will come impatiently looking for you."

"Don't act so innocent with me, my friend. I saw how you looked at Mr. Hollingsworth while you were dancing. From where I stood it looked like he did the same thing," she teased, stepping out of the heavy satin dress. She quickly donned the sturdy linen traveling suit with Tilda's help, changed pearls for a locket on a chain and put on her hat. Standing back, she looked at herself in the floor-length mirror.

"Well, do I look all grown up?"

Rebecca laughed, carefully laying the wedding gown across the bed. "I wager you'll be asking me if you look different when you return from your wedding tour in a few weeks."

"I hope so. I'll be a woman that has been repeatedly made love to by her husband."

Rebecca covered her cheeks with her hands. Elizabeth's words had unthinkable thoughts about Mr. Hollingsworth running through her head. "I shouldn't be hearing this."

Her friend laughed, applying a drop of fresh perfume behind her ears.

"Come, let's go back down so you and Mr. Hollingsworth can travel behind our carriage into town," she urged. "Tilda, please bring down Miss Davis' bag from the guest room."

A few minutes later, the two friends descended the staircase to find an array of guests waiting below. Mr. and Mrs. Calhoun and Elizabeth's three sisters and brother were at the front of the crowd. Near the door waited Mr. Cooper and Mr. Hollingsworth. While the bride bid farewell to her family and friends, Rebecca joined the gentlemen before they boarded the carriages.

Mr. Hollingsworth offered her his arm and escorted her outside. His touch had the strangest effect on her. A warmth like she had never felt before flowed through her and she again wondered what it would feel like to have him kiss her or whisper his desire into her ear. Rebecca already knew it felt heavenly to be held in his arms while dancing.

The driver opened the door for them, and Mr. Hollingsworth helped her into the open carriage. Once she settled on the seat, he joined her.

"Give Lucas a big hug from me." Elizabeth called as the bridal carriage rolled past them.

Rebecca's smile faltered. *Oh why had Elizabeth said that?*

"Who's Lucas?" Mr. Hollingsworth asked as the driver eased their carriage forward behind the newlyweds' coach for the journey.

Rebecca hesitated only slightly before answering. "My son."

Chapter Two

"Your son?"

"Yes." Rebecca's palms sweated and she hesitated a moment, not sure how he would react. "He's six months old."

His jaw twitched as he stared straight ahead. He remained quiet for several moments. When he did speak his words lacked emotion. "My wife died giving birth to *my* son."

Again, Rebecca's heart ached at his loss, and she regretted not successfully correcting him earlier about being a widow. There hadn't been a day since she lost Mariah that she hadn't prayed to have her sister back. They'd been close growing up, the four-year age difference never coming between them.

Remorse overcame her and she laid her gloved hand gently on his. "I'm terribly sorry. I didn't know."

"Don't apologize, Miss Davis. There was no way for you to have known how I lost my wife."

"I can tell you loved her very much," Rebecca said softly.

"I did."

He turned to face her, glancing down at her hand. Flushing, she removed it, regretting her boldness.

"What about your husband?" he asked. "Did you love him dearly?"

Rebecca blinked unsure how to respond having never been in love or married. She regretted not correcting the misunderstanding immediately, but how would she now explain having Lucas if she did? *Oh what a tangled web. How would she get herself out of it?*

"You don't have to answer. I know that every marriage isn't love based. And since you prefer to be addressed as Miss Davis it is clear that you wish the union never happened. But I do not judge you, Miss Davis. Many marry for security. Others through an arrangement. Those who marry for love are lucky indeed," Mr. Hollingsworth said, taking her hesitance to respond as her answer. He looked at the passing scenery, ending the discussion.

The knot that formed in her stomach twisted tighter and tighter as she stewed over a way to explain to him about Lucas. But there wasn't one without divulging Mariah's naivety. And now with the confusion over her title it would be even more difficult.

She sighed and opened her purse, unfolding the note from the day before. She glanced down at it and reread the lines. *I will contact you shortly after your arrival.*

Why hadn't Mr. Hollingsworth spoken to her about the mission? Was this his first as well? Or had he thought better of speaking to her in public about their orders, especially after Mr. Wimple's declaration? She'd nearly fainted when the man mentioned the runaway. Refolding the note, she put it back in the hidden pocket and closed the purse strings.

As they rode in silence, she studied her companion more closely. She knew why she was involved with the

Anti-Slavery Vigilante Committee, but why would a plantation owner risk everything? *What could he possibly gain?*

The carriage slowed to a stop at her hotel. Not waiting for the driver, he opened the door and stepped down before turning and offering her his hand.

She took his hand and again felt a spark of awareness from his touch as he helped her out of the carriage. "Thank you for seeing me into town."

"I've enjoyed our time together, Miss Davis. Would you care to join me for dinner in the hotel dining room?"

She couldn't help smiling at the invitation. "I'd be delighted to have dinner with you, Mr. Hollingsworth," she said. "May I have a few moments to check on Lucas first?"

"Of course." He handed her small bag to the driver before seeing her inside. "I'll reserve a table in the dining room."

"I won't be long," she assured him, turning toward the large staircase. She took the stairs at a proper pace, but at the mid-point landing stopped and glanced below. To her surprise he was still standing there, watching her. Smiling, she quickened her step, anxious to return to him.

Nearing her suite's doorway, she heard crying and her aunt's voice clear into the hallway. Her smile faltered.

"Oh Charlotte, can't you make him be quiet?"

"I'm trying my best, Miss Josephine."

Rebecca opened the suite door and found her aunt lying on the fainting couch with a compress to her forehead. The maid bounced a fussy Lucas as she walked back and forth across the room.

"What's wrong with my boy?" Rebecca asked, taking Lucas and handing her discarded gloves to Charlotte. He immediately hushed and laid his head on her shoulder. "Have you missed Mama?"

"Thank heavens, you've returned" Josephine sat up, holding a compress to her head with one hand and her rosary in the other. "I've a splitting headache. He hasn't stopped crying since you left."

Behind her, Charlotte grinned and opened the small bureau drawer, putting away the gloves.

"Goodness. I think we have a spoiled little one on our hands," Rebecca soothed, kissing Lucas' auburn hair as she sat in the rocking chair.

"You better take this or he'll soil your dress, miss," Charlotte insisted, rushing back with a cloth for her to put between his head and her dress. "He's been drooling this evening. I believe he's starting to teethe."

Nodding, she rocked him as he snubbed. "I've thought the same for the last day or two. Will you prepare him a warm bottle? I'll get him to sleep before I go to dinner."

"Dinner?" Frowning, Josephine came up off the couch. "You're going to dinner? With whom? You don't know anyone in town besides *that* Calhoun girl."

Rebecca sighed, rubbing Lucas' back. "I'm having dinner downstairs with Mr. Hollingsworth. He's a friend of Elizabeth's husband. He saw me back to town after the wedding."

"I don't like it." Josephine paced in front of the settee. "If I didn't have this horrible headache, I'd dress and go down with you. But I really don't feel well."

She silently counted to five before responding to

her aunt. She didn't want a fight on her hands, but good heaven's Josephine could be a prude at times.

"Then go lie down and rest. Lucas will sleep until I return and Charlotte can bring you something from the dining room," she assured her. "There's nothing to worry about."

****

Jared requested a private table and ordered a bottle of wine to be chilled as he waited for Miss Davis to return. He'd expected her to be gone no more than ten minutes. He hadn't anticipated it would take her half-an-hour.

"Would you like to order, sir?" the waiter asked.

"Not yet. I'm waiting…" he said, finally spotting her enter the dining room. The gas-light cast a lovely glow on her auburn hair, reminding him of the first time he'd seen her at the post office.

He waved and her face lit up with a smile. She spoke to the Maitre d' and followed him across the room to the table.

Jared stood and pulled out the chair for her to sit.

"I'm sorry to have taken so long. Lucas was fussy. I stayed to feed him before putting him down for the evening."

"Is he all right?"

"He's teething."

"Not a pleasant experience for him then." He remembered the pain he'd experienced the last time he'd had a toothache. "Would you like some wine?"

In the dim light, he could see her facial features brighten and he thought she looked exceptionally lovely. In fact, he found he enjoyed looking at her far too much.

"I'd love a glass. Thank you."

He motioned for a waiter. As the man approached, Jared noticed the Maitre d' attempting to seat a couple. However, they refused the table next to them. Miss Davis glanced at him with a questioning look.

"How odd."

"Are you ready to order?" the waiter asked, uncorking the bottle and pouring them each a glass.

Jared cleared his throat and glanced over the menu once more. "What would you like, Miss Davis?"

"The pot roast with carrots, potatoes and peas."

"And for you sir?" the waiter asked.

"I'll have the steak with boiled potatoes and green beans."

"Excellent choices." The waiter took their menus and left.

"Did you want him? Lucas, I mean? Since your marriage wasn't a love match." The question shocked him as soon as he asked it. "Please forgive my rudeness. I didn't mean to offend you."

"None taken," she replied, smiling. "I loved him from the moment I first saw him. I'll never forget how soft he felt when the doctor laid him in my arms."

A smile tugged at his mouth for a moment as she described that experience, feeling the joy of the new life through her enthusiasm. However, the joy soon faded to pain as he recalled how he'd longed to hold *his* son, but the child had been breech, the doctor inexperienced, and Charisse too weak from a difficult delivery for either of them to live.

He clutched at the cloth napkin lying on the table in front of him a little too tightly. Miss Davis' green eyes widened with acknowledgement. Embarrassed, he cleared his throat and placed the napkin in his lap.

"Have you always lived in Jackson?" she asked, adroitly changing the subject.

Jared silently expelled a sigh of relief. "Yes. Oak Hill has been in my family for many generations. It started out as ten acres and over the years each generation acquired more land until it now stands at over two thousand acres. I love the land. The history it holds."

"It sounds lovely," she said. "I'd enjoy seeing your plantation before I return to Memphis."

"I'd be honored to show it to you."

She smiled. "Wonderful. Do you ever imagine living anywhere else?"

He shook his head. "The only time I've not lived at Oak Hill is the four years I attended West Point and the four years of military service in Texas after graduation. Nowhere else comes closer to my heart than being home at Oak Hill."

"I think having a home of your own is very important in life. That's why I want to see Ruth reach her family again."

Ruth?

Jared was about to ask what she meant when their meal arrived. The waiter sat the hot plates before them then refilled their wine glasses.

"Can I get you anything else?" he asked.

"No, thank you," Jared said and the waiter disappeared as quietly as he'd appeared.

"How's your pot roast?" he asked after he'd taken several bites of his own meal.

"Delicious. The roast is very tender."

He watched as she carefully placed a small

combination of carrot, potato and pea on her fork with the pot roast before taking a bite. She closed her eyes, chewed slowly and savored the experience. Her movements made eating appear an art form and her facial expression as she chewed made him long to taste the flavorful palate as well.

He watched as she repeated the action with each bite until she put her fork down and reached for her napkin. She touched the corners of her mouth with it then replaced it in her lap. "Is something wrong, Mr. Hollingsworth? You've hardly touched your food."

Jared blinked, embarrassed at being caught staring. "No—no. I've never seen anyone find so much enjoyment out of eating before."

She flushed and looked down at her plate. She loaded her fork with a precise portion to create the perfect bite then looked up at him. "It's a terrible habit I have I know. It bothers my aunt immensely."

He smiled and they continued their meal in pleasant conversation. When the waiter offered dessert Miss Davis declined.

"I need to get back to Lucas," she explained. "Thank you for inviting me. I've enjoyed our afternoon together."

Jared nodded, wishing there was a way to detain her from leaving. "Be sure to contact me at Oak Hill if you need anything while you're in Jackson. I will be honored to assist you in any way I can."

The waiter returned with their bill, and Jared paid him.

They stood and she leaned forward. "Then we shall meet again about *Ruth?*" she whispered.

"Ruth?"

"About getting her home?" She smiled and looked hopeful.

He found her comment odd. "Tomorrow is Sunday. Shall I call on you and Lucas after church services? We can have a picnic."

"That sounds wonderful, but would you mind if I invited my aunt? I hate to leave her at the hotel alone again."

"The more the merrier," Jared said, as they walked to the stairs. He lifted her hand to his lips and brushed a kiss across her knuckles. "Until then."

Rebecca bit her lower lip as she watched him walk away. Tingles lingered across her hand from his kiss. Warmth pooled in her stomach and she smiled. She couldn't remember when she'd spent a more delightful day.

Chapter Three

"Rebecca! I can't believe you'd agree to a picnic without even consulting me," Josephine complained the next morning, as they dressed for Mass.

"If you don't want to go, I'll make your excuses for you, but I'm going," she said firmly. "Mr. Hollingsworth is being very hospitable by inviting us to a picnic and tour of his plantation. The least you can do is join us."

Josephine muttered something under her breath as she put on her dove-gray bonnet. She looked older than her thirty-six years in the outfit.

"What did you say?" Rebecca picked up Lucas unable to hide the grin that crept to her mouth. She knew her aunt well enough to know the woman stewed behind her cool demeanor.

"I'll go, but if my headache returns then I will insist we leave." She headed toward the door. "Come along, Charlotte. Don't dawdle."

"Yes, Miss Josephine." The maid hurriedly followed her out the door.

During Mass, Rebecca went through the motions of the service, but her mind was on Mr. Hollingsworth. She couldn't stop thinking about the kiss he'd placed on her hand last evening, or the way it had warmed her flesh. Having never been kissed, she found her reaction to the simple gesture frightening. Yet exciting. If she wasn't careful, she might lose her head and do something foolish. They were working together. She had to try to remember and not fantasize like a schoolgirl. Neither of them could afford for the mission to go awry. It would put everyone in jeopardy.

"Rebecca?" Josephine called to her from the end of the pew. "Aren't you coming, dear?"

Startled, she stood, following the parishioners outside.

"Are you all right?" Josephine asked. "You're cheeks are flushed."

"I'm fine," she assured her. "It's a very warm day. Let's go change into something cooler for our outing."

"It's not proper to appear so eager to see a man," her aunt scolded, "especially one you just met."

"I wa—," Rebecca began, but realized she *was* eager to see him. Mr. Hollingsworth had made an impression on her. Taking a deep breath, she silently chastised herself then conceded, "You're right. I need to hold my enthusiasm so he doesn't get the wrong idea."

"Enthusiasm is good, but not too much. I can't endure another Mariah incident." Josephine pressed fingertips to her temples as if another headache brewed.

Rebecca bit her tongue and ignored the comment, not wanting to spoil the day. She wished her aunt would forgive Mariah. It would make their lives together so much easier.

****

Jared hesitated before climbing down from the carriage as it stopped in front of the Bakersfield Hotel. His housekeeper had outdone herself preparing the picnic lunch, and he wondered if his invitation to Miss Davis wasn't a rash decision. If Mitchell hadn't suggested he consider remarrying, would he even be contemplating spending time with her?

Yes. He believed he would. His interest in her had nothing to do with Mitchell suggesting he remarry. He wouldn't mind if their acquaintance turned into more.

"Mr. Hollingsworth!" Miss Davis called, startling him out of his reverie as she came out of the hotel.

Despite her pretty smile, he recognized a note of concern etched on her face. "Miss Davis, is something wrong?"

"Aunt Josephine has come down with a dreadful headache. I was just going to get her a tisane when I saw you arrive. I'm afraid she won't be joining us after all."

"I'm sorry to hear that. Should we have our picnic inside so she can at least eat with us and then proceed on to Oak Hill for a tour?" he asked, motioning to the basket on the carriage seat.

"What a splendid idea. That would be lovely."

He turned to his driver. "Change of plans, Higgins. I'll be staying in town for a while. You can go around to the carriage house." He lifted the basket from the carriage seat. "I'll send for you when we're ready to leave."

"Yes sir," Higgins replied.

Once inside the hotel, Jared waited while Miss Davis ordered the tisane to be delivered to her suite, then he followed her upstairs.

He watched closely as she took the stairs before him, trim hips swaying as she moved, exposing a tiny glimpse of her ankle with each step. Her hair, swept into a chignon showed off the slender scope of her neck. She was a fine specimen of a woman. Whenever she was near he couldn't stop watching her closely.

When they reached the suite door, Miss Davis stopped and looked at him apologetically. "I had better go in first and prepare Aunt Josephine that we have company. I won't be but a moment."

He found waiting in the hallway odd while she announced him, but thought better of it when raised voices came from the other side of the door. He tried not to eavesdrop, but when a high-pitched shriek sounded, he dropped the basket in the hall and burst through the door.

"Aunt Josephine!" Miss Davis exclaimed, kneeling before the woman on the floor. She patted her aunt's pale cheeks quickly, but it did not rouse the woman.

"What happened?" he asked.

"She fainted." Miss Davis looked at the maid who held an infant. "Charlotte, bring Lucas to me and hurry down and see if there's a doctor near."

"Yes miss," the maid replied.

"I'll go," Jared said. "I know where Doctor Gordon's office is. That's where he's likely to be on a Sunday afternoon if he isn't at home."

Miss Davis looked at him, their gaze locking for a moment, her gratitude evident for his assistance. "Thank you, Mr. Hollingsworth."

He gave a quick bow and backed out of the room, reappearing with the picnic basket. He quickly set it inside the suite and left again.

"Charlotte, please get me a wet cloth," Rebecca reached for Lucas, then set him on the floor next to her. "I don't know why Josephine has these spells."

The maid shot her a look.

"All right. I do know," Rebecca admitted. "I just wish she wouldn't overreact. What's wrong with inviting Mr. Hollingsworth to our suite to have the picnic indoors? How can that be improper? Isn't he the one taking a chance being alone with three females and a baby?"

Charlotte snickered. "That he is, miss."

Josephine stirred and tried to sit up. "Oh my head," she muttered. "What am I doing on the floor?"

Rebecca supported her aunt and helped her to the chaise.

"You passed out, dear. Just lay still until the doctor arrives."

"Doctor! I don't need a doctor. Why…Who is fetching him?" Josephine asked, glancing around the room.

"Mr. Hollingsworth ran to get Doctor Gordon for us," Rebecca explained.

Josephine raised her hand to her head and moaned. "Are you trying to kill me?"

"Kill you?"

"Yes," she whispered. "Bringing a man you hardly know to our suite. Wasn't it bad enough you accepted an invitation from him for a picnic without a proper chaperone?"

"But you were going to be there. What more of a chaperone would I need?" Rebecca asked, leaning forward and pulling Lucas away from the rocking chair where he tried to pull up.

Josephine moaned again. "I feel an attack of the vapors coming on."

"Vapors?" a gruff voice barked, causing Josephine

to stop in mid-swoon.

"I beg your pardon. Who are you?" she asked, her eyes enlarged at having a strange man enter their suite unannounced.

Rebecca watched her aunt closely as she got to her feet, surprised the woman didn't faint dead away.

"Doctor Ancil Gordon at your service, Madame," he answered. "What seems to be the problem?"

"My aunt is a very delicate lady, Doctor Gordon. She doesn't take to excitement well," Rebecca explained, bouncing Lucas on her hip. "She's been suffering with headaches since we arrived in town a few days ago."

"Are you prone to fainting?" Doctor Gordon looked over the rim of his spectacles.

"Not as much as she's taken with the vapors," Rebecca replied.

"Rebecca, I can speak for myself," Josephine said tightly, accepting Doctor Gordon's help to stand.

"Yes. You most certainly can," Rebecca remarked. She turned and acknowledged Mr. Hollingsworth's return with a smile. "Charlotte, help my aunt into the bedroom so Doctor Gordon can perform his examination."

"Yes, miss."

"Mr. Hollingsworth, let's have our picnic at the table here," Rebecca said. "Would you mind holding Lucas while I set out the food?"

"N—no, not at all," he stammered, taking the boy from her.

"Good, we'll be eating in no time," she assured him, picking up the basket and placing the food onto the small dining table on the far side of the suite.

****

Once inside her bedroom, Josephine settled on the bed, never taking her eyes off of the doctor. She didn't like doctors. Never had. And she despised the whole profession ever since that charlatan let her precious Mariah die.

"Your niece said you've been having headaches for a few days. Is that correct?" Doctor Gordon asked.

"Yes. Since we arrived in Jackson," she responded.

"And where do you call home?"

"Memphis."

The doctor nodded, and opened his worn leather bag.

"Did you suffer from headaches there?" He glanced at her over the rim of his spectacles again.

"Occasionally. I have a very full schedule. I do volunteer work in the local parish," Josephine said. "The work can be tedious, but those of us who are more fortunate are expected to give our time to help those in need."

"Do you always wear your hair pulled back so tightly in a bun?" he asked, digging in his bag.

"What does the way I wear my hair have to do with my ailment?" she demanded, shooing Charlotte away as the maid tried to fluff the pillows and make her more comfortable on the bed.

"Everything if you're suffering from headaches as badly as you claim," he informed her. "Are you always so high-strung? Your facial expressions indicate you're suffering from tension. What do you find so worrisome?"

Indignation at his questioning prickled up Josephine's spine. She clenched her fists and remained silent, looking away from this annoying man she'd met less than five minutes ago. *What made him think he could read her so well?*

"From the looks of you, I'd wager you wear the latest fashions in women's undergarments, which isn't advisable in this climate. Do you also wear your corset as tight as you coif your hair?"

"Well! Is that the way you talk to ladies?" Josephine leaned away as he tried to put a bell-shaped object at the high collar of her dress.

Stopping in mid-examination, the doctor eyed her over his spectacles. "It's not just talk, Madame, its practicality. There is nothing wrong with you that a little softening of your garments, hair style, and demeanor will not cure."

"I didn't ask your opinion. I didn't ask you to come here. I do, however, ask that you leave at once," Josephine said, swinging her legs over the side of the bed and standing up as quickly as she could.

The sudden movements made her sway, and she found herself clutching at the doctor's arms as he steadied her.

"Miss Josephine!" Charlotte rushed to her side.

"Hush girl," Josephine snapped, staring into the doctor's amber-colored eyes. The room seemed to spin, and her breathing became shallow as he slowly eased her to a sitting position on the bedside.

"I'd suggest you refrain from sudden movements until you loosen your corset."

"Yes, doctor." She swallowed hard and took a closer look at him. Despite his salt and pepper hair around the temples, he wasn't as old as she'd first thought when he entered the suite.

"I'll leave you a few packets of powders you can take if the headaches become too unbearable. But I'd recommend my other suggestions first."

"Yes." She slowly nodded. "I'll consider your suggestion."

"You do that. I'll check on you later in the week." He closed his bag.

Josephine watched him leave and then fell back on the pillows, covering her mouth with the back of her hand. *Heavens above!*

Chapter Four

Heat from the summer sun beat down upon their heads as the open Victorian carriage pulled up outside the manor house at Oak Hill. Rebecca stared in awe from beneath the shade of her parasol at the splendor of the large two-story home before her.

"Amazing," she breathed, counting the windows on the upper floor. The house had two circular verandahs, one on each level.

"Did you say something?" Mr. Hollingsworth asked.

"I thought the Calhoun's home was the most elaborate I'd seen, but Oak Hill is astounding," she explained as the carriage slowed to a stop.

"Is that a fact?" He grinned. "Bigger isn't always better, but the extra room is helpful when holding a ball or barbeque."

"I can imagine the elegance of a ball given at Oak Hill."

He descended the carriage step and helped her down. "Yes. When my mother was alive, she was the best hostess around Jackson. Let's have a bit of refreshment and get Master Lucas out of the sun."

"That sounds divine." Rebecca slipped her arm through his as they walked to the verandah. "Perhaps Charlotte can use your swing to rock Lucas to sleep?"

"Certainly," he agreed. "If you'll wait here, I'll go see about something to quench our thirst."

While he was gone, Rebecca explored the perimeter of the house as she walked along the portico. Studying the large baskets of ferns hanging from the eaves and the inviting, yet protective, foliage planted close to the porches' edge, she wondered how many gardeners it took to keep the grounds looking so perfect. She knew Mr. Hollingsworth used hired labor on his land, which did not come as cheap as purchasing laborers at auction. If appearances meant anything, Mr. Hollingsworth was a wealthy man. Yet he risked it all to help those in bondage by the color of their skin. That fact alone held her in awe of him.

With all the excitement over Josephine's ailment she'd almost forgotten to discuss Ruth's plight further with him. She had to keep her head about her and mention it to him again at the first opportune moment.

Walking back to the front of the house, she smiled at her maid who held a sleeping Lucas in her arms.

"Couldn't you imagine living here, Charlotte?" she asked, stopping about a yard away.

"That I could, miss." The young maid looked relaxed as the swing moved back and forth. "The cottage is nice, but living on a plantation would be a world different for us."

Rebecca nodded. "Lucas could run and play to his heart's content during the summers."

"That he could."

She sighed, leaning her back against the stoop post. "A place like this comes with much responsibility. I suppose that is why I have a small place in Memphis. It's enough to keep a body from being weary."

"Being weary from what?" Jared asked, coming up behind where she stood staring out over his land. Tightness formed in his chest at the memory of his late wife doing the same on many occasions. He suddenly missed her desperately. And he wondered what he'd been thinking bringing Miss Davis and her son to Oak Hill. Was he really ready to forge forward and put his past behind him?

"Goodness, Mr. Hollingsworth, you startled me," Miss Davis said, her cheeks flushed. "I was being wistful. Speaking my thoughts aloud and no doubt, boring poor Charlotte with my prattle."

"Ah, I see," Jared replied, smiling. "My housekeeper will be out shortly with lemonade."

He pushed his previous thoughts away as he offered her his arm and led her to the wicker settee. He couldn't live in the past forever, and living *alone* at Oak Hill was not the answer either. He had to move on. Mitchell was right. It was time he began thinking about remarrying and living a normal life again. Not just to replenish his coffers, and keep the Hollingsworth bloodline going, but because he was lonely. He needed a companion, someone to make him feel alive again. Meeting Miss Davis had proven that to him. Besides, he couldn't expect the duty of producing respectable heirs and carrying forth the Hollingsworth name to fall upon Rory.

"I want to thank you for your hospitality, Mr. Hollingsworth," Miss Davis said, bringing him back to the present. "You've gone beyond what would be expected of an escort at a friend's wedding."

"It has been my pleasure, miss... Shouldn't we dispense with the formalities, Miss Davis?" He took a seat in the wicker armchair. "I know we only met yesterday, but I feel as if we are going to know each other for a long time to come, being Mitchell and Elizabeth's friends. Won't you please call me Jared?"

She smiled and her green eyes sparkled. "Then please call me Rebecca."

Jared reached across the table for her hand as a gesture of camaraderie. She slid her fingers along his; heat reverberated from their silky touch, jolting him in his seat. He pulled back his hand, abruptly breaking the contact.

Still smiling, she tilted her head and closed her eyes slightly. *Had she felt it too?* He watched her closely for several moments, but she gave no sign.

"Here you go," a plump woman in a gray dress and crisp white apron said, sitting down a glass pitcher of pale liquid on the table before them. "There are cookies cooling in the kitchen if you get a sweet tooth later on."

"Thank you, Mary," Jared replied, glad for the momentary interruption.

"I hope it isn't too tart." Mary poured three glasses and took one to Charlotte.

Rebecca accepted the glass he handed her and took a sip. "Just tart enough, don't you agree, Mr.…I mean, Jared."

"Just right."

After finishing their lemonade, they left Charlotte and Mary to visit on the verandah while Lucas slept. Jared escorted Rebecca around the grounds. On the far side of the stables he showed her the empty bins awaiting the late summer harvest of cotton. Then he took her down to where the field hands lived, boasting of the improvements that he'd made to the two rows of quarters in the six years since his father passed away.

"Why'd you decide to change from your father's way of running the plantation?" she asked, twirling her lace parasol, as they strolled past the small houses.

A few field hands lingered nearby under shade trees, taking advantage of the lazy Sunday afternoon. They called to their employer, and Jared acknowledged them with a courteous nod before answering Rebecca's question.

He picked up a small twig and snapped it in two as they walked. "I neither liked nor respected my father. He abused my mother as well as those who worked his land. His drinking only made things worse."

He stopped and stared across the field before continuing. Despite his resolve, his voice cracked when he spoke, recalling the unhealed pain of his youth. "My father's hand was responsible for my mother's early death. A body can only heal so much before it is broken."

He pulled at tall grass near his knees. "After my mother died, I vowed I would be different. No matter what it took, I would not become like my father and would never raise a hand to another."

Her silence was expected, but he wouldn't stand for her pity. Jared glanced at her. Instead of pity he thought he saw admiration in her eyes.

"You're very brave to take this stand when your neighbors cling to the accustomed way of life. Do they treat you differently?"

"Brave? Is it really brave to live by your convictions?"

"It takes courage to go against the grain. Not many men would do it, yet you have made it your way of life.

Is that why you decided to help Ruth?"

"Ruth?"

Rebecca nodded and pointed to the larger house on a small hill in the distance. "Who lives there?"

"My foreman. Mr. Paxton and his family live in what once was the overseer's home. He has three daughters and another child on the way. They're…they're praying for a son."

Rebecca laughed softly. "You don't sound like you have faith his prayer will be answered."

Jared shook his head. "Women get a look about them when they're expecting as if you can tell they'll have a son or a daughter."

"You could be wrong." She stopped under the shade tree.

"The joy would go to Paxton if I am." He pointed at a stream a few yards ahead. "Let's take a break from the heat and go wading."

The idea of taking off her shoes and stockings and pulling up her skirts to mid-calf to go wading tempted greatly. However, the thought of Josephine having another "spell" if she found out made her think twice before she finally answered him.

What harm could a little wading do?

Rebecca closed her parasol and offered him her hand in response. They ran like children, laughing on the way to the stream. Once there, she sat down on a nearby log to unlace her boots.

"Here, let me do that." He knelt before her on one knee and her heart skipped a beat as she watched him meticulously unlace each. He gently held her calf in his hand as he removed the boot. Tingles of gooseflesh shivered up her leg from the bottom of her foot as his fingers gently brushed along the underside. Her sheer stockings provided little protection from his intimate caress.

Her throat went dry because his actions were highly improper. She should stop him before she found herself enjoying his touch. Her heart fluttered and foreign warmth spread through her. "I—I better do the rest."

He looked up, his blue eyes darker than she recalled. She quivered at his intense stare and shyly looked away.

"Last one in has to kiss a salamander," he challenged.

She laughed and hastened to remove her stockings, determined not to kiss a salamander unless it had blue eyes, blond hair and looked like Jared Hollingsworth. She wasn't sure what had come over her, but if this was living dangerously, she liked it.

To her delight, she reached the water's edge first. She lifted her skirt and dipped her toe in to test the water when he caught up to her.

"I said *in* the water, not *on* the edge," he teased, grabbing her hand and pulling her along with him into the cool stream.

"Jared!" she shrieked, her feet landing in the icy water, toes sinking into the muddy sludge.

"Jumping in is more fun than dipping a toe." He kicked the water with childlike abandon.

Cool droplets splattered the front of her already damp dress. "You do *not* play fair, sir," she accused with mock indignation. She couldn't remember the last time she'd had as much fun. It had been years since she and Mariah had slipped off to a nearby stream to frolic without Aunt Josephine being the wiser.

A fleeting sadness engulfed her for a moment as she missed those cherished times with her sister. However, Jared's chuckle brought her back to the merriment at hand.

"Playing fair isn't fun." He sidestepped her attempt to splash him with water.

"Is that why you decided to help Ruth?" Rebecca raised her skirt higher than before so it did not drag in the water any more than it already had. Then she carefully stepped on a medium size smooth rock in the middle of the stream. Planting her feet firmly on the rock's sides, water rushed over her toes and she wiggled them, tipping her head back to enjoy the sun.

"Help?" Confusion evident in his voice, she looked over and saw his brow furrowed as if he didn't know what she meant.

"Yes. I'm most anxious to help Ruth reach her family. Don't you share this desire?"

****

Jared frowned. Why did she keep talking about a woman named Ruth? And why should Rebecca want him to join her efforts? They had only just met, but it was clear that whoever Ruth was Rebecca was sincere in her desire to help.

"Exactly what do you have in mind?" he asked.

She puckered her lips. Damn, but she was a vision of loveliness with the sun cascading down around her.

"I would assume *you* had a plan," she said slowly.

A plan? Why would he have a plan?

Confound it! He found her talk confusing. But that really didn't matter because right now he was far too tempted to kiss her when she turned her face from the

51

sun and smiled at him.

"How else will I take her with me?" She slipped her feet from the rock back into the water. "That is, as soon as you tell me where I can find her. Do you have her hidden on your plantation?"

He laughed at her prattle until her last statement sank in. "Hidden here? Why on earth would I do that?"

She shrugged. "I suppose that would be risking your livelihood to bring her here. I pray she is safe awaiting my introduction."

Their conversation became more peculiar by the moment as if he should know more about Ruth than he did.

"I'm afraid—" A burst of laughter interrupted him as his foreman's daughters came running from the tall grass and into the water.

"Can we join you, Mr. Jared?" the oldest of the three girls asked.

"Plee-eaze," the two younger ones chimed, kicking up water around them.

He smiled. "Just don't get Miss Davis wet," he warned, but it was too late. In an attempt to side step the girls' frolic, Rebecca stumbled over the rock she'd previously stood on and fell back, sending up a splash of water.

The girls began to squeal with laughter.

"Rebecca!" Jared sloshed through the water as quickly as possible to help her to her feet. "Are you all right?"

"I'm—I'm fine. I'm fine." She laughed accepting his help up. "Just wounded pride and some damp clothing. I'm sure I'll survive."

"Harmony. Eliza. Sue Ellen." George Paxton's

booming voice sent the girls scrambling out of the water.

"Ah I should have known." Paxton scowled, planting his fisted hands at his hips. "How many times have I told you to stay out of the water? Especially, when neither ya ma nor me is around?"

"They weren't exactly alone, Paxton," Jared said, drawing attention away from the girls to himself and his wet companion.

"Ah, Mr. Hollingsworth, I didn't see you, sir," Paxton's features relaxed slightly. "I hope my girls haven't been a bother to ya or caused any harm."

"Don't be too hard on them. They were having a little fun is all," he replied, helping Rebecca out of the water. "Miss Davis, this is George Paxton my foreman. Paxton, this is Miss Rebecca Davis, a friend."

"It's a pleasure, ma'am," Paxton said.

"Nice to meet you, sir," Rebecca said. "You have three precious daughters."

"Thank you, ma'am. Their ma and me are right proud of them." He shifted his weight awkwardly. "Why don't you both come back to the house and have some tea? Isabella was putting on a pot when the girls left. It will give Miss Davis a chance to dry off."

Jared looked at Rebecca and she nodded her consent.

"Thank you, Mr. Paxton for the offer. I'm afraid I'm quite clumsy at times," Rebecca said.

"So my girls didn't cause your fall?" Paxton asked.

"No, sir," she assured him.

Jared gathered their shoes and her parasol then offered her his arm as they walked barefoot through the field toward Paxton's house. He hadn't paid a visit to them in a while. In fact, he rarely saw his foreman's family except on holidays or special occasions these days. He could already see Miss Davis had a life altering effect on him in the short time he'd known her.

A brown spotted mongrel greeted them as they approached the small yard with a stone path and a rose trellis at the entrance by the door.

"I didn't know you had a dog," Jared said as the girls ran ahead to play with the pup.

"Simpson found him a few weeks back wandering the road and brought him to the girls. I reckon' someone had tried to drown a litter and he got away. Mind you, I didn't take a fancy to him at first, but he grows on ya," Paxton said, grinning.

"A pet is good. I had a little chick when I was young," Rebecca said.

"A chick? Now that would be an odd pet. Did ya get your hand pecked?"

She nodded. "All the time. That's why I didn't cry when it was big enough for my father to kill for Sunday dinner."

Paxton guffawed. When he sobered, he beckoned, "Come on in and meet Isabella."

Jared allowed Rebecca to go ahead of him into the house. Down the hallway, he spotted Isabella by the stove in the kitchen, pouring steaming water into a china pot.

"I'm back," Paxton called.

"Did ya find them?" she asked, not looking up.

"Aye. Down at the stream," he replied. "I brought some guests for tea."

Isabella glanced their way and smiled.

"It's good to see you again, Mrs. Paxton," Jared

called in greeting, noticing her normally trim figure swollen with child. "This is my friend Miss Rebecca Davis." He realized he'd referred to her twice as his friend. Perhaps that was the best way to describe their current relationship.

"It's a pleasure, Mrs. Paxton," Rebecca said.

"Call me Isabella. Everyone does." She placed a supportive hand to her back and collected two more cups from the cupboard.

"Let me get that tray for ya," Paxton said, then carried the tea service to the table. "I'll call the girls."

"No. Let them play so we can have some quiet," Isabella said, stopping and staring at Rebecca's dress. "Goodness! You're soaked."

"I had a little accident down at the stream," Rebecca explained. "The walk here took care of the dripping. I'm almost dry."

"But you could catch a chill," Isabella sounded concerned. "Tea can wait a few more minutes. You must come with me and change into something dry. Mr. Hollingsworth, I'm surprised you didn't see to it the moment you arrived. And Mr. Paxton, is this anyway to treat our guest?"

Jared grinned as he watched Isabella usher Rebecca away from the kitchen.

"We're in the dog house now," Paxton grunted.

Jared nodded, and realized he still held Rebecca's shoes and stockings with his own. He laid them in the seat of a nearby rocking chair, then donned his socks and shoes.

****

"You have very pretty hair, Miss Davis," Isabella said, opening up a chifforobe.

"Thank you." Rebecca patted at the back of her hair, wondering what it must look like in its damp state. She moved closer to a mirror hanging on the wall of the bedroom to take a look. A few hairpins had come loose, and she easily rectified that. Using her fingers, she reshaped the few ringlets around her face hoping Aunt Josephine did not notice her mussed state when she returned to the hotel.

"I'm afraid all I have that will fit you is a simple cotton day dress. Will you mind wearing that until your clothes dry?"

"Not at all. I appreciate your kindness," Rebecca assured her taking the dress. "When are you due?"

"In about a month or so. The mid-wife says this one could come sooner than later since it's my fourth."

"Mr. Hollingsworth said you are hoping for a son." She stepped behind a small dressing screen and began removing her wet garments.

"Aye. Paxton wants a son. But I've learned you take what you're given. It doesn't matter what we may want in life. We just make do with what we have," Isabella said. "I know nothing about boys. And after having three girls I suppose the change would be good. But I won't be sad if we have another daughter. The main concern I have is that the baby comes into the world healthy and whole."

"I'll pray you have a safe delivery," Rebecca assured.

"Thank you," Isabella replied. "It's nice to see Mr. Hollingsworth keeping company again. He's been alone since Charisse died."

Rebecca stepped from behind the screen, tying the belt in the back. She draped her wet dress over the screen for it to dry. "Losing a loved one is tragic."

"Yes it is. And I know he has to feel alone living in that big house without family around. Mary tries her best to make it comfortable for him, but I know it isn't the same as having loved ones with you."

"It sounds as if Jared has a champion," Rebecca remarked as they headed back to the kitchen."

"That he does."

Chapter Five

"You're very quiet this morning," Josephine said over coffee. "How was your outing?"

Rebecca studied her aunt. Something was different, but she couldn't pinpoint exactly what. She'd expected the inquisition this morning over her soiled dress. Yet, Josephine hadn't said a word.

"It was pleasant and most enjoyable. I wish you could have come along."

"I'd have only been in the way." Josephine spread a generous amount of butter over her biscuit.

If you only knew.

"Perhaps if I'm invited to visit Oak Hill again you'll come with me?" she said.

"Perhaps." Her aunt picked up her coffee cup and sipped.

"You sound as if you are feeling better. No headache this morning?"

"No headache." She stared off into the distance and remained silent for a few minutes before she sat her cup down and announced. "I think I'll do some shopping this morning. Do you have plans?"

Rebecca nodded. "I have a few errands to run for Elizabeth, but I should be finished before noon. Shall we plan on lunch?"

"Elizabeth? The girl is on her wedding tour. What

could she possibly need your help with?" Josephine asked.

"She's having her first tea as a married woman when she returns next month," Rebecca said. "I'm seeing to the invitations."

"Doesn't she have a mother or sisters who could do this for her?"

Rebecca hid her smile. This was the Aunt Josephine she knew so well. "She's married now. She wants to do this on her own. It's important to her."

"It sounds to me as if she's foisting the job on you."

"Think what you wish. I'm happy to do it since I couldn't help her before the wedding," she said. "What about lunch?"

Josephine shook her head. "There's a midday Mass at the church. I thought I'd drop in on the ladies auxiliary afterward to see if I could be of service while we are here."

"That sounds like a wonderful idea." If her aunt found something to occupy her time, then she'd have more time to see to her own business without making excuses.

"Well, it's either find something to do or stay in this suite, as you put it yesterday," Josephine said. "I found I didn't like being here alone while you were away, even if I wasn't feeling well."

She pushed her chair back from the table and stood, her blond hair tumbled from the loose chignon that had replaced her usual bun. She absently patted it and said, "I'd better go change and redo my hair."

"I'll see you this afternoon." Rebecca carried her coffee over to the small secretary.

Sitting down, she took out her stationary and wrote a letter to Isabella, thanking her for her hospitality. Then she struggled with one to Mr. Hollingsworth in regards to their mission. Their conversation about Ruth yesterday had ended abruptly and she needed to know where they stood. She felt antsy about completing her assignment. The longer it took, the more she feared for Ruth's safety. Yet she also feared for Lucas and what might happen to him if she were caught transporting Ruth to Memphis.

Her hand trembled and she considered her words carefully.

Dear Mr. Hollingsworth,

It is with utmost haste that I write regarding our association. I must speak with you again on the matter at the first opportune time. We must settle it quickly.

Miss Davis

Putting thoughts of danger out of her mind, she folded the letter and sealed the envelope before going to check on Lucas. Charlotte was almost finished bathing him and he splashed the water with his hands.

"Now Luc," Charlotte scolded, causing the child to laugh.

"He's feisty this morning," Rebecca observed.

"A little too much to complete his bath."

"Here, let me help you." Rebecca picked up a towel, scooped Lucas up and carried him over to the bed. "I'll dress him. It'll give me a little time with him before I go out for the morning."

"Yes, miss." The maid took the tub of water out of the room.

The child cackled as Rebecca played peek-a-boo with him and dried him. She sprinkled a sweet smelling powder on his body and rubbed it on him so he wouldn't chafe from the heat. Jackson was definitely much warmer in June than Memphis.

"Oh Lucas, what would I do without you?" she asked and kissed the top of his head, his chubby cheeks and the tip of his nose.

In response he blew spit bubbles at her as she dressed him for the day. Overcome with thoughts of a failed mission to get Ruth to safety, she cradled him against her body, enjoying the warmth.

"M—m—m," he cooed, stuffing his fist into his toothless mouth.

She smiled, laying him back down and continued to play with him until Charlotte returned with his bottle.

Rebecca scooped him up and handed him to the maid.

"I should be back by lunch," she called, disappearing behind the dressing screen to quickly change into a fresh day dress before she left.

The first stop on her to do list was the post office, then the engravers to place Elizabeth's order for invitations. While there she also ordered new calling cards for her friend. Coming out of the store she was startled to see her aunt leaving the dress shop across the street in a dress and hat she had never seen before. Rebecca watched as the woman headed toward St. Anna's.

First, she'd had a new hairstyle and now a new ensemble. What had gotten into Josephine?

Rebecca headed toward the dress shop determined to see what the latest styles offered in Jackson. Her aunt did not make hasty purchases unless they were *haute couture*. It was her one vanity.

****

Beneath her gloves, Josephine's palms were damp as she entered the church. She spotted the confessional and it beckoned to her to repent, because she was there on a carnal mission rather than to reverently worship God. She felt sinful in her actions, but she couldn't stop herself.

In a chance conversation with the hotel clerk she'd learned that Doctor Gordon attended midday services regularly. He also worked with the ladies' auxiliary, putting them in touch with families in need. Two factors that appealed to her faith and charitable work, and gave her reason to speak with him.

Taking a deep breath, she took her rosary from her purse and genuflected, crossing herself before sliding into a pew among the other parishioners. She knelt and nervously adjusted the collar of her new dress and touched the chignon underneath the short lace veil to make sure it was still in place. She prayed her efforts would not go unnoticed by the good doctor and he'd be pleased to see she'd taken his advice.

Before the service began, she saw him slip into a pew near the front, on the opposite side of the sanctuary.

Oh dear Lord, forgive me, but he's better looking than I remembered, she silently prayed, clutching her rosary to her breast. His dove gray suit stretched across his broad shoulders, but looked rumpled as if he'd slept in it.

He'd been rude to her. Yet she couldn't put him out of her mind. She abhorred his profession, believing his kind were nothing more than charlatans. So why did she want to learn more about him? Who was the man behind his rough exterior? And why did her heart beat so rapidly when he was near?

She went through the motions of Mass, repeating the litany and praying the decades of the rosary without much conviction. Squeezing her eyes shut, she willed herself to put Ancil Gordon out of her mind and concentrate on God and her service to Him. But the more she tried, the less it worked. Every time she closed her eyes she saw the doctor's handsome face, and her cheeks heated at an alarming rate.

Rising from her knees, she settled once again on the seat and listened as the priest spoke before beginning Holy Eucharist. Feelings of unworthiness soared through her as she partook of the Host. Walking back to her seat, she made brief eye contact with Doctor Gordon. He smiled, and joy rippled to her core. The jolt shook her and she took a seat in the nearest pew.

When Mass concluded, she approached the priest to introduce herself and inquire about the ladies' auxiliary.

"Miss Davis, it's a pleasure to have you with us at St. Anna's," the priest expressed. "I know that Mrs. Fletcher will be glad to have your assistance. Let me find her. Oh, there's Doctor Gordon. He can help you get started."

"No, you don't have to—" but her words fell on deaf ears as the priest motioned to the doctor to join them.

"Doctor Gordon, this is Miss Josephine Davis. She's visiting Jackson for a while and would like to aid the ladies' auxiliary. I looked for Mrs. Fletcher, but it seems she has already left the chapel. Would you be so kind as to show Miss Davis to the canteen? I'm sure you'll find Mrs. Fletcher there."

"Certainly, Father Bohannon," Doctor Gordon replied and glanced at her as the priest walked away.

She held her breath, noticing a woodsy scent, as his eyes looked her up and down.

"Why doesn't it surprise me to see you here, Miss Davis?"

Josephine hoped the warmth surging through her cheeks wasn't apparent. "I think I mentioned my devotion to working in my home parish. It's only natural I'd want to be of service to the church while I'm in Jackson."

"Of course you would." The doctor half-grinned and she could feel his gaze rove over her again. "If I may be so bold to say, you look much improved today, Miss Davis."

"Thank you, Doctor Gordon. Are you going to look for Mrs. Fletcher?"

"Oh yes." He sounded startled by her question as if he'd forgotten the priest's request. "Come with me. I'm sure Constance will be able to use your help."

Constance?

Josephine followed him outside to the breezeway that led to a mid-size building. Two women, carrying bundles of cloth swatches, were going inside as they approached and the doctor introduced her.

"Miss Davis, I'd like you to meet Posey Reynolds and Matilda Bradbury," He said. "Miss Davis is visiting Jackson and would like to be of aid to the auxiliary while she's in town."

"Can you sew?" Mrs. Reynolds asked.

"Yes, I can," Josephine assured. "One of my quilts came in second at the county fair."

"Good. We can always use an extra pair of hands. Mr. Haggerty at the mercantile just donated these bundles of cloth samples for our use in making quilts for St. Benedict's Orphanage in Mobile County," Mrs. Reynolds said.

"We do it every year for Christmas," Mrs. Bradbury explained.

A woman in a blue dress and white gloves joined them and Josephine assumed she must be Constance Fletcher. She was about ten years older than the other women and her hair was black as pitch. Her demeanor spoke volumes about her and Josephine felt inferior.

"Hello, Ancil. Who do you have here?" Mrs. Fletcher asked in a superior tone.

"Constance," he acknowledged with a slight nod. "I'd like you to meet Miss Josephine Davis. She's visiting Jackson and would like to help the auxiliary."

Mrs. Fletcher nodded but her smile suggested she was not entirely pleased. "We're always in need of extra hands. We're beginning a sewing project today. Are you handy with a needle?"

"Yes I am." Josephine wondered what kind of connection Ancil and this woman had that they'd used their Christian names so freely. He certainly hadn't called *her* Josephine.

"I'll leave you in Constance's capable hands, Miss Davis," Doctor Gordon said.

"Thank you." She gave him her warmest smile, looking straight into his eyes.

He looked startled for a moment, then cleared his throat and smiled at those around him. "Ladies, if you'll excuse me I have patients to see."

The women went about their business while

Josephine watched him go. Her heart beat a little faster as she feared he had a love interest with Constance Fletcher. She desperately wanted to know if he did. She would not allow herself to be made a fool.

Slowly turning to join the others, Josephine noticed Mrs. Fletcher's close cold stare. Chills ran up her spine and for the first time in her life she felt she'd just entered the lions' den.

But she wouldn't cower. She didn't care how hard Mrs. Fletcher stared or how cold her smiles were. As far as Josephine was concerned Ancil Gordon was fair game and until she knew otherwise she'd pursue getting to know him. It didn't matter how much Mrs. Fletcher dyed her hair, she was younger and she could turn on the charm when she wanted. And she wanted Ancil Gordon.

Chapter Six

Jared sat at his desk a few nights later going over the plantation ledgers. His lamp burned low as the wick soaked up the last of the oil. He closed the book and rubbed his face. When the light went out, he stood and walked over to the French doors and stared up into the midnight sky.

The accounts balanced. Every month since the three bad seasons of crops, he feared there wouldn't be enough money to cover the expenses and pay his men. It brought a small measure of comfort he could do so. But being in balance did not take away the looming threat Stuart Delaney made to Oak Hill. His letter said he'd be here by the end of the month with an auctioneer.

Jared wasn't sure if Delaney seriously planned to force him into auctioning Oak Hill to cover Rory's debts, or if he'd referred to the action as a threat to show power. Either way he wasn't looking forward to Delaney's arrival.

His options were minimal and he'd been giving Mitchell Cooper's suggestion he remarry more thought, especially since meeting Miss Davis. He'd enjoyed their time together far more than he'd ever imagined he would. A feeling of guilt...no remorse nagged at him, but he couldn't cling to his marriage vows with

Charisse forever. What they'd had together was special, but she was gone. Surely she'd want him to move on, to find happiness if the opportunity rose.

"Mr. Hollingsworth!"

"Mr. Hollingsworth!"

The faint call of a child's voice came from the darkness and he stepped further out onto the upper verandah to get a better look.

"Mr. Hollingsworth!"

"Who's there?" he called, finally spotting a moon shadowed form in the darkness.

"It's Harmony, sir. Papa sent me to get you." Her voice trembled with agitation and urgency. "Come quick."

Jared raced down the verandah stairs and into the front garden where the young girl stood barefoot in her nightgown. "What's wrong?"

"It's Mama. She's having the baby. The midwife says she needs the doctor to come," Harmony explained. She tugged on his hand urging him toward the barn. "Papa needs you to go to town and bring back the doctor. He'd go himself, but Mama doesn't want him to leave the house. She's awful scared." The girl's voice faltered and she cried, "We're all scared."

"I'll go." Jared knelt and squeezed her shoulders lightly for reassurance. He looked directly into her eyes. "Don't you worry, your mama will be fine. I want you to go wake Mary and take her back with you to watch your sisters."

Harmony nodded and raced to the main house. Jared watched her disappear into the shadows before he went into the stables. To his surprise, Higgins had a horse saddled waiting for him.

"I heard the child, sir. Should I go for you?"

"Thank you, Higgins, but no. I'll go. You can go back to bed now." He'd sent Paxton to fetch the doctor that fateful night when Charisse went into labor, so it was only right that he return the favor.

"Yes sir."

Jared forced the horse into a gallop in the moonlit darkness. The heady scent of honeysuckle perfumed the summer air, but a skin crawling anxiety soaked his shirt, chilling him as though it was winter.

Low-hanging branches from a nearby tree scrapped his face and arms as he leaned over the horse's neck. He pushed them out of his way, but he couldn't do the same with his old painful memories of Charisse and their child crowding his brain.

Fear for Isabella and remorse for his own loss prompted him to push the memories aside and drive the horse to go faster. Doctor Gordon was the town's physician now. Isabella would be fine. She wouldn't suffer like Charisse. Jared had to believe that.

When he reached the darkened town, he headed to the doctor's small house. He pounded on the door, guessing he'd have to wake the man from a sound sleep. He waited; then, he pounded again, harder this time. Still no answer. Panic dried his mouth. If Gordon was away attending someone, then he'd never find him in time.

Jared turned and quickly scanned the area. A dim light shined in an upper window of the hotel at the end of the street. Praying the doctor was there, he jumped on his horse and headed to the hotel.

The night clerk dozed behind the front desk, but jumped to his feet when Jared burst through the doors.

"Wh—what's going on?" the clerk stammered.

"Have you seen Doctor Gordon?" Jared demanded.

The clerk nodded, rubbing sleep from his eyes. "H-he's upstairs with a guest."

"Thanks," Jared called over his shoulder and raced toward the stairs.

"Wait, you can't go up there," the clerk said, following close on his heels.

Jared paid no heed to the man as he took the steps two at time. There was no time to waste.

At the second floor landing he stopped and looked down the hallway in both directions.

"Which room?"

"I'm not at liberty to give out that information." The clerk stiffened his back to appear taller than his stubby frame. "If you persist, I'll have no choice but to call for the sheriff."

Jared grabbed the clerk's shirtfront, pulling him close. "Listen, there's a woman in childbirth needing Doctor Gordon. Are you going to tell me which room he's in, or do I have to knock on every door, waking your guests until I find him?"

"There's no need to get violent," the clerk blustered, backing down. "He's in the suite at the end of the hall."

Jared released the man and stalked to the door. It wasn't until he reached it that he realized this was Rebecca's suite.

Further alarm engulfed his senses and he rapped on the door, fearing the worst. No one answered. Taking a deep breath he leaned his head against the door and knocked again. On the other side he heard the sound of Lucas's cry and perspiration broke out on his forehead.

Please God, don't let Lucas be ill. Not now.

After what felt like an eternity, the door opened. He staggered inside, his strength drained.

A wide-eyed surprised Charlotte stared at him. "Mr. Hollingsworth! What brings you here at this late hour?"

"Jared, are you all right?" Rebecca entered the room, carrying a whimpering and diaper clad Lucas in her arms. She looked like a heavenly vision wearing a white silk dressing gown with her auburn hair hanging loose around her shoulders.

For a moment, he found it difficult to speak. He swallowed hard and stumbled to the nearest chair before his legs buckled beneath him.

"Charlotte, get him some water," she ordered.

"Yes, miss."

The maid returned and offered him a tumbler. He drank the tepid water in several gulps. "I'm sorry to barge in, Rebecca, but I was told Doctor Gordon could be found here." Sitting the glass on the small table he spotted a red rash all over the child's back. "What's wrong with Lucas?"

"He ate something that didn't agree with him. At least that's what the doctor believes," she explained, looking more concerned about him than Lucas at the moment.

"Jared, what seems to be the problem?" Doctor Gordon asked, coming into the front room with Rebecca's aunt.

"My foreman's wife has gone into labor before her time and the mid-wife has sent for you. We need to hurry."

"Oh my heavens!" Rebecca exclaimed.

Doctor Gordon handed her a small jar. "Rub this salve on him and let him sleep in loose clothing tonight. I'll check back tomorrow."

She nodded, rubbing her cheek against Lucas'.

"Thank you for coming." Josephine followed the doctor to the door.

"It was no problem," Gordon replied, then looked at Lucas. "No more strawberries for you, young man."

"Good night, ladies," Jared said, starting to back out of the room.

"Wait." Rebecca rushed to the door and touched Jared's arm to stop him. "Do let me know how Isabella does. We'll be praying for her."

He nodded, covering her hand with his own. His earlier panic washed away and was replaced by a comforting peace. He again swallowed hard, not understanding how she had such an effect on him. "I'll do that."

As the men left, Charlotte closed the suite door and leaned against it. "Do you want me to take Lucas and get him to sleep, miss?"

Rebecca shook her head. "You go get some rest."

"I can stay up with you," Josephine offered.

"No. We'll be to bed shortly." She settled in the rocking chair with Lucas

When the room was quiet, she laid Lucas on her lap, applied the salve then wrapped him loosely in a thin blanket. She rocked him until well after he'd fallen asleep. Her mind wandered to Isabella and the difficult time she must be having. Jared's concerned expression told her he feared the worst. He'd experienced it firsthand losing his wife and child. She recalled the night Mariah gave birth to Lucas and the unforeseen complication that took her life. She didn't understand why bringing life into this world had to be so dangerous.

Lucas whimpered in his sleep as she slowly rose from the rocking chair. She nuzzled his cheek with a kiss and put him in his crib.

She turned the wick low in the oil lamp until the light dimmed and crawled into her own bed. Her heart ached with worry for Isabella and concern for Jared. She silently prayed the night would be easy on both. *Please God let Isabella and the baby survive.*

****

Jared paced the front porch of his foreman's house in one direction while Paxton paced in the other. The sun slowly rose in the sky, announcing a new day. Their eyes meet briefly as they passed the other.

"Something's wrong. I know it." Paxton muttered, swinging his arms and balling his fists. "The baby should be here by now."

Jared stopped in mid-stride and caught Paxton by the arm. "It should, but for some reason this time's different."

"But it shouldn't be. She's healthy and strong."

"And that will go in her favor," Jared said wishing he had total faith in what he said, but for Paxton's sake he added. "We have to believe that."

The words had not left his mouth until they heard the sound of a newborn's cry.

A smile spread across Paxton's face. "The baby's here."

"Go find out if you have a son or daughter." Jared laughed, slapping the man on the back. *Thank you, Lord.*

"Aye, I think I will."

A few moments later Mary came out carrying a steaming cup of coffee. "It's a boy."

"How is Isabella?" Jared took the cup.

"She had a rough time. The baby was breech and the mid-wife couldn't get him turned. Doctor Gordon had a difficult time of it himself." Mary placed her hands on her ample hips and stared out into the sunrise. "If you don't object, I'm going to take the girls back to the house with me, Mr. Hollingsworth."

He nodded. "Of course. Keep them there as long as you see fit."

"You don't look well," Mary remarked. "A body would have thought you were awaiting the birth of a child too the way you paced out here with Paxton."

Had his worry been so evident? "I remember what it was like, the waiting," he said, not wanting to elaborate.

Mary nodded. "And now that all is well you can put that fear to rest."

Jared drained the cup and handed it back to her. "I'd better see to the field hands this morning. I don't think Paxton will be in any shape to carry on his normal chores today."

Mary gave him a worry-filled glance. "And what about you?"

"I'll be fine," he assured her. Heading for the walk, he added. "I've worked on much less sleep before."

He was halfway down the stone path when Mary called, "I'll have breakfast waiting when you return to the house."

"Thank you." Heading toward the field, Jared figured he could work for at least two or three hours on the adrenaline coursing through his veins. He found most of the hands preparing their tools and water buckets for the long day ahead.

"Good news, men. Mrs. Paxton delivered a healthy boy this morning," he announced.

Cheers erupted, and gratitude at the men's loyalty for their foreman surged through Jared.

"It's about time he got a son," Simpson shouted, and the other men called varying agreements.

"I don't expect you'll be seeing Paxton today. It was a long night of waiting and worrying. Simpson, I'm putting you in charge," Jared said, and they nodded in understanding. "I want all men in the fields today. I'll see to the stables. That should make the work go faster."

When he reached the stables, Higgins was already grooming the horses. The man looked up and stopped mid-brush when Jared entered.

"Everything all right, sir?" Higgins asked.

"Yes. It's a boy." Jared grabbed a rake and went to muck out the stalls before using the pitchfork to line them with fresh hay. They worked in silence until Mary rang the bell, calling them in for breakfast.

Wiping sweat from his brow, Jared left Higgins to go wash up. As he approached the main house, a briskly moving carriage entered the driveway and surprise halted his steps. Rebecca and Josephine Davis were sitting in the back of the hired hack. Grabbing his handkerchief, he quickly wiped his hands and stuffed it back into his pocket. The vehicle pulled to a stop by the front steps and he lengthened his stride.

"Rebecca! Miss Davis. What brings you out here?"

She gave him a shy smile. "I hope you don't mind

our showing up uninvited, but I was so worried about Isabella. I sent Charlotte to check at Doctor Gordon's this morning, but he hadn't returned. This news didn't set well with me. How is she?"

"In the doctor's capable hands. You'll be happy to know I was wrong. They have a son after all."

"Marvelous!" Her smile broadened, and Jared's weariness vanished.

"Mary has just put breakfast on the table. Won't you both join me?" he asked, offering Miss Davis his hand.

"Thank you, Mr. Hollingsworth." Her smile was as wide as Rebecca's

Jared looked up at the sky to see if it was falling. Josephine Davis had not been pleased with him since their first meeting. Even their last meeting had been strained, and he wondered what had changed.

"We've already had breakfast," Rebecca explained.

"But coffee would be nice," Josephine added.

"Certainly," he agreed, offering her his hand again.

After Jared had helped them both descend, Rebecca fished in her purse for some coins and paid the driver. "Can you return for us in a few hours?"

"That isn't necessary," Jared said. "I can have Higgins drive you and your aunt back to town."

"We wouldn't want to impose," Josephine interjected.

"I insist." Jared offered Rebecca his arm.

"Thank you, Mr. Hollingsworth," her aunt said and followed them up the walk to the verandah.

Mary appeared at the front door as they approached. Despite her smile, she looked flustered. "I began to wonder where you got off to, Mr.

Hollingsworth. Your guests are waiting."

Jared nodded. "Please set two more places, Mary. Miss Davis and her aunt will be joining us. If you'll excuse me ladies, I must wash up."

"It's a pleasure to see you again, Miss Davis," Mary said, and showed them into the dining room. "Girls, Doctor Gordon, we've got two more additions to breakfast. Miss Davis and her aunt."

"Good morning, Doctor Gordon," Rebecca greeted. She glanced at her aunt who had stopped in the doorway and just stared. Slowly Josephine reached up and touched the back of her neck before coming into the room. Twin patches of color bloomed in her cheeks.

"Miss Davis, Miss Davis." Doctor Gordon stood and bowed to them both. "How is Lucas fairing today?"

"Better, the rash is almost gone. He's also stopped fretting so much," Rebecca said, taking the chair the doctor pulled out for her. "Thank you."

"My pleasure," he said, pulling out a chair for Josephine.

She quickened her pace to the table, allowing him to seat her. "Thank you," she murmured.

"You're welcome," he said, returning to his seat. "I'm glad to hear Lucas is doing so well. I'll drop by this afternoon to see him if you don't mind."

"Certainly," Rebecca agreed. "How's Isabella doing?"

"I left her resting." He turned his attention to Josephine. "How's the ladies' auxiliary work going?"

"Very well. I've almost finished the front panel of one quilt. Mrs. Thackeray is doing the back."

Rebecca watched the interchange between her aunt and the doctor. Josephine was actually smiling at the man.

Oh my goodness. She's flirting with him.

Fascinated, Rebecca watched the exchange between the two. Awareness dawned and she understood the many subtle changes in her aunt's appearance. The new hairstyle, the new dresses and even the softening of her posture was because of Doctor Gordon. She hid her smile for fear they'd notice her observing them. She couldn't wait to tell their maid.

Chapter Seven

Ancil Gordon found himself enthralled with the bewitching woman sitting across from him at the breakfast table. His first impression of Josephine Davis had not been favorable when he rushed to the Bakersfield hotel when they met. He'd found her prim and extremely tense. In fact, looking back, he'd have to say his behavior toward her had been downright rude. Yet, something he'd said must have made an impression to cause such a remarkable transformation in her.

He now saw a beguiling creature he couldn't take his eyes off. The tension around her mouth was no longer evident and her harsh expressions had softened. She smiled and her violet eyes twinkled. She laughed and his weary heart beat with a new passion.

He found his reaction to her startling. Instead of putting distance between them, he wanted to draw her near. He wanted to learn what had made her frosty cocoon melt away.

"I'm glad you're enjoying your service to the ladies' auxiliary," he said, lifting the coffee cup. He took a slow sip and watched her over the rim.

She poured cream and sugar in her cup. "A finer group of ladies I haven't met. They've taken me in as one of their own. You don't often find that kind of acceptance. It's a true testament to southern hospitality."

"I'm sure Constance would enjoy hearing your opinion. She's devoted many years to the group."

"I can tell the organization would fall apart without her instruction," Josephine said.

He noted a forced smile on her lips as she spoke. He'd seen that smile before whenever he'd mentioned Constance to her. *Could Josephine be jealous of Constance?*

Ancil pondered the notion, reaching for another biscuit. Surely he was wrong.

"Sorry to have taken so long." Jared stopped before his chair and shot the Paxton girls a look of disappointment. "You started without me?"

A peal of giggles rippled from them. Each sported a milk mustache above their upper lips. Their blond heads bobbed.

Ancil half-grinned. They were quite adorable. He'd missed out on the chance to have a family, devoting himself to his profession. Being a doctor didn't give much time for a man to pursue a personal life. He'd learned that the hard way almost fifteen years ago. No woman wanted to play second fiddle to the sick. She wanted a man who'd be home every night, all night, to warm her bed. A man who wouldn't miss their engagement party because he attended an ailing widow's deathbed.

He looked back at Josephine, wondering if she'd tolerate the demands on a doctor's life. She appeared too practical with her charity work to not understand the call of his profession, but could he take the chance to find out for himself?

He slowly breathed in the aroma of fresh coffee and lemon verbena. He'd noticed both Miss Davises favored the fragrance. Looking up, he admired how the color of Josephine's dress complemented her beauty. His gaze locked with hers. He expected her to look away. Instead, her eyes twinkled over her cup, her mouth's curve suggested a smile.

Unexpected heat crept up his neck and the collar of his shirt felt tight. Unsettled, he set his cup down rather hard, spilling the liquid on his hand and the tablecloth.

"Doctor Gordon, hold still and I'll get that for you." Mary pulled a dishtowel from her apron band as she brought in Jared's hot plate of food.

"Did you burn yourself, Ancil?" Josephine asked, using his Christian name. Was it a slip? Or did she do it on purpose?

"No, I'm fine, thank you." Annoyed at his clumsiness, he shooed Mary away and stood. "Thank you for breakfast, Jared. Ladies, I've enjoyed your company." He looked at Josephine again and held her gaze longer than he should before speaking. "Perhaps I'll see you at Midday service again, Josephine. If you'll excuse me, I need to go check on Isabella and the babe before heading back to town."

Nodding, Josephine watched the doctor leave, and silently exhaled. *He'd called her by her Christian name.* Never had she found the sound of her name more lyrical than when he spoke it.

"Would you like more coffee, Miss Davis?" Mary asked, drawing her attention away from her thoughts.

"No, thank you. I believe I've had enough." Josephine sat back in her chair, clasped her hands in her lap and relaxed. She watched the young girls enjoy their breakfast. The oldest, Harmony, reminded her of Mariah at that age.

She sighed, and continued to watch the girls until Mary shooed them off to the kitchen to help make cookies, leaving the adults alone. Emptiness filled Josephine when they left and she realized she missed Mariah dearly. The poor girl had lost her life too young without learning the truth. A truth Josephine wasn't certain she could ever confess.

Shaking her head, she turned her attention where Rebecca and Mr. Hollingsworth were exchanging quiet conversation on the other end of the table.

"Mr. Hollingsworth, I noticed you have a lovely flower garden. Would you mind terribly if I leave you and Rebecca to finish your breakfast and go for a walk?"

Jared looked up and smiled. "Please feel free to enjoy the garden to your heart's content, Miss Davis. We'll join you shortly."

"Thank you." Josephine stood and touched Rebecca on the shoulder before she left them.

Once her aunt was out of the room, Rebecca covered her sudden laugh with her hand.

"What's so funny?" Jared asked.

"I think my aunt is smitten," she said in a low voice.

"Smitten?" He frowned.

"With Doctor Gordon."

"Ancil Gordon?"

"Yes." Rebecca held in her exasperation. "Haven't you noticed a difference in her since you first met her?"

He nodded. "Yes, but I thought it was because her headaches had gone away. I never would have imagined she fancied Doctor Gordon."

"I know. Isn't it miraculous?"

He furrowed his brows. "Do you think the feeling is mutual?"

Rebecca toyed with her napkin. "I'm not sure. Didn't you see him watching her over his coffee cup?"

"You mean to say you were *spying* on them?" Jared's warm smile was infectious and she returned it with one of her own.

"Of course," she admitted. "She is my aunt. She's lived a guarded life for far too long. I'd hate to see her feelings hurt the first time she's ever allowed herself to show interest in a male companion that I know."

"As would I." He covered her hand with his own. The heat from his touch radiated up her arm and filled her chest with warmth. Their eyes met and he held her gaze with his own far longer than he should.

Rebecca felt her cheeks flush warm and she looked away lest he see the effect his touch, both physical and visual, had on her. She didn't understand the perplexing effect he had on her either. Sometimes she felt as if she'd burn to an ember on the inside from an innocent touch or glance.

Jared pushed his chair away from the table. "Would you like to have a tour of the house?"

"Yes," she said far too eagerly, but she...they...needed a distraction, if he felt anything like she did when they were alone.

She waited as he stood, pulled back her chair, and offered her his arm before leading her into the foyer. His golden hair still hung in wet curls around the collar of his crisp white shirt. Standing this close she could not help but inhale the clean, spiced soap scent and heat threatened to flame her cheeks once more as she imagined him in his bath.

"Let's start upstairs. I'd like to show you the library. It was my mother's favorite room in the house. She loved to read. The shelves are stocked with all her first editions of the classics."

Rebecca smiled, her heart beating faster with each step. She naughtily thought about him bathing, water glistening on his rock hard body. Even though he was dressed, she couldn't stop sneaking a look at him. She imagined his skin was just as tanned underneath his clothing as above. He no doubt removed his shirt when working in the hot fields, letting the sun bake him. Her desire to touch him was strong. Her mouth felt dry and her heart beat a little faster.

She missed her footing on the next step and stumbled forward, but he caught her, helping her right herself.

"Are you all right?" he asked when they reached the landing.

Embarrassed, she looked away and nodded. She didn't understand what made her lose all propriety when she was around him. They'd just met, but she'd simply die if he didn't feel anything for her. She felt like a silly goose allowing herself to hope that he did. She stepped closer to him and laid her hand on his chest.

He blinked and she saw the surprise in his eyes that she'd touched him.

"Do you like me, Jared?"

Her unexpected touch seared his flesh and he hesitated a moment trying to read her thoughts before he answered. "Yes. I like you. Why do you ask?"

He could feel the rise and fall of her breasts as she stood so close to him. Her emerald eyes were dark and her lips were pink, inviting him to taste them if he dared.

My God yes, I like you. Inwardly he groaned, but did he dare to confess his desire to her?

"Come with me." He entwined his fingers with hers and led her quickly into the library past the many bookshelves of leather bound volumes. He walked over to an alcove for privacy. Turning around, he pulled her close until she was pressed against him. "I like you far more than I should for the time I've known you, Rebecca."

She swallowed. "You do?"

With his free hand he cupped her cheek, caressing it gently. He rubbed the pad of his rough thumb over her lips. They trembled in response and he lowered his head, nibbling at her mouth with small kisses until she responded in kind. Without warning, he parted her lips with his tongue and captured her mouth, exploring its depths.

Her hand crept up his arm to his neck, holding his head so he couldn't pull away. Her fingers speared through his damp hair, sending shivers down his spine.

His body hardened and he groaned, pulling away before he lost his head completely. He walked toward the French doors on the opposite side of the library afraid she might see what had started out as an innocent kiss had done to him. He didn't want to frighten her, or make her think he was on the verge of losing control.

Startled by her reckless behavior, Rebecca calmed her breathing and admired Jared as he stood facing the French doors. She didn't know what had gotten into her asking such a question. But she'd received her answer. It frightened—yet excited her—that he felt the same about her after only meeting a few days ago.

She smiled and wondered if it could finally be happening for her. Had she met the man with whom she'd spend the rest of her life?

Still staring at him, she noticed how nicely he filled out his clothes and her naughty mind went to wandering again. She recalled his kiss and her knees trembled. She never imagined a kiss could drain her of her strength. But then, she'd never kissed a man before, and not just any man, a man like Jared Hollingsworth.

You're supposed to be a widow. A widow with a child who has had experience kissing a husband, sharing his bed, making love to him and bearing him a child.

Silently, she groaned at the thought of her lie to Jared and she worried that she'd revealed herself by her reaction to his kiss. *Had that been the reason he'd pulled away? Had he suspected her inexperience?*

As if sensing she stared at him, he turned and held out his hand to her. She walked toward him, moistening her bruised lips with the tip of her tongue. He pulled her close against his chest, lifting her hand to his mouth. He brushed his lips across her knuckles and shut his eyes.

Rebecca's cheeks warmed. *Was he as shaken by their kiss as she?* Closing her eyes, she breathed in his manly scent. She wanted to stay in his arms for the rest of her life, but that was a dream. She couldn't abandon Lucas.

What about Ruth? Have you forgotten about her?

Frustrated by the thought, she tensed. Why was getting this poor woman to her family becoming such a problem? Her attempts to complete the mission had been halted by one factor or another. He hadn't even acknowledged her last missive. How much longer could she wait before pursuing the mission at hand?

She took a deep breath. "Jared?" Her voice cracked as she spoke his name.

"Yes?" He slowly opened his eyes. His warm smile of contentment nearly took her breath away.

"I think it's time we started discussing our plans for Ruth. I must get her out of Jackson soon."

His brows furrowed and he stepped away from her. "I'll do anything for you, Rebecca, but I really don't see how I can help you with this."

"You don't?"

He shook his head, opened the French doors and walked out onto the upper verandah. He glanced at her over his shoulder before he spoke again. "No."

"B—but—" His words made no sense. How couldn't he help her with the mission? He was her liaison after all, wasn't he?

With the force of a bolt of lightning realization dawned and she felt a sickly churning form in her stomach. She thought back to the first missive from her liaison. He'd said he'd be in touch and he'd be wearing a yellow rose.

Jared had worn a yellow rose, so why had he never discussed the mission with her? She'd been the one to initiate talk of Ruth and it had led to nothing.

The churning in her stomach tightened and she couldn't breathe. She opened her mouth to speak, but no words would come. The horror written on her face reflected in his eyes and she knew her knees would buckle underneath her.

Oh my God! He's not Hollingsworth. He's not my liaison. What have I done?

She'd wasted all this time, possibly putting Ruth and her real liaison in danger. Bile filled Rebecca's mouth as the thought of what could happen if they were caught during the transition. Her temples throbbed and she took a few deep, steadying breaths, which made her feel that much more light-headed. She swayed.

"Rebecca! Are you all right?" Jared caught her before she collapsed.

She laid her head against his chest and breathed in the spicy scent of him until she regained as much of her composure as possible. Tears of frustration formed in her eyes and she couldn't stop them from streaming down her face. The committee had put their trust in her to complete this mission and she'd failed.

"No, no!" she cried.

"Rebecca, what is wrong?" The urgency in his voice made matters worse because she knew she couldn't tell him the truth.

She wiped her eyes with the back of her hand. "Jared, I must return to town at once." She stepped out of his arms to the railing and looked down into the garden until she spotted her aunt near the rose bushes. "Aunt Josephine! Aunt Josephine! We must leave now."

"Rebecca, what the devil is going on?" he demanded, coming up behind her.

She tried to smile, but failed. "I'm sorry to frighten you. But, I must return to town and take care of a matter immediately."

"Does this have anything to do with Ruth?"

She nodded, stepping away from him. "Please

don't ask. I can't explain."

Jared watched as she turned and rushed from the library, disappearing down the hall.

What the hell had just happened?

Chapter Eight

Jared stalked to the railing and watched Josephine join Rebecca in front of the house. She was still deeply upset. Josephine looked up at him with an icy glare.

Jared jammed his hands in his pockets and went down the back stairs out to the stables. He avoided Mary and the Paxton girls. He wasn't in the mood to speak to anyone.

Inside the stables, he spotted Higgins brushing a young colt. "Miss Davis and her aunt need to return to town. Please prepare the carriage at once."

"Yes, sir," Higgins replied, dropping the brush into a nearby bucket.

Jared did an about face and joined the women at the edge of the garden where Josephine tried to calm Rebecca.

"The carriage will be ready for your departure shortly, ladies."

"What have you done to my niece, Mr. Hollingsworth?"

"He hasn't done anything," Rebecca said, pacing.

"Well something happened to upset you," Josephine declared.

"Rebecca—" He tried once more to speak with her, but the carriage rolled up and Higgins jumped down to assist them inside.

"Thank you for your hospitality, Jared." Rebecca spoke the formal, expected words, but there was no warmth.

How could she dismiss him so easily? Damn it, she owed him an explanation of some kind. He wanted to demand she explain herself, but his pride wouldn't allow her to see she'd affected him. Nor did he want to discuss it in front of her aunt

"Good day, ladies."

"Good day, Mr. Hollingsworth." Josephine's curt nod and clipped tone irritated him further as the carriage drove away.

His jaw clenched. How dare the woman assume the worst when he'd done nothing wrong. He'd welcomed them into his home. His only fault was he'd allowed himself to be manipulated by Rebecca's beguiling smile. Her beauty. She made a complete package of temptation wrapped up with innocence.

Too much innocence for a widow.

****

As soon as they returned to the hotel, Rebecca rushed upstairs to check on Lucas.

"How's my boy?"

"He's napping, miss." Charlotte looked up from the settee where she folded diapers.

Rebecca crossed to the bedroom. She stood at the crib in silence and watched Lucas sleep. Soon her breathing slowed, matching his. Her heart ached so badly at the feared ruined mission that she turned away. She went to the bed, fell across it, and cried until the tears fell no longer.

She'd failed miserably at her first assignment for the Vigilante Committee. It had all seemed so easy when she accepted this task.

"Now, now," Josephine soothed, sitting down on the corner of the bed and rubbing Rebecca's back. "Why don't you tell me what's wrong?"

Rebecca looked up, wiped tears from her face, and sniffed. "There isn't anything you can do to help me. I've made a terrible mistake. A terrible mistake."

"Did he try to take advantage of you?"

She pushed herself to a sitting position and stared. "How can you even think he'd lay a hand on me?"

Josephine patted her hand. "I did leave the two of you alone in the house without a chaperone. I know the housekeeper was preoccupied with those darling girls so it was possible he took liberties."

Rebecca's cheeks flamed. How could Josephine assume Jared's guilt so easily? "The mistake I speak of is my own doing. Jared had nothing to do with it, unfortunately. And that is the problem."

Josephine gaped at her, covering her heart with her hand. "Are you saying you acted the wanton and he refused you?"

"No!"

"Then I don't understand."

In spite of the tears flowing down her cheeks, Rebecca threw back her head and laughed.

"What's so funny?"

"You. Not everyone finds intimacy outside of marriage as scandalous as you do."

Josephine crossed herself. "I'm going to pretend I didn't hear that. Surely you wouldn't consider going to a man's bed that wasn't your husband's."

"If the moment arose and I loved the man deeply and he loved me the same..."

Her aunt clutched her hands together and looked up to the ceiling. "Heavenly Father please forgive her for saying these things which she surely doesn't mean."

She shouldn't tease her aunt, but she couldn't help it when the woman frustrated her so much. She wiped the remaining tears from her eyes and got up from the bed, knowing what she had to do. "I have some letters to write. Thank you for the talk."

"But you haven't told me what's wrong," Josephine called after her.

Rebecca ignored her, going into the sitting room. There was no need to explain. She'd said more than enough already.

Sitting down at the secretary, she took out a sheet of stationery and began writing the hardest letter she'd ever written, and yet the simplest. It was the Vigilante Committee's code for defeat.

By sending it, she'd be admitting failure on her first mission to her superiors. But what more could she do? She'd been unsuccessful in meeting her liaison. She'd never reached Ruth.

Dearest Ophelia,

I hope this letter finds you well. I, however, am at my wits end. Please send assistance before I drown.

Your dutiful servant,

R. J. Bingham

*****

Josephine watched Rebecca struggle with her letter. She didn't understand what had gone on between her niece and Mr. Hollingsworth. But if Rebecca said it was her mistake, she would have to accept that explanation.

She knew all too well about making mistakes

where love was concerned. She'd lived the last eighteen years repenting for her youthful transgression. Finding solace in her conviction to serve the church, she had never questioned the Almighty for taking her Charles away at a young age.

Josephine took out a handkerchief and her lace prayer veil from the top dresser drawer. She checked her hair, fixing a few pins to secure the chignon before putting on the veil.

"I'm going to Mass. Would you like to join me?" she asked.

Rebecca looked up and shook her head. "I don't want to leave Lucas for too long."

"Very well. I'll see you later."

It bothered Josephine that Rebecca didn't practice their faith more diligently. She'd tried to set a good example for her niece after her brother and his wife had died. However, she feared she'd failed, especially now that she had proclaimed she'd have no regret taking a lover before marriage if she desired.

"Youthful folly." Josephine murmured. She stepped out of the hotel onto Main and spotted Doctor Gordon coming toward her. He waved and she waited for him at the corner.

"Good afternoon, Doctor Gordon. Are you going to Mass?" she asked.

"I am after I check on Lucas," he replied.

"He's napping at the moment."

"Well, then perhaps afterwards." He offered her his arm. "Do you mind walking over with me?"

"I'd like that." She felt her cheeks warm when she took his arm. "How are Mrs. Paxton and the baby doing?"

"They're good after the ordeal. Her coloring has returned and the boy is eating heartily. Paxton's puffed up like a bantam rooster."

"That's wonderful. I'm so glad you were able to save that family from heartache. My d-niece died in childbirth last year."

"I'm sorry to hear that, Josephine."

"Thank you, Ancil."

He reached across and patted the hand that lay in the crook of his arm and they walked toward St. Anna's. She relaxed beside him, matching his step with her own. She smiled when Constance Fletcher and two other women from the ladies' auxiliary came out of the mercantile. Constance didn't look pleased and that made Josephine smile even brighter.

****

Shading her eyes from the noonday sun Rebecca stepped out of the hotel. She waited a few moments for her eyes to adjust to the sun before she headed to the post office to mail her letter. She wanted to return before Lucas woke.

Down the street she saw her aunt and Doctor Gordon going into St. Anna's for Mass. It looked like things were progressing nicely between them. Good. Her aunt needed love and it wasn't too late for her to have a family if she desired.

Josephine as a mother! What a thought.

Rebecca entered the post office and waited in the short line for her turn.

"Good afternoon, Miss Davis," the postmaster greeted when she stepped to the counter. "I have a letter for you."

"You do?"

He nodded. "It came this morning."

She looked down at the envelope in her hand and decided against mailing it just yet. She shoved it back in her purse.

The postmaster handed her the letter and she stepped away to read it.

Dear Miss Davis,

Please forgive my delay. Unforeseen circumstances have kept me from procuring the item in question. Will notify you within the week.

Your faithful servant,

R. Hollingsworth

A thrill of delight filled her. Ruth was safe. Her liaison had been delayed. She hadn't failed the mission. She held the letter to her chest and said a silent prayer to heaven that she hadn't put the woman in jeopardy after all.

Her liaison would be in touch within the week. And her liaison was R. Hollingsworth.

R. Hollingsworth? Could he be related to Jared? Only time would tell.

****

Crouching low in tall grass, Rory surveyed the surroundings and waited for the mocha-skinned woman in a faded red dress to come closer. He'd spoken with her briefly a few weeks earlier in this very spot. She'd been alone that day, and he'd expected today would be no different. Yet, he was having a devil of a time snatching her. Three other women waded in the water nearby washing a mound of homespun clothing.

Perspiration beaded his forehead and upper lip as the morning sun beat down on his head. He had to get the woman's attention without alarming the others.

There would be hell to pay if the women saw him and could describe him to the authorities.

"You there," a large man on a horse called, riding up and stopping near the water's edge. "You're wanted at the house."

Rory's brows arched as the woman he'd been watching picked up a basket of clothes and started toward the main house at a brisk pace. When the man on the horse was preoccupied, Rory slowly inched his way toward a thicket of bushes and trees that ran along the path she took. He'd already scoped out the area and knew no one watched.

He grabbed a handful of pebbles along the way and began throwing them in her direction, hoping to distract her so she'd stop. She paid little attention at first, but when he threw a stick that landed a few inches in front of her she slowed.

"Ruth," he called, keeping his voice low.

The woman's head jerked, but she moved a little slower.

"Ruth."

Finally, she stopped and looked around. Her eyes grew large and worried as she scanned the area.

"Over here."

She turned in his direction, acknowledgement evident in her brown eyes.

"It's time." He reached out his hand to her.

Silently, she jumped into the bushes where he waited. "Leave the basket hidden here. We haven't got a minute to waste. You'll be with your family soon."

Ruth nodded.

He took a huge risk seizing her during the day. Normally escapes were at night. No one would be expecting it to happen in daylight. Though, when she didn't immediately arrive at the main house as requested a search would begin.

Adrenaline pumped through his veins as he silently led her through the wooded area, careful to avoid stepping on twigs or fallen limbs. Searing pain shot through his abdomen with each move he made. He winced and touched his side. Blood seeped through the rudimentary stitches in the flesh he'd haphazardly sewn last night and stained his shirt. He never should have agreed to one last round of cards when he'd already won the pot. A sane man would have cleared out of town. Instead, he'd followed greed and the loser pulled a knife to regain his losses.

The wound was yet another headache he had to contend with as he tried to complete the mission. He was over a week late in meeting with his contact, but he'd been thrown in jail after a brawl. He'd sent word upon his release explaining the delay, something he rarely did, not living by traditional standards. He enjoyed living dangerously. The higher the risk, the more he enjoyed the gamble.

When they reached the black carriage that awaited them, Rory opened the door and helped Ruth climb inside.

"There are clothes for you to change into in the box. I'll ride on top with my driver until you are dressed. Use the cane to rap on the roof when you're finished, and I will join you," he explained before closing the door behind her.

"Did you run into trouble?" his driver asked.

"None, thankfully." Rory grimaced at the twitch in his side as the carriage headed toward Jackson.

He placed a handkerchief over the blood stain and donned a full waistcoat to cover the soiled shirt. He tied his blond hair back in a queue at his neck. No one would deny he looked like a gentleman traveling with his lady friend.

A few moments later they heard the rap of the cane and the carriage slowed to a near crawl. He opened the door, filling the inside with light before he joined her. Then he closed the door and pushed the velvet curtains all the way open.

"My, but don't you make a pretty picture." He settled on the bench across from her taking note of the way the yellow dress hugged her scrawny frame, enhancing her features. "From now until I say otherwise, you are Delia, a fallen dove from New Orleans. Do you understand what I mean by 'fallen dove'?"

She nodded.

"You'll be staying with a friend of mine and *her* girls. She'll protect you until I can safely get you to the next leg of the journey."

"I won't be one of *her* girls," Ruth protested, indignation thick in her voice.

A deep rumble escaped him at her misunderstanding and he held his side until the pain subsided. "You'll be hidden away. She won't make you work for your room and board. I'll be your only visitor."

Rory watched her brown eyes widen. The girl was frightened, as expected in her current situation. It was his place to make her feel more at ease, but he did a poor job of it.

He picked up a medium size box lying on the seat

beside him and removed the lid. "Here, you'll need a wig to pull off your disguise. Try this on."

The wig of ebony curls glistened even in the dim light of the carriage and it made her skin look more sallow than mocha against the pale yellow of the dress. He studied her for a few moments then handed her a pouch.

"You'll need to learn to wear this as well. Lip and cheek rouge will draw attention away from your dark eyes. The face powder will make you look whiter," he explained, recalling the detailed technique Monique had showed him before he left Jackson a month ago. "We might just pull this off."

She shook her head, but he pushed the pouch into her hands.

"We made a deal when I first found you. You agreed to do everything I said in order to get you to your family."

She nodded. "I remember."

He opened a secret compartment underneath the opposite carriage seat and withdrew a summer weight cloak. "You'll wear this over your dress to help cover your arms as we exit the carriage and enter the *house*. Gloves will cover your hands. Your skin must always be covered. Do you understand?"

She nodded her head, the curls of the wig bouncing on her shoulders.

"How do the shoes fit?" he asked, reaching to lift the skirt of her dress, but she slapped his hand away.

"I ain't never worn shoes before."

"I know, but you must try."

"They hurt."

"Sorry. They were the closest I could get to the

measurements I took. You won't have to wear them long," he assured her.

"Now, try to relax and I'll tell you a tale about Madame Monique and her girls."

Chapter Nine

"What do you think of this pattern?" Josephine held up the quilt topper she'd been sewing for the last few days.

Rebecca examined it from her place on the floor by Lucas. "Very pretty. Do you think they'll give it to a little girl?"

"I can only hope."

She smiled, refolded the missive from Jared she'd received earlier that afternoon, and slipped it into her pocket.

"You've read and reread that since it came by messenger today. I can only assume it is from Mr. Hollingsworth?"

Her cheeks warmed. "Yes."

She picked up one of the blocks on the blanket, and turned it over, thinking about Jared. She longed to see him and apologize for her behavior the last time they were together. His letter indicated he was eager to see her again and hoped they could meet later in the week.

"Rebecca, are you in love?" Josephine asked.

Caught off guard, Rebecca's head jerked up and she stared at her aunt, "In love? I—I…"

"No need to answer, dear," her aunt amended. "It was a silly question. You hardly know the man. I can see you're troubled by the mistake you think you made.

If it has nothing to do with him, then I suggest you put it behind you and go forth with the relationship."

If you only knew how much I wanted to do just that. Rebecca stacked the block on two others, making a small pyramid. Lucas squealed in protest, knocked them down, and laughed.

"Oh really, sir?" she said, gently ruffling his hair. "Do you really want to do that?"

He grinned. She glimpsed the first signs of a tooth underneath the gum. He reached his arms out for her to take him. She obliged and he cooed, blowing spit bubbles.

"You spoil him, Rebecca."

She wrinkled her nose at her aunt. "Isn't that what children are for? To love and spoil?"

Josephine mumbled something under breath and went back to her sewing. Rebecca loved Lucas and she'd dote on him all she wanted, no matter what her aunt thought.

"How's Doctor Gordon?" she asked, breaking the momentary silence.

Josephine dropped her needle, but recovered it without looking up. "How should I know?"

"I thought he attended Midday services with you."

"Yes, he does." Her voice took on a defensive note. "But that doesn't mean I speak with him regularly."

"Really?" Rebecca managed not to smile. She'd watched from the hotel window and seen them meet at the corner before walking to the church together almost daily. If that didn't suggest a developing friendship, what did?

"Weren't you going to pay a visit to Mrs. Paxton this afternoon?"

Rebecca jostled Lucas on her lap and gave her aunt full points for smoothly changing the subject. She'd put off going to Oak Hill for a few days, but now that she'd heard from Jared she didn't have to worry about accidentally seeing him while there.

"I guess I should go on if I want to return before supper. Charlotte, will you put Lucas down for his nap?"

"Yes miss," Charlotte said, coming into the room with a spool of thread Josephine had requested.

Rebecca kissed Lucas good-bye, and handed him to the maid. "Mama will be back soon. Have a good nap."

"M-m-m," Lucas cooed.

"Enjoy your visit, dear," Josephine called.

****

Frowning, Jared exited the bank. He'd expected the news he'd received, but had hoped for better. Even though he'd paid his monthly note on time for the last year, he'd been turned down on a further note to cover Rory's gambling debts. It had taken the bank three weeks to make this decision leaving him little time to come up with an alternate solution and prevent Delaney from claiming Oak Hill.

Mitchell's inquiries into Rory's whereabouts had produced nothing. It didn't look as if his cousin would resurface in time to make good on his markers to Delaney either. For that, Jared vowed to do bodily harm to Rory when he saw him again despite his resolve not to strike another human being.

He crossed the street to where Higgins waited. Mitchell had also suggested at their last meeting that he consider remarrying a wealthy woman. But to marry for money wasn't something he wanted to do. And even though he had met Rebecca and found her extremely desirable, he was hesitant to enter into a marriage with her just to save Oak Hill. He knew of marriages based on financial need, and they were rarely happy unions. He felt it was only right that Rebecca have love in *their* marriage.

The thought stopped him dead in his tracks, and he stared off into the distance as he thought about what he wanted. *When had he started thinking about marrying Rebecca?*

"Where to sir?" Higgins asked.

Did he really want to marry her?

He'd married for love the first time, but losing his wife and child had left him cold. It had taken several years for him to even allow another woman to get close to him again. But Rebecca had. He'd realized that whole-heartedly when he'd kissed her. She'd been so soft and trusting in his arms.

He felt in time he could love her the way a husband should his wife. There was no question about it. This realization made him feel hope was within reach. Oak Hill could be saved and he wouldn't have to compromise his principle to do it.

"Mr. Hollingsworth?" Higgins called again.

Hearing the concern in his driver's voice, Jared looked up. "Wait here. I have another errand to run."

"Certainly, sir."

Jared turned and headed toward the Bakersfield Hotel. Rebecca hadn't invited him, but his letter had said he would call within the week.

He straightened his waistcoat as he walked down the street imagining what he would say. That is, if she would accept his call. She must. He would not go away until he spoke to her. He needed to know whether she had developed feelings for him or not before he spoke of marriage. He knew he was rushing this, but if he gave himself too much time to think he'd back out.

"Jared?"

He looked up at the sound of her voice. Grinning at his own folly, he hurried toward her. "Rebecca, I didn't see you."

"You looked as if you were on an important errand." She tilted her head to the side. Her emerald eyes twinkled.

"Yes I was. In fact, I was on my way to see you." He took her hand, and she stepped closer. "Why is it you look more lovely every time I see you?"

Her cheeks flushed. "Do I?"

"Oh yes." He lifted her hand to his lips, brushing them gently across her gloved knuckles. "Where, may I ask, were you going?"

"I was on my way to hire a carriage so I could pay Mrs. Paxton a call. I didn't see her the last time I was at Oak Hill as I had planned."

"Were you? How fortunate for you that I'm in town on business. Would you consider sharing my carriage so we may talk...privately?"

She nodded.

"Excellent." He placed her hand in the crook of his arm and led her back to his carriage. "How is Lucas doing?"

"Very well. The rash is gone and his first tooth is visible under the gum."

"Good for him." He smiled and stopped beside the carriage. Motioning for Higgins to stay put, he opened the door and helped Rebecca inside. Instructing the driver to return to Oak Hill, he settled next to her.

He took her hand in his again. "I've missed you."

"You have? Even after I…"

"Yes." He turned to face her. "I didn't like the way our visit ended. Something upset you, dear Rebecca, and I apologize if I somehow caused it."

She smiled. He'd called her dear. Her pulse quickened and she covered his hand with her other.

His blue gaze met hers. Heat radiated off his body, enveloping hers in a warm cocoon. Her mouth dried, and she yearned for him to pull her into his arms and kiss her like he had in the library.

"You said you wanted to speak to me in private?" Her voice wobbled.

Abruptly, his smile vanished. He released her hands, and leaned back, his shoulders squared as if preparing for battle.

"Oak Hill is in danger. I'm afraid I'm about to lose the plantation."

His flat tone sent a chill racing along her skin. "Surely not."

"The bank refuses to extend any further loans on the property to cover a new debt I've accrued at my cousin's negligence," he continued, staring at the opposite seat. "He's gambled and lost a small fortune, and he's signed my name to cover the note. To make matters worse, a river boat gambler holds Rory's markers and is coming at the end of the month to auction Oak Hill if I don't come up with the money to purchase the markers back."

"How awful." She reached for his hand and held it tight between hers. "Is there any way I can help?"

His mouth set in a grim line. "No, there isn't. Oak Hill and the Hollingsworth name are facing ruin. I dare say you will not want to be associated with me once the plantation is gone."

"Don't say that. There has to be another way. Isn't there someone you can approach to borrow the money from? A friend? A relative?"

He stared at her. "That isn't an option."

"Surely there is someone? What about Mr. Cooper?"

He shook his head. "I couldn't ask him to make that kind of sacrifice. He has to support Elizabeth now."

"There has to be another option," Rebecca insisted. "Your land alone has to be worth the bank's interest."

"It's more complicated than you can possibly understand."

"How?" She asked as the carriage rambled along.

"Do you remember the wedding, when those around us were talking in whispers, giggling behind their fans?"

She nodded.

"And how Mrs. Calhoun turned when I spoke with her?"

"Yes," Rebecca said slowly, remembering the slight. "Perhaps she was preoccupied with Elizabeth's wedding."

"No. That wasn't it," he said. "Did you not notice when we were at the hotel dining room later that evening and the couple asked to be seated at another table?"

Again, she nodded, trying to make sense of these clues and what they meant.

"I'm not accepted among the other plantation

owners because I use hired labor instead of slaves. If it weren't for Mitchell being my friend and attorney, I wouldn't have been invited to the wedding. Mrs. Calhoun was showing her guests that even though I was there, I wasn't welcome."

"So that explains it," Rebecca said slowly. "I'd wondered why they treated you so. How perfectly awful." A wave of tender affection for this man surged through her. She couldn't change the town's opinion of him, but she could save Oak Hill.

"Let me help you, Jared. I want to buy Rory's markers."

Jared's lips parted in surprise. "That's out of the question. I couldn't possibly—"

"—lose Oak Hill?" she interrupted. "That is exactly what will happen if you don't come up with the resources. I want to do this, Jared. I want to make a difference. Let me help you."

He took hold of her forearms and looked her square in the eye. "I didn't tell you about Oak Hill to solicit money from you. The fact that you would offer proves you are so very special, Rebecca."

Her cheeks warmed, and she thought she would wilt at his scrutiny. The way his gaze raked over her made her feel faint.

"I know this isn't the most opportune time to ask. Not when I'm facing total ruin. But—"

"Yes?" Her voice caught in her throat.

"I want you to be a part of my life, Rebecca. I want you and Lucas to come live at Oak Hill. I'd be honored if you'd agree to be my wife. Will you marry me?"

She had waited for so many years to hear those words spoken by a man she loved. It was all she could do not to fling herself into his arms and shout yes. But she couldn't. She couldn't accept his proposal. There was too much at risk for her to seek her own happiness and pleasure when she still had to see Ruth to safety.

"Oh Jared, I think I could be falling in love with you. And even though I want more than anything to say yes, I can't. Not now."

"Because of Oak Hill?"

"No. I love Oak Hill. The first time I saw it I knew I'd love living there."

His brow creased and he searched her eyes with a long look. "You've just come out of mourning. Is it too soon?"

"I don't care about that."

"Then what?"

She cupped his cheek with her hand. She couldn't risk telling even him about her involvement with the Vigilante Committee. If she were caught during her assignment, it would be far better for him not to know. For him to answer truthfully to not being aware of what she was really doing in Jackson.

"Darling, I can't tell you. I wish I could, but I can't."

He flinched out of her reach, as if her words stung him. "Don't you trust me?"

"I'd trust you with my life."

"Then why won't you tell me why you can't marry me?"

She shook her head.

"Is it Ruth?"

His accusing stare pierced her to her core and she swallowed back a sob. "I'm sorry. You must accept my answer without questioning me."

A moment of silence passed between them and she watched his jaw tighten.

"Higgins!" Jared yelled.

His driver pulled them to an abrupt stop and dismounted, hurrying to Jared's side of the carriage. "Yes sir?"

"Take Miss Davis to the Paxton's, then see she gets back to town," he ordered, opening the door and stepping to the ground. "I'll walk the rest of the way to Oak Hill."

"Jared, please, you must understand," Rebecca pleaded, reaching to touch him.

He stepped away, his gaze cold and hard. "I thank you for your company, Miss Davis, and your offer to aid Oak Hill, but like you I cannot accept the offer."

His tone stung and she bit back tears as she watched him turn and walk away. He had every right to be upset by her refusing his proposal. She wasn't happy about it either, but she couldn't agree to marry him and endanger Ruth. She shivered at the thought.

"Are you all right, miss?" Higgins asked, closing the carriage door.

She forced a weak smile. "Yes. Thank you."

"Then we'll be on our way." He gave a nod and disappeared to the front of the carriage.

After he was gone, she covered her face with her hands and gave into her anguish and pain, letting the tears of frustration flow. Why did this have to happen now? Jared's timing couldn't have been worse.

This wasn't the way things were supposed to happen.

Chapter Ten

Josephine tied her bonnet and reached for her gloves. She turned when the maid entered the parlor.

"Charlotte, I've run out of thread. I'm going to the general store to get another spool. I hope I can get the right color. The quilt will be ruined if I don't."

"Yes, Miss Josephine." The girl carried an empty bottle to the wash pan on the dining table by the window.

"I won't be long." Josephine closed the suite door behind her still worried over the color of the thread. She had just enough left on the spool to make a match. If the mercantile didn't have the color, then perhaps one of the women in the Ladies' Auxiliary would.

"Josephine Davis."

She looked up and forced a smile when she saw Constance Fletcher and two other women from the auxiliary coming down the corridor.

"Good afternoon ladies."

"Good afternoon to you, Josephine," Constance said, stepping closer. "We were just coming to pay you a call."

"Were you?"

"Oh yes." Sybil Macklin confirmed.

"We apologize for not sending word ahead of our arrival," Constance offered. "But the matter is of the utmost urgency."

Josephine nodded. "I understand."

"It's about your niece," Sybil spoke in a low voice.

Her niece? Josephine's spine stiffened. *How could they have found out about Mariah and Stuart Delaney?* "What about my niece?"

"We really hate to be the bearers of bad news," Constance began, "but we feel it our Christian duty to help a fellow sister out when we see danger approaching."

"Danger? What kind of danger?" Josephine's voice rose. She took a step back and bumped against the door.

"Now, now. Don't get excited," Jenny Silvers, the other woman in the trio, soothed.

"We really only wanted to warn you. We just saw Rebecca getting into a carriage with Mr. Jared Hollingsworth." Constance looked pleased at the pronouncement.

"Without a chaperone!" Sybil interjected in a whisper.

"Not to mention the man is less than desirable as a suitor," Jenny added.

Josephine swallowed, slightly relieved it was Rebecca and Mr. Hollingsworth they meant. She didn't find being cornered friendly in the least. "I see. And what makes the man less than desirable?"

Constance touched her arm. "Since you are new to town we realize you have no way of knowing what kind of person your niece is associating with. Perhaps we should go inside where we can talk more candidly."

"More candidly? How can you be *more*?" Josephine asked.

Sybil and Jenny snickered.

"May we come in?" Constance asked.

She pressed her lips together and reached behind her to open the door.

"Charlotte, change of plans. I'll be having company for a while. Will you run down to the store and see if you can get me the spool of thread?"

"Yes, miss." Charlotte dipped a curtsey. "Should I order a pot of tea sent up from the dining room?"

Josephine looked at her guests and when they nodded in agreement she consented. "Yes, please do."

"Anything else, miss?" Charlotte asked, taking the spool from her and a coin.

"That will be all." Josephine removed her bonnet and turned to the ladies. "Please, have a seat."

"You're servant is well mannered," Constance commented.

"You were saying about Mr. Hollingsworth?"

"It's really quite simple," Constance continued. "He's not accepted in polite society."

"And why is that?"

"Really, Josephine," Jenny scoffed. "Do we have to spell it out for you?"

"Yes, I'm afraid you do. What has Mr. Hollingsworth done to receive such disapproval from the *Ladies' Auxiliary*?"

"It isn't just the auxiliary," Jenny pointed out.

"Have you been to his plantation?" Constance asked.

"As a matter of fact I have."

"Did you notice anything *strange*?" Sybil inquired.

"Strange?"

"Yes, strange," Jenny added.

Josephine thought on this a moment. She'd been in

his house and then in the garden. She drank coffee. Then his driver brought her and Rebecca back to town.

"Nothing peculiar comes to mind."

"Nothing peculiar," Sybil and Jenny said in unison and giggled.

"The servants...?" Constance prodded, sounding impatient.

"What about *the servants?*"

Constance pursed her lips together. "Most of his servants are like *your* Charlotte. And we won't speak of the others."

My Charlotte? The others?

"Oh, you mean..." Realization dawned on Josephine and she didn't like it. "What's wrong with that?"

Jenny folded her hands in her lap. "What's wrong with it is no other plantation is run that way."

"It just isn't done," Sybil remarked.

A knock on the suite door stopped Josephine from commenting.

"Come in," she called and a waiter rolled in the tea trolley then exited, shutting the door.

Her ire with the women for their narrow mindedness rose. The audacity that they came to visit her out of Christian duty was laughable.

"Frankly ladies, I don't think it is any of our business how Mr. Hollingsworth chooses to run his plantation." She poured tea. "If he prefers hired labor to purchasing—"

"But—but," Jenny sputtered, taking the cup from Josephine. "It can lead to unrest at other plantations."

"There's even been word around town that a plantation over in McCleary County had a girl run off in broad daylight. They've not even been able to find her," Sybil added.

"Do you think other owners want this to happen to them?" Constance asked. "I know my Hiram opposed it when he was alive."

"No, I'm sure they don't. But it doesn't mean it will happen. Surely the *good* people of Jackson aren't going to hold this against Mr. Hollingsworth?"

The three women exchanged glances, set their untouched cups on the table, and stood in unison to leave.

"I thought you'd see reason, Josephine. You didn't appear to be so naïve when Ancil brought you to the auxiliary. I'm afraid in lieu of this revelation we will no longer need your services."

Josephine stared at the women. "Constance, you don't mean that?"

"Yes I do. And if you or your niece continues to associate with Mr. Hollingsworth, you will no longer be welcome at St. Anna's for worship. I will see to that."

Jenny and Sybil nodded in agreement.

"You can't do that. I don't believe Father Bohannon would allow it."

"We can and we will," Jenny assured her.

"We'll also need your sewing project back, if you don't mind." Sybil picked up the quilt topper lying on Josephine's sewing basket and examined the material. "Nice stitching. I'll finish this for you."

Josephine grabbed the topper out of Sybil's hands. "No you won't. If the *good* ladies of the auxiliary won't allow me to finish this for the orphanage then I'll do it on my own. I know the perfect plantation where they'll appreciate true Christian charity."

She marched to the suite door not believing the lengths these narrow-minded biddies were taking. "Ladies, before you go I must ask where in the Good Book does it say you have replaced God on *His* throne and man should now live by your rules?"

The trio gasped and crossed themselves.

She jerked open the door and stepped out of the way. "I bid you good day."

The clicking sound of their self-righteous heels filled the hallway as the women descended the stairs.

Josephine slammed the door and stormed across the room, pacing back and forth. *Who did they think they were, coming into her suite and telling her whom Rebecca could or could not see?*

"Are you all right, Miss Josephine?" Charlotte asked, returning from the errand.

Josephine ignored the girl. Realization of what she'd done shook her. By defending Mr. Hollingsworth, she had no doubt labeled herself a pariah. If word spread of this then she could be run out of Jackson.

"Miss Josephine?"

"I'm fine," She answered through clenched teeth.

"Are you sure?"

She swung around, fixing her stare on Charlotte. "Yes I'm sure. I don't want you saying a word about this to Rebecca. She doesn't need to know I've been banished from working with the Ladies' Auxiliary."

"*Mon Dieu!*" Charlotte crossed herself.

Josephine faintly smiled at the young woman. "Help yourself to tea if you like. No one touched it. I'm going to take a walk to clear my head."

"Are you sure you'll be all right by yourself?"

"Certainly," Josephine grunted. It would take more

than a walk to cool her temper, but she needed to regain composure before she warned Rebecca.

As she walked along the street, she contemplated how she would approach the subject with her niece. She would make it clear she did not oppose Mr. Hollingsworth. Heaven knew they'd butted heads enough on the issue of Mariah to last a lifetime. She longed to bare her soul to Rebecca about her past. However, until Rebecca married it would have to wait.

More importantly, she would no longer live her life in fear of what others thought. Being a part of a women's charity society did not have to be her calling, especially if the women who comprised it were like Constance and her followers.

"Hello, Josephine," a deep, male voice broke through her thoughts and she looked up, surprised to find herself standing in the small yard outside of Ancil Gordon's house.

"G-good afternoon, Ancil."

"Is everything all right?" he asked and set down a toolbox. He wiped his hands on a rag and closed the screen door he'd been repairing.

"I'm out for a walk," she explained and noticed his sleeves rolled up to his elbows. The sinewy veins on his tanned forearms spoke of his strength. The bronze coloring of his skin piqued her curiosity. Why had she never noticed this before?

Her pulse quickened at the thought of him shirtless standing before her and she wondered if he worked with his shirt off when no one was around.

"And you ended up at this end of town?"

"What? Uh- yes. Imagine that."

"The mind can cause a person to do peculiar and

even unexplainable things. Your walking this way had to be for a reason. Are you sure I can't help you with something?"

"No, thank you." *Nothing that's proper for an unmarried woman.*

"Everyone's fine?"

"Yes."

He shoved his glasses onto the top of his head, rubbed his eyes, and let the glasses fall back into place. "The sun sure is hot this afternoon."

"Yes it is." She felt perspiration begin to bead at the back of her neck. Whether from the heat of the day or her illicit thoughts she didn't know.

"Would you like to have dinner with me tonight?"

"I beg your pardon?"

"I said would you like to have dinner with me? I hear the dining room at the hotel is having an Italian extravaganza tonight. I thought about going. Would you like to join me?"

"Well—I—I suppose I could join you." Her spirits lifted and her turmoil over Constance faded. "Yes, that would be lovely."

"Good. I'll call on you at seven," he said, grinning.

"I'll be looking forward to it. Thank you for asking," she said, unable to stop smiling. "I'd best be running along now."

She turned and headed back down the street with more vigor in her step than she'd felt earlier. If Constance objected to Rebecca's association with Mr. Hollingsworth, then how would she react to Ancil's invitation for her to have dinner with him?

Josephine laughed. Yes, she was certain Constance would be fit to be tied when she learned the good doctor was having dinner with a pariah.

****

Rebecca let the driver help her down from the carriage outside the hotel. "Thank you for driving me home, Higgins."

"It was my pleasure, miss," he said. "I hope you feel better soon."

"Thank you."

"Good day to you now." Higgins climbed back up in the driver's seat.

Rebecca watched Jared's carriage roll away and a tightness in her chest formed anew. The pain of seeing it leave reminded her of the emptiness she felt inside as he'd left her earlier to proceed to the Paxton's alone.

Why did he have to propose today? Why couldn't he have waited a few more weeks? If she'd completed her mission, she could have accepted, and they'd be happily planning a future together.

She needed finality. She needed to see her assignment finished. Turning away from the hotel, she walked the short distance to the post office.

"Can I help you, miss?" the clerk asked as she entered the building.

"Yes. Are there any letters for Davis?"

The clerk nodded and handed her an envelope. "Came this morning."

"Thank you. Have a good day."

She hurried outside and sat on the bench where she could read the missive.

Miss Davis,

Please plan to meet me at ten in the morning on June twenty-eighth in the Lady's Chapel at St. Anna's. I've been assured we'll have total privacy.

Your dutiful servant,
R. Hollingsworth

Tomorrow! Blasted postal service! It was always so slow. She refolded the letter and tucked it safely inside her purse. Her pulse quickened. She'd finally meet the illusive Mr. R. Hollingsworth.

Excited, she headed back to the hotel to begin making plans for her return to Memphis. By the time she returned from her trip, Elizabeth would be home from her wedding tour. She looked forward to hearing her friend's romantic musings. Perhaps Elizabeth could give her advice on handling the situation with Jared.

Rebecca quietly entered the suite so not to wake Lucas if he were napping. The scent of lavender filled the air. She could hear Lucas' gurgles and Charlotte reciting a nursery rhyme to him in the servant's quarters.

"I'm back," she called.

"Rebecca, I'll be finished with my bath shortly. I need to speak with you if you have a moment," Josephine's voice rose from behind the dressing screen. "How is Mrs. Paxton?"

"She's doing well. Little William is adorable."

"What do the girls think of him?"

She grinned, recalling how they'd doted on him. "They adore him, especially the youngest one."

"That's nice. Will you hand me a towel? I left it lying on the bed."

She crossed the room and picked up the downy towel. She noticed a dress she hadn't seen before on the bed. Josephine had been shopping again. "Are you going somewhere?"

"I've been invited to dinner this evening. Will you

be able to get along without me?"

She handed the towel around the screen. "Certainly. Will you need a chaperone? Should I send Charlotte with you?"

"Absolutely not!" Josephine exclaimed, and then more calmly spoke. "I mean...there really isn't a need for a chaperone. I'll be downstairs in the dining room."

"With anyone I know?"

"Yes."

"So, you're going to the Italian extravaganza with Doctor Gordon?"

"Don't sound so smug. It isn't becoming of a lady."

"I'm glad the doctor has finally taken notice. I'd hate to see you throw yourself at him."

"Rebecca Kathleen Davis!"

The splashing sound of her getting out of the tub covered up the later mumblings. "I have never thrown myself at a man and I do not appreciate you even uttering those words. I'm a God fearing Catholic woman who has worked hard to walk in the right path..."

"And I expect the same from you." Rebecca finished the litany she'd heard more times than she could count. Josephine threw her wet towel at her.

Rebecca laughed so hard her side began to hurt. "I was only teasing."

"I don't find the subject funny." Josephine stepped from behind the screen in her robe and glared at Rebecca. "Shut the door. I need to speak to you in private."

She did what Josephine asked and perched on the edge of the bed. "I apologize for making light of your reputation."

"Making light of your reputation can lead to serious consequences," Josephine began.

"I'm sorry for doing so."

"Rebecca, I'm not talking about my reputation, but yours. After you left a few of the women from the Ladies' Auxiliary paid a call. They saw you getting into Mr. Hollingsworth's carriage without a chaperone."

Rebecca winced. She decided to explain her actions before Josephine assumed the worst.

"I ran into him on my way to hire a carriage, and he offered me a ride. Since I was going to Oak Hill I didn't see why it would hurt joining him."

"The ladies informed me that Mr. Hollingsworth's reputation is not stellar. In fact, they find him unsuitable as a suitor," Josephine explained crossing her arms. "I, on the other hand, do not hold the same opinion. In fact, I find more favor with him for standing firmly on his principles using hired labor than bending to society's rules."

Rebecca nodded. "And he's ostracized by the other plantation owners for it."

"Exactly. It's a pity. I think he'd make you a suitable match. But there could be consequences if you are inclined to pursue it. There will be talk and heaven help us if they should somehow learn about Mariah and Lucas' parentage."

She blinked, not believing her ears. *Had Josephine just declared her approval of Jared?* She turned away and tried not to show how pained she was to learn of her aunt's favor with him. It made her refusal to his proposal even harder to bear. She quickly sought a way to change the subject.

"I—I'll be making a trip back to Memphis tomorrow evening to take care of some financial business with my attorney. Since I'll be returning for the remainder of our stay, I don't see any reason to put you and Lucas through the journey. Will you mind staying in town?"

"Can't the business wait?" Josephine asked, sitting down at the dressing table. "I don't feel right about you leaving right now."

"I'm afraid not. Normally I'd take Charlotte with me as a companion when I travel, but I feel she is needed here to help you with Lucas."

Josephine turned around, looking as if she were about to protest, but nodded. "I think that would be wise."

"Thank you for understanding. I hope you enjoy your dinner with Doctor Gordon."

"Thank you dear, I plan on it."

Chapter Eleven

Josephine was ready and waiting when Ancil arrived for their dinner date. Yet she stayed in her room until Charlotte answered the door and announced his arrival. She immediately noticed he'd paid a visit to the barber. His hair looked trimmed and he wore pleasant smelling cologne.

"Do you enjoy Italian?" he asked as they descended the staircase to the hotel lobby.

"Yes. I spent two months in Rome many years ago. I became fond of the region's food."

"Have you traveled extensively?"

"I've enjoyed two trips to Europe. Once in my youth and two years ago with my d-niece Mariah."

"Mariah?"

She saw questioning in his eyes as the waiter showed them to a table.

"Rebecca's sister. I mentioned her the other day. She passed on last Christmas."

"Yes, I remember. I'm sorry for your loss, Josephine." He pulled out a chair for her.

"Thank you, Ancil."

The waiter handed them both menus and poured water in two glasses. "I'll give you a moment to decide what you'll have."

Josephine made her choice and laid the menu on

the table in front of her. She casually glanced around the dining room, noting the change in décor to resemble an Italian Bistro. Tables were draped with red and white plaid tablecloths. A display of Chianti bottles wrapped in twine lined one wall and a single violinist roamed the dining area playing an exotic tune, entertaining the guests. In her perusal of the room, she recognized a few faces as others staying at the hotel. The rest she knew from around town. She'd come to enjoy her visit to Jackson and for many reasons she wasn't looking forward to leaving. However, Constance Fletcher and her followers could make it impossible for her to stay.

"Is something wrong, Josephine?" Ancil asked, concern a little too heavy in his voice. To her surprise, he reached across the table for her hand. His touch was light, but warm.

"Why do you ask?"

"Your walk today. You were clearly preoccupied with something or you wouldn't have ended up at my house."

Josephine sighed and nodded. "Ancil, do you believe that a church official would bend to the desires of one parishioner over the good of the whole congregation?"

He drummed his fingers on the table top before answering. "I've seen it happen before, but the outcome was not good. Why?"

"I'm not one to spread gossip or even start it. I'm concerned by what I've heard though. Do you think Father Bohannon is the type who would?"

"Father Bohannon is a good man. He is faithful in his service to the Lord. I've known him as long as I've lived in Jackson."

"That's the opinion I have of him as well, but I haven't known him that long so you see why I would ask."

He nodded.

The waiter returned and took their order. When he left, she asked, "How well do you know Constance Fletcher?"

"Quite well. Her mother married my father when I was a young man."

Josephine's mouth suddenly felt dry and she was sure her cheeks had flushed at his revelation. *Constance Fletcher was his step-sister.* The thought was extremely unnerving. She reached for her glass of water and took a long drink. "I had no idea," she finally said.

"Few make the connection without being told."

The waiter returned quickly and set down their food, refilled their water glasses and left without a word.

"Has Constance done something?" Ancil asked.

She didn't want to admit she'd been handed an ultimatum, but she couldn't pretend nothing had happened either. "Constance and her friends have their opinion on how certain people should carry on with their lives. In the same accord, they feel others should not associate with those who live outside social barriers. If they do, then they should be banned from attending church or participating with church functions."

"Like the auxiliary?" he asked.

She nodded.

"Constance opposes Jared Hollingsworth's preference of using hired labor and she has seen Rebecca with him, am I correct?"

Josephine blinked and put down her fork. How had he suspected the reasons for her questions? She wiped her mouth on her napkin feeling less ill at ease with the subject. "Yes. She also claims if I do not discourage Rebecca from seeing him then she'll go to Father Bohannon and we'll no longer be welcome at St. Anna's. I hate to imagine what Constance would do if she learned you and I have become friends."

A grim smile formed at his mouth. "Constance has a high opinion of herself and the lofty standing she claims within this community. Much of this came from her husband's position before he died. However, please know that she doesn't dictate how I view others. Especially those I choose to associate with and call my friends. Is that clear, Josephine?"

She slowly nodded. Knowing he considered her his friend should have made her happy, but she wanted desperately to know he considered her more.

"Good. And while we're speaking on this, I wouldn't worry about Father Bohannon giving one fig as to what Constance has to say either. He admires Jared's stand and has said so to Constance's chagrin."

"I'm so glad to hear it, Ancil. I've worried all afternoon on what I was going to tell Rebecca if we should be turned away from the church."

He reached for her hand again and squeezed it. "Don't worry further. As for our seeing one another, I'll have a talk with her myself and make sure she understands my feelings on the matter."

"Your feelings?"

Ancil half-grinned and squeezed her hand again. "I like you, Josephine. I hope the feeling is mutual?"

She nodded. Her stomach did flip-flops and she

couldn't eat another bite. "Very mutual."

"Good. I'm not one to beat around the bush either. I'd like to call on you for a drive Sunday afternoon. Have you seen much of Jackson other than your visit out to the Hollingsworth plantation?"

"No. I haven't. I'd enjoy going for a drive with you."

"Excellent."

She pushed her food around on her plate for a few moments and tried to contain her excitement. She looked up and found him watching her. "Rebecca will be out of town for a few days. Would you like to have Sunday dinner with me before we go for that drive?"

"That would be nice."

"I think so too."

After coffee and dessert of gelatos, Ancil invited her for an evening stroll before he walked her back to her suite.

"Will I see you at Mass tomorrow?" he asked.

"Yes."

"Until then." He said, taking her hand and brushing a light kiss across her knuckles.

"Until then."

She lingered in the hall watching him descend the stairs until she couldn't see him anymore. When she entered the suite Charlotte was preparing a bottle for Lucas.

"Would you like anything, Miss Josephine?"

"Hmm? Oh. No, Charlotte. I'm fine. See you in the morning."

"Good night to you."

"A very good night."

Chapter Twelve

Rory checked his pocket watch and rechecked it a few minutes later as he waited for Miss Davis to arrive at the Lady's Chapel located off from the High Altar inside St. Anna's Church.

In the distance he heard the clicking of heels only a female's shoe would make. He ducked behind the statue of The Virgin Mary and watched as she stopped momentarily before the stoup, dipped her fingers in the holy water and crossed herself before entering the chamber. When she had seated herself in the back of the chapel, he imitated a cricket's call.

In answer, the woman sneezed three times. He approached slowly, admiring her profile and fair complexion. The color of her hair was hidden beneath a dark lace prayer shawl.

"Miss Davis, I presume?" he whispered.

She nodded without looking in his direction. "Mr. Hollingsworth?"

"At long last."

"Yes, I—" her words stumbled as she turned, emerald eyes widened. "Jar—Jared?"

Puzzled by her calling him his cousin, he settled in the pew beside her and asked the simple question, "You know Jared Hollingsworth?"

"Yes. But you look like—"

"I know. It's a curse, I assure you," Rory explained.

She stared at him for a moment and then her features changed as if she suddenly realized something important. "It was you. You sent me the letter when I first arrived to town. You were supposed to have met me at Elizabeth's wedding. Not Jared. Yet he was there because he and Mitchell are friends. Not because of our mission. It all makes sense now. No wonder he didn't know about Ruth."

Rory stiffened as her babbling made sense to him. "You told Jared about Ruth?" He reached out and grabbed her by the arms and shook her. "Good God, woman. What were you thinking?"

"I thought he was you!" She glared at him and flinched away from his hold causing the prayer shawl to drop to her shoulders. "Your letter said *you'd* be contacting me soon, and *you'd* be wearing a yellow rose. How was I supposed to know the man I later met wearing the flower in his lapel wasn't you? He was introduced to me as Mr. Hollingsworth so naturally I thought he was my contact."

"What irony!" Rory exclaimed rising from the pew. He leaned over her and demanded in a softer voice. "How much did you tell him about Ruth? Is the mission in jeopardy?"

Her back stiffened at the question and she shook her head, boldly looking him in the eye. "What about you, Mr. Hollingsworth? You were several days late upholding your end of the bargain. How do I know you didn't jeopardize the mission?"

"Touché. I ran into a little problem, but I assure you it did not put Ruth in danger." His hand went to his side where the cut still smarted even after a few days of being stitched.

"Are you certain my brilliant cousin didn't figure out what you were talking about?"

"Yes. I dropped a few hints about her, but when he didn't comprehend, I ended the conversation. I was certain I'd put her life in danger until I received your letter a few days later about the delay. I was ready to send an abort letter to the committee." She shook her head. "He must have thought I was daft, and yet, he still wanted to marry me."

"He wanted to marry you?" Rory looked at his cohort more closely. He could understand why his cousin would want to marry her for she was a beauty and she had spunk. "You must be an amazing woman, Miss Davis. The last time I saw Jared, he was heartbroken over losing his wife and child. All he could talk about was throwing himself into making Oak Hill prosperous and turning a profit without using—"

"You're quite the scoundrel, double-crossing your cousin. Oak Hill's facing ruin because of you and your gambling debts," she spat, her emerald eyes growing dark.

He smirked. "Good to know my cousin spoke so highly of me."

"Don't pride yourself in your folly. He confessed his financial burden to me so I'd know what I was getting myself into if I accepted his proposal."

"And did you?"

"Not that it is any of your concern, but no. I couldn't. Not when I didn't know how this assignment would turn out. I couldn't risk connecting him more than I possibly had. Now knowing you too are associated with him proves I was right in my hesitation."

Rory nodded, grateful for her admission. Women who worked for the Vigilante Committee were always courageous and compassionate for those in need of assistance. Her commitment to the cause was worthy. And yet she obviously loved his cousin. Why did Jared have all the luck? First, Charisse and now Miss Rebecca Davis loved him.

He mentally shook himself and refocused his attention on the matter at hand. "About the assignment, have you made arrangements for your passage?"

She nodded. "We leave tonight. There's a late train departing at eleven that will take us to Grenada. From there we will go on to Memphis."

"Perfect." He took a piece of paper from his pocket and handed it to her. "Meet me at this location no later than ten and I will deliver the package to you. Do you have a cloak? If not, get one. You will not want anyone seeing you at this establishment."

"Then why—"

"Sh-h-h. Someone's coming."

The sound of approaching footsteps grew louder. The murmur of voices faded into silence and the footsteps retreated. When he was certain they would not be overheard he answered her question.

"Because no one will expect it."

Miss Davis stared at him before speaking again. "You take pleasure in this don't you?"

Rory grinned. "It's the chase that makes the game pleasurable. Just like chasing a woman. The pursuit is more satisfying if there's a challenge. You'll find Delia waiting for you."

"Delia?"

"Her new name. It fits her disguise."

Rebecca watched as Rory turned and left the chapel. A chill crept over her as she waited a safe amount of time before she followed, replacing her prayer shawl on her head. Once again she feared for her safety and Ruth's as she passed through the corridor leading into the sanctuary.

Out of the corner of her eye she saw a priest approaching her. Alarm that he'd overheard her conversation with Rory filled her and she turned her head in his direction.

Her sudden movement startled the man. He stopped at the end of the pew. "Are you troubled, my child?"

She swallowed. How could this man take one look at her and read her soul? She slowly nodded.

"Father, I know it isn't the appointed hour, but will you hear my confession?"

"Of course."

Taking a deep breath, she followed him to the nave and the nearest confessional, going inside.

Kneeling, she bowed her head. "Bless me Father, for I have sinned. It has been four weeks since my last confession. My life is a lie. I pretend to be a mother when I'm not for the good of the child. Now, I must journey for the sake of another to have freedom. I seek guidance and deliverance for my deception."

"Kindness, compassion and humility are virtues to seek. Do you love this child?" the priest asked.

"Oh yes, with all my heart."

"And where is the true mother?"

"She died shortly after giving the child life. She

asked me to take him."

"Then where is the lie? One day you can tell the child of his mother."

"But others believe he is mine."

"Giving birth is not always the true sign of being a mother. Loving and nurturing a child is the true form of motherhood."

"Yes, Father. But this journey I'm about to make... I'm risking everything. I thought I could do this...but—but I'm not sure now." She'd known the gravity of the consequences when she took on this assignment, but now that the time had come, she didn't know if she could go through with it. Meeting Jared and falling in love with him had not been in her plan.

"Tell me about this journey. Are you being forced to take this path?"

The priest's words startled her. "N-No, Father," she stammered again. "I chose this journey to help another."

"And you must deceive for the safety of this person?"

"Yes."

"How long will this deception continue? What will happen if you are unable to succeed with this lie?"

Rebecca closed her eyes and took a deep breath before she answered his questions. She'd expected censure not possible understanding from him. Moisture formed at her eyes. "Many lives are at risk, Father. Mine, my family's, and the person I'm trying to help. It's a heavy burden. One I thought I was prepared to carry."

"And now you are not sure?" he asked.

"Yes, Father. What am I going to do?"

"Risking your life for another is a noble act. You should have faith that you will see your goals accomplished. Trust that God will give you the strength to see it through. Keep your rosary with you and pray to the Blessed Virgin daily."

She nodded, prepared to rise, but stopped when he spoke again.

"But know this, a lie is a lie no matter the reason you tell it. I cannot absolve you for this sin when I know you are going to continue in this path until your journey is complete."

"I understand, Father." She took a handkerchief from her bag and dried her eyes. "Thank you."

"You're welcome, my child. Go in peace." The priest made the sign of the cross then closed the portal between them.

Go in peace. The thought was difficult when accompanied by an image of her swinging from the end of a rope. The image was so real in her mind she felt herself suffocating, and she gasped for air.

"Stop it, Rebecca," she told herself. "You can't start doubting your resolve now."

The priest was right. She'd chosen this journey. It was a noble act. She'd accomplish her goal and return to raise Lucas. There was no need for her to worry.

Still, she had a nagging feeling that tonight would not play out the way she imagined.

****

"I do wish you'd allow me to see you off at the train station," Josephine complained as Rebecca gathered her things later that evening.

"It isn't necessary. I'll be fine. I'd like to know you are here in case Lucas should awake. This is the first time I'll be away from him for more than a day. It makes me nervous just thinking about leaving him even for a short trip."

"Then you need to be away from him more," Josephine said, startling her. This was not the same woman from a few days ago. Her aunt sounded more confident. It made Rebecca feel better about leaving the child in her care.

"There's nothing to worry about," Josephine continued. "I think I can handle the boy while you're away. We'll be just fine."

Rebecca hugged her one last time, tighter than she intended. "I know you will. I love you both very much."

When she broke away from the hug, her aunt gave her a questioning look. "You're not eloping are you?"

"No."

"This sudden trip has nothing to do with Mr. Hollingsworth?" Josephine crossed her arms over her chest, looking stern.

"Absolutely not. I told you I have some financial matters to attend, and I must see my lawyer immediately. I'll be back within the week if all goes as planned."

Her eyes narrowed as she continued to study Rebecca. "All right. You have a safe journey. I'll see you when you return."

Rebecca kissed a sleeping Lucas on the cheek as Charlotte held him. "Mama loves you dearly, little one. Take care, Charlotte."

"Yes, miss. There's nothing to worry about. He'll be fine."

Nodding, she took a deep breath and without

further delay, she turned, picked up her bag and cloak, and headed to the door.

A knock sounded before she reached it. She stopped and her heart skipped a beat. What if Rory had been caught after he left St. Anna's and somehow the authorities had linked them together?

"Heavens, who could that be at this late hour?" Josephine said.

"I don't know." She still didn't move toward the door as another knock came.

"Aren't you going to open it?" Josephine asked, impatiently.

When she hesitated further her aunt implored, "Rebecca, did you hear me?"

"Yes. Yes. I'll get it." She forced her feet to take the remaining two steps to the door. She opened it wide and was stunned seeing the man on the other side. "Jared!"

"Hello, Rebecca."

Goose flesh prickled her skin as his gaze roamed over her, taking in her attire. "Going somewhere?"

"As a matter of fact, I am. What are you doing here at this late hour?"

"I need to speak to you. May I come in?"

The polite gesture would have been to invite him inside, even at this late hour, but she didn't have time to spare. She had to meet Rory by ten o'clock. She waved to her aunt and stepped out into the hallway, closing the suite door behind her.

Jared backed away, frowning.

"I'm afraid not. I have a train to catch. I'll be back in a few days after I take care of important business. Can't this wait?" She asked, heading toward the stairs with her one bag.

"Rebecca, please. I want to apologize for my reaction yesterday. I wanted your answer to be yes, but I realized my proposal came too soon. You shouldn't have to explain why you turned me down."

"I'm sorry, I really have to go, or I'll miss my train. Can we talk more about this when I return?" *If I return.*

"At least let me carry your bag and see you off," he said, catching up to her as she went down the stairs.

She stopped at the bottom landing and whispered. "I don't think this is a good idea. People are already talking about us."

His brows knitted together. "Who's talking?"

"I'll be back in a few days, and I'll pay a call to Mrs. Paxton," she said loud enough for the night clerk to overhear. He'd been straining his neck as she descended the stairs, trying to hear their conversation.

"Good night, Mr. Hollingsworth," she called over her shoulder.

Jared watched as she stopped outside of the hotel, sat down her valise and donned the garment she had draped over her arm. From the distance it looked like a cloak, which he found odd since it was late June. Yet, she wore it, covering her person from head to toe. He could only see her dainty hand as she reached out to hail a hired cab.

Curiosity demanded he discover what she was doing. He stepped out of the hotel and motioned for Higgins to bring the carriage, and climbed up beside his driver instead of getting in back. He was not surprised at all when the cab he followed turned down Brewerton Street instead of going to the train station.

"Slow down, Higgins. We don't want Miss Davis to spot us following her," he ordered.

"Yes, sir. Do you mind my asking why we're doing so?" The driver pulled back on the reins.

"I suspect she's headed for trouble."

"Then she needs our protection."

Jared grinned at his faithful servant. Taking care of Rebecca was something he was prepared to do. And he might as well get used to doing so if they were going to marry.

His brow furrowed and he thought back to what she'd said on the staircase in the hotel. *People were talking about them.* He clenched his hands into tight fists. His personal reputation being in question was old hat. He had accepted the murmurings behind his back long ago. But to drag Rebecca's reputation down by association was something he wouldn't allow to happen. He *would* find out who was doing the talking.

His carriage slowed even further as Rebecca got out of the cab and turned down an alley.

"Looks like you'll have to walk," Higgins said, pulling the Victorian to a complete stop.

"Wait right here," Jared ordered, and jumped to the ground. He quickly walked down the street and stopped at the alley entrance. He could barely make out her silhouette at the other end of the dim passage. She turned left which took her to Amherst. The only establishments there were a few gaming halls and a brothel. Not a place you'd expect to see a lady visit.

What in the hell are you up to, Rebecca?

The night was quiet except for the sound the click of horse hooves made on cobblestone as Higgins slowly approached with the carriage disregarding his orders.

"Meet me over by the river, but don't let her see you. She's headed toward Amherst."

"Aye, sir."

What's she doing? It's the middle of the night. No woman in her right mind would even consider walking down by the river alone. This explains her wearing the cloak. She thought no one would recognize her if she hid herself.

Jared's breathing grew labored as he walked quickly down the darkened alley. He came out at the other end just in time to see Rebecca pass under a gaslight and enterer *Madame Monique's House of Delights* with his cousin Rory.

Rory!

If someone had kicked him in the gut Jared wouldn't have been more surprised. Or angered. He hurried to the front stoop of the establishment and knocked rapidly until the door opened.

"Well hello, love. You looking for some company tonight?" a painted woman in a snug fitting red dress asked, leaning on the door.

"I believe a well-dressed woman just entered here. Can you show me to her?"

"Ah, I see. You interested in a little ménage á trios?"

"No."

"You want some special pleasure, but you don't know exactly what? I'll get Madame Monique for you. Follow me, love."

Jared watched her saunter into another room and slowly followed, noticing several small parlors where women in silk wrappers entertained gentlemen or served drinks. But he did not see Rory or Rebecca among them.

He didn't get any farther than the stairs when the painted lady returned with a woman wearing a transparent black dress, leaving little to the imagination. Her breasts, round and plump, looked as if they were about to burst forth from the black lace bodice. Sparkling jewels graced her neck and earlobes.

"What can I do for you?" she asked, taking a drag on a cigarette and blowing out a puff of smoke.

Jared coughed. "I'm looking for a couple who just entered this establishment together. The man is my cousin, Rory Hollingsworth."

"Ah, dear Rory." The woman blew smoke rings over his head and winked naughtily at him. "He's busy at the moment, but if you'd like to have a seat I'll be glad to tell him he has a visitor when he finishes."

Jared took a step backwards, finding her words hard to swallow. Rory busy.

"The woman who came in with him. Is she with him now? Does she work for you?"

"What woman?"

"In the cloak."

"Ah, the cloak. Rory likes his women to be mysterious. They must be playing out *la petit chaperon rouge*. This could take hours. Rory is a notorious big, bad wolf. If we listen closely we might hear his triumphant howl as the deed is completed. Won't you have a seat?" She gestured toward a vacant chaise. "We can have a few drinks while you wait."

"I don't want to sit down. I don't want to have drinks." He roared. "I want to see that woman!"

"I can wear a cloak for you," the painted lady in the red dress wrapped her arms around his neck. "I can be anything you want, honey. You don't need Rory's used goods."

He wrenched himself free of the woman's hold and glared at them both. He didn't like their innuendos about Rebecca. There had to be some mistake. "If he's laid one hand on Rebecca, I'll kill him."

Monique snuffed out her cigarette on the stairwell banister and flicked it into a nearby potted plant.

"Chérie, leave the man alone. Go fetch Rory." Monique's tone changed and so did her features. Her smile was gone and now she looked bored. "Tell him the Master of the Plantation is here to see him. We'll be in my suite."

"Oh, so you're the master of Oak Hill? Rory talks about you all the time." The painted lady gave a yearning look and vulgarly blew kisses in the direction of his crotch.

Jared recoiled back a step.

"Come with me." Monique put her hand on his shoulder to draw his attention back to her. "I'm sure you'll wish to speak to your cousin in private. It'll be a nice little reunion."

He followed her down a corridor and up a second staircase into her suite. He'd expected the room to have gildedmirrors, bold colors and gaudy draperies. Instead, the room was soft blue with sheer drapes cascading at the windows and bed frame, giving the room a peaceful and innocent feel much like Charisse had decorated the nursery. The low burning candles around the room added to the serenity.

"Rory said you looked alike, but you're nothing like I imagined." Monique smiled. "Clearly you're the more handsome cousin."

"What else did he say about me?" Jared looked around the room. "Are they here?"

Monique laughed, going to a drinks table. "Oh, not much. Rory's as cunning as a fox. What's your poison?"

"Rory."

"Touché." She poured herself a splash of Bourbon then looked up at him. "Are you sure you'll not join me?"

"I want to see Rory. More importantly I want to see the woman who is with him."

"Patience. Have a seat. Chérie will be along with him momentarily," Monique purred, settling on a chaise. She stretched out on her side letting her hand run down her leg from hip to knee and back again, bringing the sheer black dress up with it. "I have an array of girls who could bring you pleasure if you don't like what you see. You're so tense, Mr. Hollingsworth. How long has it been since you've been cradled between a woman's legs?"

Jared clenched his fists, trying to keep his breathing normal as he silently counted to ten. The very thought of Rebecca entering a place like this sickened him, and to think that she knew his cousin Rory all this time without even saying a word to him infuriated him. She'd deceived him. He'd made a fool of himself thinking he was in love with her. It was obvious he didn't even know her. How could he ever trust her again?

"I've waited long enough. If I have to tear this place apart to find Rory, I will."

A side door opened and his cousin sauntered into the room. "That won't be necessary, Jared. You really should use a little more control. I could hear your venomous voice all the way down the street."

Jared took three long steps toward the younger man and grabbed him by the open shirt collar. "Where is Rebecca? I saw you bring her in here."

Rory laughed, jerking free. "I thought that was you lurking in the shadows out front. But I'd never have guessed you'd stoop to spy on your lady friend. You nearly frightened the poor woman to death. She thought...well never mind what she thought. It isn't important."

"Where is she?" Jared shouted.

Rory sidestepped Jared's second attempt to grasp his collar. "Gone."

He lunged toward Rory and knocked him into a side table. It broke beneath their weight as they toppled to the floor. With a right hook, he slammed his fist into Rory's jaw, then grabbed him by the collar and shook him. "What's your business with her? How long have you known her? Are you lovers?"

His cousin broke free and scrambled away, giving him a look of utter contempt. "If you think any of that is true about Miss Rebecca Davis, then I say you know nothing about her at all."

Chapter Thirteen

Rebecca's heartbeat raced as if she'd run down a road instead of sitting in a private compartment on a northbound train. Rory assured her she'd only imagined seeing Jared follow her down the alley to Madame Monique's. But if it had been him…what he must think of her going into a brothel. *And with Rory.* A man she shouldn't even know. How would she ever explain it all to Jared?

"Are you feeling all right, miss?" Ruth spoke slowly and softly in unbroken words, laying a gloved hand on Rebecca's arm.

"I will be soon."

"Maybe you should get some rest?"

Rebecca shook her head. "I couldn't sleep if I tried right now."

The young woman carefully rearranged her skirts and smoothed her cloak of any wrinkles. "M'neither."

Rebecca watched her companion take pride in her clothing. "You look beautiful, Ruth. The soft butter color compliments your complexion."

Ruth smiled. "Madame Monique made up my face and fixed my hair."

"She did well."

A knock sounded on the sliding wooden, glass paned door and the ticket master stuck his head inside the private side chamber. "Tickets please."

Rebecca handed him their passage stubs and he glanced at them before he smiled and punched the tickets. "Changing trains in Grenada to Memphis. Enjoy your travels." He nodded and closed the door before proceeding down the corridor.

Ruth let out a breath and smiled faintly at her once they were alone again. "Ain't you scared?"

Rebecca nodded. "More than I can express in words. But let's not think about it. We'll be in Memphis in the morning and no one will be the wiser if all goes as planned."

"I hope you're right."

"Here, I brought something to help occupy our time." She reached into her small valise and produced two hooks and two skeins of yarn. "I find crocheting relaxing."

"M' too, miss," Ruth said, taking a hook and skein.

An awkward silence engulfed the chamber, but neither began a project. Rebecca couldn't stop thinking about Jared, and she assumed Ruth was consumed with thoughts of her new home.

"Perhaps we should turn down the lamps and try to get some sleep after all if we can."

She nodded.

Rebecca stood, turned the wicks down on both lamps, and settled herself in the corner. She pressed her cheek against the cool windowpane and watched as the dark night passed. Somewhere between the mingled tree limbs, the moon and stars, her thoughts returned to Jared and his proposal. She'd thought many times about what life they'd be able to build together once this mission was complete. Silently she prayed he'd understand her involvement with Rory, and the need for secrecy. Surely there would still be a possibility for them when she returned. *If she returned.*

****

The sound of a match striking flint and the smell of sulfur stung Jared's nostrils. Sharp pain shot through the center of his head as he slowly opened his eyes to the blinding light shining in his face. Blinking, he held up a hand and shielded his eyes from the white light until he was more awake. His surroundings were foreign, but the fragrance that filled the air seemed familiar, strong and faintly exotic.

He sat up quickly. A little too quick. The room began to spin and he slumped back against the silken sheets, their coolness against his skin startling. "Where the hell am I?" he muttered to himself, not expecting an answer.

"Don't you remember, honey?" a sultry voice spoke to him from across the room, and then the pungent scent of cigarette smoke assaulted his nose. *Monique.*

He recalled coming here looking for Rebecca because she'd been with his cousin.

"Rory!" Jared bellowed, pushing himself up off the bed. He landed on his feet and staggered toward the direction of the voice.

"How about a drink? Bite that dog that bit you last night to cure what's ailing you, honey." Monique caught him before he fell to the floor.

"What am I doing here? In your room?"

She laughed, helping him sink to a sitting position on a step leading to her doorway. "You and Rory tied one on last night, sugar. Don't you remember? After the two of you beat the hell out of each other, you both drank until you passed out."

"But I was on a bed?"

"I couldn't very well let you boys sleep on the floor, now could I? Though I was tempted. Very tempted after the way you carried on. And over that little goody-good when you could have fought over me."

Jared's vision slowly cleared as she spoke and he saw the disheveled state of the room. Chairs lay on their sides, pillows were scattered everywhere, a few with stuffing coming from the sides. Pictures in pewter frames hung askance on the walls. He found her attitude toward what they'd done to the place peculiar. Of course, all the events of last night had been strange. He still didn't know why Rebecca had come here in the first place.

He rubbed the back of his aching head, then his sore jaw and winced when he touched his cut lip. Looking down, he saw his hands were bruised, knuckles skinned. "Where's Rory?"

"Having breakfast downstairs with the girls. Would you like to join him?"

Jared shook his head, but stopped as the room began to spin again from the sudden movement. "I don't think I'd keep anything down."

Monique laughed; patting him on the back then returned to the chaise, her filmy wrapper dancing in her wake. "How about that drink?"

"No."

"Black coffee?" She asked, discarding the cigarette butt in a nearby ashtray.

"Yes."

She pulled twice on a white velvet cord hanging from the ceiling. Within minutes the door opened and a maid rolled in a cart with a coffee service.

"Can I get you anything else, Madame?"

"Please tell Mr. Rory to join us when he's finished."

"Yes, Madame."

Once the maid left, Monique lit another cigarette. She took long draws on it and blew smoke rings into the air.

"When you feel up to it there is fresh water behind my dressing screen and a razor if you wish to clean yourself up. As for your state of dress I cannot provide new, but I can have them cleaned and pressed if you like."

"And then what?"

Monique smiled saucily and wet her lips. "Then you and Rory are going to make compensation for the damages to my establishment. I feel I've been more than tolerant to you boys."

"How much will it cost to compensate you?"

"Tsk—tsk, I thought you to be a smart man, Mr. Hollingsworth. I don't want your money. I want you. And Rory, of course, but I can have him whenever I like."

The door to the room swung open and Rory waltzed in, clean-shaven, sporting bruises and a black eye. "Monique! You look ravishing as always."

"Ravishing," she repeated and smiled. "See Mr. Hollingsworth, Rory knows what I like to hear."

He grinned and winked at Jared. "Monique, what are you up to? He looks mortified."

She chuckled, went to Rory and wrapped her arms

around his neck. She planted a kiss on his mouth. "I think he needs to go back to his plantation and wait for his goody-good to return. I'm too much for him to handle."

"Exactly where has she gone?" Jared asked, getting to his feet, this time without the need of support. He slowly walked to the beverage cart and poured black coffee into a china cup.

"Sorry, Jared. Her destination is something I cannot tell you." Rory pulled Monique snug against him, running his hand slowly down her back and cupping her bottom before squeezing. "As for you, you saucy wench, leave him alone."

Pouting, Monique pushed Rory away. "Then both of you get out before I think better of it. And if I see either of you here again I'll have you thrown out."

"You heard the woman, Jared. Let's go." Rory grabbed his waistcoat from an overturned chair. He put it on then winked at their hostess. "Until later."

The men walked outside into the brightness of the new day. Jared frowned, hurrying to keep up with Rory. "Exactly where do you think you're going?" he asked as they walked down Amherst toward the more respectable side of town.

"Home, of course."

"And where is that?"

"Oak Hill." Rory stopped and grinned, holding up both hands. "Surely all is forgiven after I saved your hide in there."

Jared snorted. "Saved me? From what?"

"Monique. She's a barracuda in bed."

"Do you honestly think I couldn't hold my own with a woman like *her*?" He began walking again.

Rory laughed. "You've never met a woman like Monique. She has mystical powders and oils she uses on men to make them a slave to her whims. Monique may be a Madame, but when she sees something she likes, she gets it, and from the way she looked at you, dear cousin, she wanted you and wanted you bad. I should be upset, but Monique is Monique."

Jared ignored him. "That still doesn't mean you're welcome at Oak Hill. There is the matter of Stuart Delaney and his hold on your markers. How do you propose to pay them off?"

Rory patted his coat pocket. "I've got it covered."

Jared scoffed. "I find it hard to imagine you being able to raise the money."

"You wound me to the core, cousin." He staggered, clutching his hands over his heart.

"Don't be melodramatic. You're a spendthrift and a gambler, not a thespian. As soon as you get your hands on any amount of money, you go through it as fast as you can. Exactly how long did it take you to spend the inheritance your mother left you?"

"I had a run of bad luck at the tables."

"Exactly my point!" Jared exclaimed.

Silence accompanied them as they rounded a corner coming upon Higgins and the carriage.

"Mr. Hollingsworth!" The man exclaimed, jumping down from his perch. "Didn't you find her, sir?"

"I'm afraid not. She was gone by the time I got there, but I did find Rory. As you can see."

"Mr. Rory," Higgins nodded. "What a surprise. Bad pennies always show back up."

He grinned. "Hello, Higgins, always the dutiful servant. Waiting on your employer, even if it means staying out all night."

Ignoring the comment, Higgins turned toward Jared. "Did you want to look anywhere else, sir?"

"No." Jared paused, getting into the carriage. "Put the cover down, Higgins, and take us home at once."

The man did as requested and climbed on his perch before turning the carriage toward Oak Hill.

Rory slouched in the corner on one side, eyes closed. Jared watched him, his mind racing over the events of the last twenty-four hours. He still couldn't figure out how Rebecca came to know Rory. When he couldn't take the suspense any longer he nudged his cousin with the toe of his boot.

"So where did you get the money?"

Rory kept his eyes closed. "Wouldn't you like to know?"

"Damn it. If I'm going to allow you to come back to Oak Hill, you owe me an answer."

Rory slowly opened one eye and grinned, clasping his hands in front of him as if in prayer. "I sold my soul and promised to be an angel from now on."

Jared crossed his arms over his chest and stared at him.

Rory chuckled, sat up and leaned toward him. "Aren't you even a little bit curious as to whom I made such a vow?"

Irritation grew in Jared as he warned. "If you say Rebecca, I'll throttle you."

"Then I won't mention it."

"And why would she give you a penny?" Jared reached the short distance between them and grabbed Rory by the collar, pulling tight. His cousin began gasping. "Can't think of a witty reply now, can you?"

He shook his head and tried to pull Jared's hands away from his throat. "Let me go and I'll try to answer.

"Let's hear it." Jared shoved him back in the seat.

Rory straightened his collar and wheezed, "When did you become so violent?"

"The day I found out you gambled away my home, my life," he retorted.

"Touché," Rory said. "But she didn't give me the money. Believe it or not, I suspect Rebecca *would* give me money, because she loves you and doesn't want to see you lose Oak Hill. And from what I've seen and felt these last several hours, I'd say you love her as well. She said you had even asked her to marry you. This explains your outraged sense of chivalry whenever I mention her name. It's also the reason I haven't retaliated. It's good to see you caring about life again."

Jared slumped back on his side of the carriage and stared outside. Even if Rebecca did love him, it didn't explain her involvement with Rory.

"How did you meet her?" he demanded.

"It's a long story which I'd prefer not to discuss with you at the moment. Let's just say it was pure dumb luck." Rory closed his eyes again and turned his face toward the sun.

Jared glared at nothing in particular as the carriage rambled back toward Oak Hill. Rory could call meeting Rebecca dumb luck if he wanted, but Jared knew there was more to it. If he wasn't going to talk, then he'd have to wait until Rebecca returned. However, he was certain a session on the rack would be preferable to waiting for the answers he wanted. Not having choices was hell enough. But to be forced to wait days was inconceivable.

"Where'd she go?"

"That's something I can't tell you. As much as I'd enjoy seeing you settled again and happy, if Rebecca wants you to know where she's gone, she'll have to tell you."

"Damn it, Rory. In all that's holy, at least tell me how you know her? And why didn't she tell me she knew you?"

"Perhaps because we'd never met before yesterday?"

"Then why'd she go to a brothel with you?"

He grinned and shook his head. "That I can't tell you."

Jared's head pounded again. The open carriage and fresh air did little to defuse the scent of Monique's bedchamber that clung to his clothing. He couldn't wait to reach the plantation, bathe, and put space between himself and Rory. The further, the better.

"Enough with these word games." He crossed his arms over his chest. "How long are you planning to stay?"

Rory scratched his chin and shrugged. "I'm not sure. I guess that depends on how well you treat me."

"Then don't unpack your bags. After you take care of your business with Delaney, you can head right back out of town. I don't need the strife your presence brings to my life. Everything was fine until I got the letter from Delaney demanding that I make good on your markers."

Rory shook his head as the carriage slowed to a stop in front of the main house. "You've turned into a bitter person since losing Charisse. I thought time would heal. Apparently it hasn't."

"What would you know about loving someone and losing them? The only person you've ever cared about is yourself."

When Higgins opened the door for them, Rory stepped out of the carriage. He looked back at Jared with piercing eyes. "You really don't know me very well cousin."

"On the contrary. I know you too well," Jared spat as Rory sauntered toward the front verandah and the open arms of Mary.

"Heaven's above. I can't believe my eyes," the woman exclaimed.

"Don't let your eyes get too accustomed to seeing him, Mary. He won't be staying."

"And what side of the bed did you get up on? Obviously not the right one," Mary harrumphed, turning away from him to fuss over Rory like a mother hen.

Jared shook his head. Mary had always taken a fancy to his cousin in a special way. He turned to his driver. "Don't put the carriage away. I'm going back to town."

"Yes, sir," Higgins replied.

Jared walked to the house where Mary still fussed over Rory. "Send up my bath water…even if it's cold, Mary."

"Certainly," she said. "I'll have breakfast on the table for you both soon enough."

"None for me. I've already eaten," Rory said.

Jared went upstairs to his study and pulled out the daily ledgers to begin going over the weekly figures while he waited for his bath water. But he couldn't concentrate. His mind kept returning to Rebecca and where she had gone. Why had she been in such a hurry to leave last night? She'd said she had to go take care of some business. Did that mean she'd returned to Memphis? If so, then why did she go to Madame Monique's? And why did she have to see Rory first? None of this made sense, but he would get to the bottom of what was going on even if he had to catch the next train to Memphis.

Slamming the ledger closed, he placed it in the desk drawer and locked it before he stalked into his bedroom and performed his ablutions. Going back downstairs, he searched for Mary and found her in the kitchen.

"Well now, that's more like it," she remarked handing him a plate of food when he came into the kitchen. "It's not like you to be out all night and come dragging in here looking like you've been in a fight."

"I didn't just look like it. Rory and I did brawl. Though I don't recall much of it."

"You boys shouldn't be fighting with one another. Rory's your blood kin. The only living relative you have left."

"No lectures. As far as I'm concerned what Rory gets, he deserves." Jared leaned back against the worktable and ate, washing the food down with hot coffee, while Mary cleaned the kitchen.

"I'll be gone for a few days. Rory has some business to take care of and can stay here until it's completed. Then he will leave. Can you see that he does this?"

Mary eyed him warily. "Your leaving doesn't have anything to do with him being here, does it?"

"No, it doesn't." He set his empty plate on the

counter. "Will you make sure Rory doesn't stay beyond his welcome?"

She nodded slowly. "If that is what you want."

"It is, Mary. Rory can't treat his family's heritage like it's nothing and expect to come home freely. He needs to earn that right."

She nodded again, but her eyes were sad with understanding. "I know you are hurt. Rory has a way of getting all over a body that makes you want to throttle him, but he is your family, your only blood family."

"Sometimes blood family can be the worst parasites of all. I consider you and Higgins my family as much as I want to forget that Rory is mine," he said. "I'll be back in a few days."

"You be safe."

"I will." Jared left the house with the one bag he'd hastily thrown together. His mind flashed an image of Rebecca wearing the cloak waving good-bye to him and a chill ran over him. Was she in danger? He feared she was.

"Where did you really go, Rebecca?" he mumbled going down the walk.

"Pardon me, sir. Did you say something?" Higgins asked, opening the carriage door for him.

"No." He climbed into the carriage. He had to stop Rebecca from doing something foolish.

Chapter Fourteen

Drizzling rain welcomed the train as it pulled into the station in Memphis. Despite the damp and muggy summer morning air, Rebecca wrapped the cloak around her and Ruth as much for warmth as protection from the wet.

They dashed across the street to the covered boardwalk.

Ruth's steady hand on Rebecca's arm kept her from falling into the mud when her booted foot slipped. The two giggled nervously as Rebecca removed the cloak and shook the rain from it, before wrapping it again around her shoulders. She noticed a well-dressed man in a white suit and plaid vest leaning against a post watching them.

"Goodness, are you all right?" Ruth asked.

"Yes. Just startled and out of breath." Rebecca turned her back to the man to shield Ruth from seeing him. "I know it is mid-morning, but do you feel like breakfast?"

Ruth nodded.

"Follow me. I know a place where we can get something to eat."

As they walked, Rebecca thought she heard footsteps following them. She stole a peek over her shoulder. It was the same man from the store not ten feet behind them. He smoked a cheroot and tipped his hat to her. She gasped and looked straight ahead.

"What's wrong?" Ruth asked.

"Don't be alarmed, but I think we're being followed. Keep close to my side and don't look back," she whispered, feeling the girl tense and clutch her arm tighter.

The rain had let up by the time the boardwalk ended, and they turned down another side street toward a church. The man passed them by, but Rebecca wasn't so certain it wasn't a move to give them false security. She quickened her pace and urged Ruth toward the small parish house to the left. Rebecca knocked on the door, and a few moments later it swung open.

"Lord love ya," an elderly woman greeted, hugging Rebecca quickly. "Come in. Come in."

"Thank you, Mawsy." Rebecca removed her cloak, took Ruth's from her, and hung them on a peg by the door. "This is my friend Delia. We were hoping to have breakfast with you."

"I've been expecting ya for nearly a week now. Was gettin' awful worried, but Ben put me at ease. Said we'd have heard if somethin' went wrong," Mawsy rattled, putting a meager meal on the small table.

"Go ahead and sit down, Delia" Rebecca urged. "Where's Ben this morning?"

"Funeral over in Wakefield for a dear friend of his. He should be back tonight. He'll be sorry he missed ya. He always likes to pray with the travelers before they go." Mawsy sat at the table, said a short prayer and helped herself to the food. "Eat up. We gotta get going soon."

Rebecca watched Ruth for a short time as she

timidly ate a dry biscuit. She wanted to put her at ease and smiled at her. "You'll be traveling with Mawsy as her companion to the meeting point."

Ruth slowly nodded. She picked up another biscuit.

"How many do you think they'll be today?" Rebecca asked, turning her attention to Mawsy.

"Hard to tell. We had a dozen last week." Mawsy finished her coffee and poured another cup.

"You do this for more 'n just me?" Ruth asked.

"Sure do." Mawsy took her dishes to the sink. "I'll go change into my spiffier traveling clothes. Be back shortly."

"I'm worried," Ruth said when Mawsy was safely out of the room.

"Try not to," Rebecca urged.

"But what about that man that followed us?"

"He passed on by when we turned down the side street. You'll be safe traveling with Mawsy."

"Aren't ya going with us?"

"No. My part of the journey is over. It's safer that Mawsy is the one who takes you to the meeting point. The less people who know about its location the better." She cleared the table.

Ruth nodded and slowly rose to help put the kitchen in order.

Once they were finished Rebecca said, "We have a plainer dress to fit the style a companion would wear for you to change into. Did they send the make-up?"

"It's in my bag," Ruth said. "Are ya sure it's safe?"

Rebecca touched her arm in reassurance. "As safe as the rest of this journey has been. There are no guarantees. We try to do what we can to ensure you reach your destination without being caught. There's danger to all involved."

She nodded and bit her lower lip. "Am I closer now?"

"Yes."

"Then why do I feel so scared?"

Rebecca hugged her. "Sometimes we can't help but fear the unknown. I'm still scared too, but I have faith we'll see victory. I've been praying for it."

The girl wiped moisture from her eyes with the back of her hands.

"Come. Let's get you changed." She led the way to the small room off from the kitchen. Touching up the make-up Madame Monique had applied the night before, she made sure it looked natural.

By the time Mawsy returned to the kitchen, Rebecca had Ruth dressed as a traveling companion. No longer did she wear the butter colored silk dress, but a sturdy, long sleeved charcoal blue with tiny black buttons down the front. Dove gray gloves covered her hands, and a matching hat hid most of the curls of her ebony wig.

A knock came at the kitchen door and the three women froze. Rebecca pulled Ruth to the side and they stepped out of view before Mawsy answered the door. She wrapped a protective arm around the young woman, and they held their breath until they heard Mawsy greet the visitor.

"Good morning, Horton. Would ya like a cup of coffee before we go?"

"I already had my fill, Mawsy, but thank ya," the man said. "Any baggage today?"

"Just one. We're traveling light for this trip. Come along, Delia."

Timidly, Ruth left Rebecca in the shadows. "Yes, miss." She handed her bag to the driver and reached for her cloak on the peg.

Rebecca waited five minutes after the door closed before donning her own cloak and leaving the parish house. She made sure the man she'd spotted earlier wasn't hanging around before walking to the other end of the boardwalk and hailing a cab. She needed to see her lawyer.

****

Stuart Delaney watched from the doorway of the bakery as the auburn-haired beauty climbed into the carriage. He didn't believe he'd seen her before, but there was definitely something about the way she looked that reminded him of the chit, Mariah, he'd bedded in New Orleans almost two years ago. The thought brought back pleasant memories. He recalled his clever manipulation at the masquerade party getting his friend to come as a priest to perform the "marriage ceremony." The chit had been his for the taking after that little ruse. He wondered what ever happened to her. Her aunt had hurried her away from New Orleans the following day, and he'd never seen her again, but that hadn't stopped him from thinking about her.

He lit another cheroot and took a few draws before heading back to the Exeter Hotel.

****

"Miss Davis, what a surprise," Colton Merewether greeted when Rebecca entered his law office. "It's been almost a year since you were here."

"Yes. Much has happened since then." She took the seat he offered.

"I heard about Mariah's passing, and I'm deeply

sorry," he said. "Please forgive me for not paying a call on you and your aunt before now."

"Thank you. That is partly why I'm here and why it has taken so long to do this. My aunt and I have stayed to ourselves at our country home while in mourning. As much as I love the home, I'm thinking of selling. Josephine and I need a fresh start. I've been looking at some property in Jackson, Mississippi."

"I'm sorry to hear we will be losing you from our fine community. I know the church will greatly miss your aunt's dutiful service," Mr. Merewether said. "What are your plans for the cottage and property?"

"It was my family's home for many years, but I do not see any reason to retain it. My aunt has become very fond of the community we have visited and I believe she wishes to stay as much as I do. That is why I've decided to sell. I was hoping you could make the necessary arrangements for me?"

"Certainly. It may take a few days to draw up the necessary paperwork for your signature."

"I don't have a few days, Mr. Merewether," Rebecca said. "I've been away in Jackson for the last few weeks and only came in on business today. I must return as soon as possible. Aunt Josephine is expecting me."

"I understand, Miss Davis, but what you are asking is highly irregular. Don't you want a detailed accounting of the furnishings, personal belongings, what you want to keep and what you want to sell and so forth before you return to Mississippi?"

Rebecca considered what he said. "Yes. I hadn't realized it might take so long to arrange."

"I can take you out to the cottage this afternoon to

look things over and begin the process. Does that meet with your approval?"

"That should be fine. I'd planned to stay in town tonight so I'll be at the Exeter Hotel. You can call on me there."

"I'll call around two," Mr. Merewether said, standing.

"Thank you very much." Rebecca stood and shook the man's hand.

When she exited the lawyer's office, the sun shined and there was no sign of the morning's earlier rain shower. She scanned the street for any unlikely characters who could be watching her, then headed to the hotel to get a room.

Safely inside her room, she relaxed for the first time since she left Jackson the night before. Even with Ruth out of her care, she was still in danger of being caught. If the wrong person saw them together, even though Ruth wore a very good disguise, it could raise suspicion about them.

Nervously, she poured some water from the pitcher on the washstand and dipped a towel in it before blotting her face and neck with it. Tired, she took off her dress and lay down on the bed. She tried not to worry about her part of the mission. It was over and she'd be safely back in Jackson as soon as she took care of business with Mr. Merewether. She also needed to make a visit to the bank and have her funds transferred to Jackson as well.

Turning onto her side, she closed her eyes and thought about Lucas. She missed him. She also wondered if Josephine and Doctor Gordon were attending Mass together today. Dear Charlotte was a

Godsend with the way she took care of Lucas and Josephine when she wasn't there. Then her thoughts stopped on Jared. He was the one she longed to see the most when she returned. She wanted to set matters right with him. If he'd still have her, she'd accept his proposal. And whether he wanted her to or not, she planned on buying Rory's markers. After meeting his cousin, she doubted he'd be so honorable as to cover them.

****

It was late in the afternoon when Jared stepped off the train in Memphis the next day. He checked with the conductor and got directions to the nearest hotel. After the long trip, he needed a bath and a shave before he started searching for Rebecca. His stomach rumbled, and he decided he'd take time to eat something as well.

At the hotel, he requested a hot bath and signed the registry book. He couldn't believe his luck when he saw Rebecca's signature a few lines above his. Fate was being kind to let him come to the very hotel where she stayed.

"Excuse me, but can you tell me if Miss Davis is still here?" He pointed to the name so the clerk could see.

The bell clerk looked at the book and turned to the alcove of slots. "Her key's not here. She must be in her room."

Jared didn't want to alarm her by showing up at her door unexpected. It was better if he announced he'd followed her to Memphis. She might not like it, but he was here and there wasn't much she could do about it. "Can I leave a message for her then?"

"Of course."

The clerk gave him some paper and he jotted down a note. He folded the paper, slid it into the envelope, and handed it back to the man. "Please see that she gets this."

"Yes, sir."

Jared turned, smelled the delicious aromas coming from the dining room to the left of the lobby, and debated whether he should eat or go to his room. Unable to dispel the need to bathe, he started up to his room, but stopped when he heard a man call his name.

"Hollingsworth. Is that you?"

Surprised, he slowly turned and came face to face with a flamboyantly dressed man. The brightly plaid vest visible underneath the white coat gave the man's preferred profession away. A gambler.

"Do I know you?" Jared asked, wondering how many people in the world would mistake him for Rory upon first glance.

The man studied him for a moment and shook his head. "I beg your pardon, sir, but I thought you were someone else."

"No harm." He sized the man up curious if he were a friend or foe of Rory's, before he continued on up to his room.

The hot bath he'd ordered arrived shortly after he entered his room. He didn't waste a moment taking advantage of the steam and he relaxed. He closed his eyes and his thoughts turned to Rebecca. Knowing she was somewhere within the hotel made him long to find her. But he'd reacted too irrationally the last few times they'd met, so he vowed to practice a little patience.

****

Rebecca woke from a nap to knocking at her door.

She slowly got up and slipped on the dress she'd worn to the bank that morning. Transferring her money to Jackson had not been as simple as she'd imagined. There had been so many documents to sign. "Just a minute."

She opened the door and a bellboy handed her an envelope. "Please wait a moment." She went to get her purse and took out a coin to hand to the lad. "Thank you."

She closed the door wondering who could be sending her a message at the hotel. The only person who could possibly need to reach her was her lawyer and they were to meet again this afternoon. Unfolding the paper, she quickly read the words, stopping when she saw the closure.

Jared. Her heart skipped a beat.

How had he found out where she had went?

Chapter Fifteen

Heart racing, she re-read the note and couldn't understand why Jared had followed her. He could have jeopardized the mission by showing up at the wrong time. Why hadn't Rory stopped him?

Rory!

She fully understood Jared's disdain for his cousin. Rory was insufferable. She was still upset that he'd taken her to Madame Monique's. He could have met her near the train depot with Ruth. If she hadn't been dazed by his resemblance to Jared, then she would have insisted upon it.

Going to the wardrobe, she selected a different dress and changed into it, preparing to meet Jared. A troubling thought crossed her mind as she repinned her hair. She'd not left Jackson on the best of terms with him. She'd turned down his marriage proposal, and then he'd no doubt seen her going into Madame Monique's with Rory. He must be livid with her. Had he followed her to Memphis to have it out with her because he couldn't wait to do it when she returned?

Taking a deep breath to settle the butterflies in her stomach, she closed the door and went to meet him.

****

Reaching the second floor landing, Stuart Delaney watched the woman he'd seen the day before come down the hallway. Her hair was swept up on her head, showing off her tempting slender neck. She truly was an exquisite creature.

"Good afternoon." He tipped his hat.

She glanced his way, and nodded slightly. "Good day."

"Pardon me, but haven't we met before?"

The woman stopped and turned back in his direction. "I don't believe so."

"I'm almost certain we met in New Orleans?"

She shook her head. "I've never been there. Sorry."

He frowned. "You look so familiar. Are you certain we've never met?"

"Positive," she said. "I think I'd know if I've visited New Orleans."

"You're right." Delaney rubbed at his chin. "Again, I beg your pardon."

She turned and began walking, but his words stopped her again. "Perhaps a sister?"

"N-No."

"Maybe it was another city?"

He'd already mistaken the identity of one man. And it confounded him how much that man looked like the fool Hollingsworth he'd won the plantation from. What he was going to do with it he wasn't sure, but maybe he'd finally settle down and become respectable. Once he did, perhaps he'd even try to find that girl Mariah and really make her his wife.

The woman turned, fixing an icy glare on him. "No. I believe I'd recall meeting you." She pursed her lips together. He could feel her gaze roaming from his head to his toes as she sized him up. "Now, if you'll excuse me."

"Of course." He tipped his hat again. "It'll come to me eventually."

She looked exasperated by his insistence. "I tell you we have not met before today."

"I think we have."

A door opened, and the man he'd mistaken as Hollingsworth stepped into the hallway.

"Rebecca, is something wrong?"

The woman quickened her pace to join him. "Jared. Thank heavens. This man believes we've met before, and I can't convince him otherwise."

The man looked at him. "First it's me, now my friend? Do you make a habit of mistaking the identity of people, sir?"

"Stuart Delaney's the name," he offered, startled to see the woman go ashen and swoon.

"Rebecca." The man she'd called Jared looked as pale, but caught her before she fell to the floor. He scooped her up in his arms and carried her into his room.

"Is she all right?" Stuart asked, following close behind.

"I'm not sure," Jared said. "But it's none of your concern. You've caused enough trouble. Good day." With his foot, he kicked the door shut.

He laid her gently on the bed and then loosened two buttons on the collar of her dress before he patted her cheeks. "Rebecca. Rebecca. Rebecca, can you hear me?"

"Jared," she murmured moving her head back and forth as she came around. Her eyelids fluttered before she fully opened her eyes.

"I'm here, darling. You're safe. No need to be

frightened."

"Oh, Jared." She clutched at his hand and tried to sit up, but he stopped her.

"Lie still." He went to the washstand and wet a towel. He came back and blotted her face and neck. "Does that feel better?"

"Yes," she murmured. "What happened?"

"You fainted."

"I did?"

"Yes. I have a mind to go after that Delaney fellow for frightening you. Why did he think he knew you?"

She slowly sat up and swung her legs over the side of the bed. Reaching for the damp towel, she ran it across the back of her neck. She looked at him and bit her bottom lip, shaking her head.

"Because he's Lucas' father," she blurted.

"What?" Jared stood and stared at her. "I don't understand. I thought you said your husband was dead."

"I never said that. I've never been married."

"Never married? But at Mitchell and Elizabeth's wedding you said…"

"No, you assumed I had come out of mourning for a husband when it was my sister who had passed."

"Then why didn't you correct me?"

She licked her lips and shrugged. "It seemed easier to let you believe I was a widow than explain being a single woman with an infant child."

Jared turned away not understanding any of this. He gripped hold of the dresser. "If Delaney is Lucas' father, how could he not know who you are?"

"Because I never met him before today," she said. "I'm not Lucas' biological mother."

He turned back and felt as if the floor had

disappeared from beneath his feet. He couldn't believe what he heard. She'd lied to him. Pretended to be something she wasn't. Yet, he'd fallen in love with the woman he thought she was, and she claimed to return his feelings. Could he believe her? Should he believe any of what she was saying?

He crossed his arms, leaning back against the dresser, and stared at her. "If you aren't Lucas's mother then who is?"

"M-my sister. Mariah."

"And she's dead?"

"Yes." Rebecca nodded, twisting the hand towel. "She died shortly after giving birth to Lucas, but before she passed, she begged me to take him and raise him as my own. Sh-she didn't want Stuart Delaney to ever know he'd fathered a child from their union."

Rebecca looked up at him and he saw moisture in her eyes, pain, and uncertainty. "You see, he's not an honorable man. He tricked Mariah into thinking they were married by a priest on a riverboat while she and Aunt Josephine were in New Orleans. She was young and too naïve. If only I'd been there—"

"You can't blame yourself for that." God help him, but he believed her for no other reason than the man he believed Stuart Delaney to be.

"Aunt Josephine blames Mariah. She said Mariah died for her sins. But how can she have sinned if she thought the ceremony real?"

Jared sat beside her. He took the towel from her and laid it aside before taking her hands in his. "I don't believe she did, and I don't believe your aunt truly believes it either. She's blaming Mariah as a way to deal with her own guilt for allowing this to happen. I should know. I blamed myself for Charisse dying."

"Oh Jared," Rebecca said, running a hand up his arm. "You must forgive me for allowing you to think I was a widow. I hated deceiving you, but I had to do it to protect Lucas. You understand that, don't you? I regretted not correcting your misconception of why I had come out of mourning, especially after you told me how Charisse died in childbirth."

Jared stood, ran a hand through his hair and walked across the room. He turned back. "Where does Rory come into the picture? Is it because he gambled away Oak Hill and Delaney bought the markers?"

She gasped. "Delaney is the one who holds the markers on Oak Hill?"

"Yes."

"You must not let him get your plantation, Jared. I cannot stand the thought of that vile man living at Oak Hill. Let me cover the markers if Rory is unable to pay his debt."

He shook his head. "Rory has the money. He showed it to me before I left Jackson."

"That is a relief. But can we trust him not to gamble it away before he sees Delaney?"

Jared felt his jaw twitch at the notion. "It makes me uneasy to think about it. But tell me, how do you know Rory?"

"Ruth. But that's another confession all together. I can't tell you everything."

He leaned against the dresser again. "Then tell me what you can."

"I wish it was that easy."

"I want to hear it all."

Rebecca swallowed and stood, clutching the skirt

of her dress. She'd confessed about Lucas, so she might as well confess about her secret life. "We're much alike in our principles, Jared. You use hired labor on your plantation, and I work with a committee that supports emancipation. I joined an organization while at the Women's Seminary in Virginia where I met Elizabeth. I know you'll find it hard to believe, but Rory works for them too."

Jared laughed, but sobered when she did not break a smile. "Go on."

"My visit to Jackson was to attend the wedding, but also to complete a mission. Rory was my liaison. We'd never met, which is the way the committee works to protect all involved. After arriving in town, I received a correspondence from him and it was signed Hollingsworth. He said I'd know him by the yellow rose in his lapel. When I met you at Elizabeth and Mitchell's wedding you wore a yellow rose. A simple mistake for me to make, don't you agree?"

He stared at her. "So our relationship has all been a charade?"

"Oh no, Jared." She rushed across the room and stood before him, taking his hands in hers. "You mustn't think that. My feelings for you are real."

His expression was unreadable and she held her breath, fearing he didn't believe her.

"Why did you agree to have dinner with me after Elizabeth and Mitchell's wedding?"

"I won't pretend I didn't hope we'd discuss our mission," she admitted, "but I was also interested in getting to know you better. If I may be so bold as to say, I found you very attractive. I still do."

A quirk of a smile formed at his mouth, but a stern

look quickly replaced it. "And the weeks that followed? Were you toying with my affections, especially after you realized I wasn't your contact?"

"No."

"But that's what happened in the library, isn't it? You realized your mistake. That's why you rushed away."

She nodded. "I'm sorry. I feared my mistake had cost Ruth her life. I'd been spending my time falling in love with you instead of getting her out of Jackson."

His brows arched at her confession. "And in the carriage that day, is Ruth the reason you refused my proposal?"

Rebecca swallowed. "It broke my heart you chose that moment to propose because the last thing I wanted to tell you was no. But, until my mission was complete, I couldn't even begin to think about a future with you. That's the only reason I turned you down. If I was caught..."

His features softened. "And is your mission over now?"

"Yes."

The beginnings of a smile formed at his mouth. "So if I knelt down right now and asked you to marry me, would you say yes?"

She half-grinned. The edge had gone out of his voice, and the talk of marriage meant he still wanted her, even after her deception. But the butterflies were back, playing havoc in her stomach. Her pulse quickened. "No," she said playfully. "I don't suppose so. I'd like the circumstances to be different."

"Different?"

She considered for a moment. "More romantic."

"I see. What would make it more romantic? A large bouquet of flowers? I'm sure I could arrange it."

"That would do for starters."

"Followed by what? A dinner by candlelight with violins playing?"

She smiled. "That would be pleasant."

He cleared his throat. "Will you be visiting any more brothels?"

She laughed. "Not if I have any say in the matter."

"Will there be any more missions?"

"If the committee needs me, I may consider it, but as my husband I would discuss it with you before deciding."

Jared nodded and held out his hand. She slowly placed hers in his and with one fluid motion; he pulled her into his arms. "Miss Davis, you utterly charm and amaze me."

"Is that a good thing, Mr. Hollingsworth?"

"A very good thing." He smiled, lowering his mouth to hers for a kiss.

"Then you forgive me?" she asked, stopping him in mid-motion.

"Yes. But you must promise to keep no more secrets."

"I promise."

Before she could distract him again, he tilted her chin upward and brushed her lips with his. Nibbling with kisses, he swiftly parted her lips and captured her mouth with his own. His tongue darted in and out joining hers in a glorious, fevered dance.

As the kiss deepened, Rebecca slid her hands up his chest, over his shoulders until she wrapped her arms around his neck. A lusty moan startled her, and she pulled away.

Breathing labored, she placed a hand at her throat and felt the open collar. She quickly buttoned it back and looked toward the door.

"My heavens! I'm in your room with the door closed. If anyone found me here..." She turned back to face him. "Or if Aunt Josephine were to find out."

Jared pulled her back into his arms. "Let her."

Chapter Sixteen

Rebecca had difficulty convincing Jared to go downstairs for lunch. He kept pulling her back into his arms for another kiss each time she broke free.

"That's enough, Jared."

"It'll never be enough," he groaned, reaching for her again.

Sidestepping him, she went over to the mirror and refastened a few loosened hairpins. When she turned, she found him sitting on the foot of the bed, watching her. He patted a spot next to him.

"Come here."

"No, Jared. I have already risked convention by being alone in your room with you for more than a minute. You forget this is my hometown. If anyone I know were to see me coming out of this room…my reputation would be ruined. And if Aunt Josephine's church friends were to find out…well, she'd disown me."

"Then that settles it. You'll have to marry me now."

She laughed and placed her hands on her hips. "As if you'd have to force me."

"Is that a yes?"

"Perhaps." She turned back toward the mirror and checked her hair one last time to make sure every pin was in place.

"What would it take to make it a definite yes?" He stood.

"A real proposal. Not one in jest. Not one after an argument. But one when I least expect it."

"Fair enough." He came to stand behind her and trailed kisses up her slender neck before nibbling at her earlobe.

She smiled at him in the mirror, enjoying the tingles running over her body. "Jared, you must behave yourself."

"Only if you'll marry me," he said.

"Jared, please," she pleaded.

He nodded. "All right. And to save your reputation, dear one, I'll exit the room first, go downstairs, and wait for you in the dining room."

"Thank you." She faced him and wrapped her arms around his neck, kissing him one last time before he left.

He groaned, pushing away from her. "Don't be long."

She swallowed and waited until he was gone before she walked over to the window and watched the hustle and bustle of the people going about their business. She spotted a few familiar faces, and then she saw Stuart Delaney leaning against the post outside the candy shop, smoking a cheroot.

She truly didn't understand what Mariah had seen in the man. Sure he was handsome to a fault with dark hair, broad shoulders, and brooding eyes. But Rebecca would take ten Jareds over him any day. She only prayed Lucas took after the Davis side of the family in looks when he grew older. She didn't fancy the idea of being reminded of Delaney every time she looked at her boy.

Sighing, she turned away from the window and went downstairs to the dining room. She found Jared at a corner table already enjoying a cup of coffee. He stood when she approached and pulled out her chair.

"I went ahead and ordered for us. I hope you don't mind. I remember you liked pot roast."

"That's fine. I have a meeting at two o'clock with my lawyer. Would you like to come with me?"

"Are you sure?"

"I wouldn't have asked otherwise." She smiled and placed her napkin in her lap.

"Then I'd be honored to join you."

"Good. I'll show you around town afterward."

Jared reached for her hand and squeezed it. "I'm glad you aren't upset with me for following you."

"I should be very angry that you didn't trust me enough to take care of my business without following me, but I understand why you came. And now that you're here, I'm glad."

"You were being so mysterious that night, wearing a cloak and going into the shadier part of town where no woman in her right mind would go during the day, let alone at night." Jared's brows arched. "What was I to think? I feared for your safety. I don't know what I would have done if something had happened to you."

Rebecca nodded and her stomach knotted with regret for her deception. "I'm sorry I worried you, but I didn't have a choice. I had to see Ruth made it safely to Memphis."

He squeezed her hand again. "Until I thought I had possibly lost you, I didn't truly understand the depth of my feelings for you. I need you in my life, Rebecca. I truly do."

"I-" she began, but was interrupted by their food arriving. Jared released her hand and they ate, but she noticed him watching her from time to time as she cut up the meat and placed it along with portions of the vegetables on her fork to make the perfect bite.

"Is it as good as you are making it out to be?" he finally asked.

"Only because I'm sharing the meal with you." She laid her knife and fork aside and picked up her water glass.

"Pot roast is one of Mary's specialties at Oak Hill," he said. "She can make it for you anytime you like."

"I'll remember that." She took a sip of her water and set the glass down.

"If you do decide to come live at Oak Hill—"

"Jared." She interrupted him. "You don't have to persuade me. In fact, I'm honored you want to marry me knowing I have a child and an overbearing aunt as part of the bargain. Though Josephine may be making her own plans for the future."

He wiped his mouth with his napkin and laid it on his plate before he pushed back from the table. "Would you consider letting me adopt Lucas?"

Rebecca's vision blurred with unshed tears. "Y-you'd really want to do that?"

"Yes. That is what I was going to say before you interrupted me. I want to raise Lucas as my own. I want to make it legal."

She quickly rose from her seat, and her napkin fell to the floor in her haste to round the table. He stood and she practically flung herself into his arms. "Yes, oh yes.

I'd like that very much."

"Of course, you'll have to marry me first," he whispered into her hair. "There would be no point in an adoption without you becoming my wife."

She looked up, her cheeks glistening with tears. "Yes. Yes, I'll marry you."

He laughed, hugging her close, and lifted her feet off the floor. Applause erupted from the occupants at the next table who'd heard their conversation.

"So much for not making a spectacle," he muttered and set her back down.

Rebecca softly laughed and brushed the moisture from her cheeks with her fingertips. She couldn't stop smiling, nor could she remember being happier in all her life.

Their waiter appeared. "May I offer you a bottle of our best champagne? Compliments of the management on this special occasion?"

"Thank you, but no, we have an appointment," Jared explained.

"Very good, sir. I'll bring the bill." The waiter nodded and hurried away.

Rebecca sat again and hand trembling, she reached for her water glass. "Goodness I'm shaking." A few more tears ran down her cheeks and she swiped them away, but more fell. She rose. "Please excuse me while I run back up to my room and compose myself."

"I'll wait for you in the lobby."

"I won't be long."

Jared paid their bill and went to wait for Rebecca. To his chagrin Stuart Delaney was standing by the front desk.

"Mr. Hollingsworth is it?" Delaney tipped his hat

and sauntered over to him.

"I am." Jared wondered what the man wanted.

"The hotel clerk tells me your name is Jared Hollingsworth, but I know for certain you're not the same fellow I played cards with and won the plantation from some months ago."

Jared's jaw twitched. "No. I'm not. In fact, that was my ungrateful cousin Rory. He holds no claim to Oak Hill, your IOU is a forgery, but he will pay you the debt he owes."

Delaney grinned. "How can you be so sure?"

"I will see to it, that is how I am sure you will be paid. He has the funds to do so and is waiting at Oak Hill for you to come collect."

"Maybe I don't want the money." Delaney sneered. "Maybe I want the plantation."

"Why? A man of your means is a free spirit. A place like Oak Hill will bind you in shackles and drain you dry. What good would come of it?"

"Ah, I see you, too, are a gambler, Mr. Hollingsworth. Your game is not at the table, but with your words." Delaney pulled a small case from his pocket, took out a cheroot, and offered one to Jared, which he declined.

"If by a gambler you mean I take a chance daily on the land to provide for my family, then yes I am one, but I do not mince words with you Mr. Delaney. Oak Hill is not for the taking and if you do not accept Rory's payment on the debt he owes I will take legal action to retain what is rightfully mine."

Delaney chuckled. "We'll see about that, Mr. Hollingsworth. We'll see."

Jared looked up and saw Rebecca descending the

staircase. Her eyes enlarged and her pallor paled at the sight of them.

"Jared? I'm ready to go now."

He nodded and glanced back at Delaney. "Remember what I said."

"Is that a threat?"

"Take it as you like." Jared did an about face and offered her his arm and they left the hotel.

Once outside, he relaxed and looked down at Rebecca by his side.

"Whatever did that man want?"

"Nothing. And that is all he will get."

Chapter Seventeen

At Mr. Merewether's law office, Rebecca settled into one of the matching Chippendale leather chairs opposite his large desk and took the legal documents he handed her. She read through the papers regarding the sale of her country home and the surrounding property on his desk awaiting her signature.

Looking up, she smiled at the man. "Will a surveyor be going out to draw the boundary line for the two acres of land and the family burial plot I wish to give to my aunt?"

"Yes, I've made all the arrangements," he said. "I'm sorry I couldn't get someone here to do it while you were in town, but your request was sudden. When those documents are ready, I will forward them to you in Jackson."

Rebecca signed the document and took a sheet of paper from her purse with Mitchell Cooper's name and address on it. She handed them to him. "Mr. Cooper, a friend's husband, will be happy to handle my affairs while I'm in Jackson."

Mr. Merewether looked over the document and nodded. "It seems everything is in order," he said. "As soon as the property sells, I'll have the house closed and the pieces of furniture you specified shipped to you."

Relief surged through her. "Excellent."

He escorted her to the outer chamber where Jared had waited while they conducted their business.

"It was a pleasure to meet you, Mr. Hollingsworth." Mr. Merewether shook his hand. "I wish you and Miss Davis many happy years together."

"Thank you."

"Good day, Miss Davis." The attorney bowed.

"Good day, Mr. Merewether."

Late June heat greeted them when they stepped outside of the brick building. "We need refreshment. Let's have tea. There's a lovely shop a few doors down," Rebecca suggested, taking his arm.

He smiled and nodded. "I think that a wise decision."

A few minutes later a smiling hostess led them to a corner table and took their order.

"I'm sorry Mr. Merewether wouldn't allow you to join us in the meeting," Rebecca said

"It's understandable," Jared said. "Mitchell is very private about my affairs as well. We never discussed business in front of Charisse when she was alive."

The waitress returned with their pot of tea. "Will there be anything else?" she asked.

"No. Thank you." Rebecca smiled as she waited for the tea to steep and realized it was the first time Jared had spoken of his beloved by name. "Your wife had a lovely name."

Jared nodded. "She was just as lovely in person. Sparkling blue eyes, golden hair, and the prettiest smile I'd ever seen until I met you. We were happy."

Rebecca laid her hand on his. "I'm glad."

After their tea, she took him to several stores she

thought would interest him. Then he insisted on going into one she'd never visited before. Michelo's Estate Sales.

"This must be new," Rebecca said.

The store had an interesting collection of antiquities. Furniture with a distinct European flair took up the majority of the store's space while the remaining contained curios, filled with figurines, and a display case with a wide assortment of jewelry.

The delighted proprietor showed them necklaces, brooches, and rings of several styles and color.

"Do you have any emeralds?" Jared asked.

The man held up one finger, stepped to another case, and brought a wooden box to the counter. "I believe you will like this."

Nested in black velvet, a three-tiered emerald and diamond choker sparkled in the lamplight.

"Oh." Rebecca let out a long sigh. "It's exquisite."

The man carefully picked it up, came from behind the counter and draped it around her neck. "You'd be the envy of all your friends," he said proudly.

Rebecca hesitated, reluctant to hurt his feelings. "I'd prefer not to evoke envy," she finally said.

"No?" the man questioned.

She shook her head, and he immediately removed the choker.

Rebecca gave him a smile of thanks, and moved to look at several items on display in the curio.

"Actually, I was thinking about something smaller," Jared said, pointing to his ring finger.

The man looked thoughtful. "And it must be emerald?"

"If you have it."

The man searched his cases and returned holding a ring with a square cut stone set in a gold band. "How would this suit?

"It's perfect." Jared took the ring and inspected it for clarity. "May I see if it fits?"

"Anything you want, sir," the clerk told him. He looked at Rebecca and added, "Though I think the lady would look lovely in any stone you chose for her."

Jared walked to where Rebecca sat on a gold brocade settee. He knelt and took her left hand in his.

"Jared? I've already said yes. What are you doing?"

"You did," he agreed. "But I didn't have a ring. May I try this on you?"

She gave a slight nod, and he slipped the ring on. It was an exact fit. "Do you like it?"

She held up hand and inspected it. "It's gorgeous. But why'd you choose an emerald?"

"It reminded me of your eyes and the dress you were wearing the first time we met. I'll never forget that day." He moved to sit beside her. "But if you'd prefer another stone?"

"No," she said, taking his hand. "It's perfect. I've always loved emeralds. I thought perhaps Aunt Josephine might have told you."

He shook his head. "Let me settle the bill and we can go."

When they left the store, Jared asked, "Will you marry me today?"

"Today?" Rebecca stopped, certain she'd misheard him.

"Yes. If we can find a parson to do the ceremony, would you marry me today? I don't want to risk something stopping us if we wait until we return to Jackson."

She slipped her arm around his. "What could possibly go wrong?" she asked.

"Stuart Delaney," he said grimly, as they continued their stroll down the street. "I don't trust him, and the less time he has to learn about Lucas the better."

Rebecca squeezed his arm. "I know a parson who'd be delighted to marry us if you are certain you want to risk invoking Aunt Josephine's wrath."

He grinned. "I think your aunt will understand."

****

Mawsy's mouth dropped open as she stared at Rebecca. "Lord love ya, girl. What brings you back again so soon?" But upon seeing Jared, her brows furrowed. "Who's that?"

"Mawsy, I came to see Ben. Is he around?" Rebecca asked.

"Sure he is. Are ya in some kind of trouble?" Scowling, Mawsy nodded in Jared's direction.

Rebecca grinned. "No trouble. This is Jared Hollingsworth. We want to get married, and I hoped Ben would do the honors?"

The old woman stared at the couple for a full minute before she moved back and beckoned them inside. "Married you say?"

"Will that be a problem?" Jared asked. When the old woman didn't answer, he suggested, "Perhaps we should go somewhere else, Rebecca?"

"No, no. Please have a seat." Mawsy gestured at the table in the corner. They took their places, but Mawsy continued to stare at them, while wadding her apron between her fingers. "Are you sure you want to marry a man like him, Rebecca? He's a scoundrel."

"Mawsy!" Rebecca protested.

"I don't reckon you'd admit to it, but I know all about you," she said, pointing at Jared.

Jared stood. "I beg your pardon?" he said coolly. "Why do you consider me a scoundrel?"

The old woman planted her hands on her hips. "You know why."

"Mawsy!" Rebecca exclaimed again. She didn't understand what had gotten into her friend, but she'd never seen her act or say things like this before. She apologetically looked at Jared, and motioned for him to sit again.

Mawsy turned away and shuffled across the floor to a doorway. "Ben, we got company. Bring your Bible."

A moment later a white haired man wearing spectacles entered the kitchen. "I thought I heard voices. Rebecca, it's so good to see you again."

She stood and hugged him. "Ben, I've come to ask you to marry me and my fiancé, Mr. Hollingsworth, if you'll be so kind."

"Don't do it, Ben." Mawsy shook her head. "He's that scoundrel that works for the committee. He no doubt hexed the child with his charms."

"You mean Rory?" Rebecca asked, glancing at Jared. His set jaw clearly indicated he wasn't happy at being mistaken for his cousin. "I don't want to marry him."

"You'll have to excuse her, she doesn't see well without her glasses." Ben smiled and patted Mawsy on the arm. "Where's your glasses, woman? If you were wearing them you'd see clearly this is not the same

191

man."

She fumbled in her apron pocket, pulled out the glasses, and put them on. She gasped. "But they look so much alike."

"You know my cousin Rory?" Jared asked. "How?"

Rebecca swallowed a laugh. "I told you, darling, he works for the same organization that I do."

"He's a scoundrel," Mawsy insisted. "I don't care how many souls he's helped with his gambling to raise funds for the committee and his wicked disguises. He's still a scoundrel."

"Ah, Mawsy." Rebecca said patiently. "This is Jared, not Rory."

"I'm sorry, Mr. Hollingsworth," Ben gave a good natured sigh, "but Mawsy speaks her mind freely. Heaven help the person who tries to stop her."

"I'm sorry, too, for not seeing you weren't that wretched man," she said. "I know it's not Christian to feel the way I do about that Rory fella. Guess I'll just have to ask for the Lord's forgiveness."

Jared ran a hand through his hair and gave her a rueful smile. "Don't worry, Mawsy, I share your sentiments."

"Let me make you some coffee," she offered. "Perhaps even a bite to eat?"

"That would be lovely," Rebecca said, "but we came for a—"

Ben nodded. "You want to get married. I'll be happy to do the honors, but first, I'd like to talk to Mr. Hollingsworth in private. Will you follow me to my study?"

Jared left the room with Ben and Rebecca turned to

Mawsy. "Is there anything I can do to help?"

"Set the table for coffee and cake. It's nothing fancy like a wedding deserves, but I baked it this morning."

Rebecca took napkins from the hutch near the door, craning her head in hopes of hearing parts of the men's conversation from behind the closed door.

"Are you certain you're ready to be a wife?" Mawsy asked.

Rebecca went back to the table, laying out the napkins. "I believe I am."

"How long have you known Mr. Hollingsworth?"

"Not long, but long enough to know I love him."

"Look at me, child."

She raised her head. Behind the spectacles, Mawsy's gaze was clear and direct. "Do you love him enough to spend the rest of your life sharing his bed? Taking care of him and his children?" she asked.

"Yes." Rebecca took spoons from the table's middle drawer for the sugar and cream. "And even that doesn't seem long enough."

"Marriage isn't always about the romance." The old woman continued her counsel. "There will be hard times as well as good ones. Remember what the vows say, for better for worse."

"Jared and I have already had some difficult moments," Rebecca admitted. "But I do know I love him heart and soul."

Mawsy continued to regard her thoughtfully, then grinned.

"What will your Aunt Josephine say? I got the impression when I met her she'd be the kind of person who'd insist on being part of the ceremony, at least be in attendance."

"She'll understand." *Or at least I hope so.* Rebecca offered a hasty prayer heavenward and added, "She knows Jared and I truly love one another."

The smile Rebecca knew so well creased Mawsy's face. "Then you marry with my blessing, child. And I pray you will be happy all the days of your lives together."

Rebecca went to hug her friend. "Thank you," she whispered. She stepped back and asked, "How long have you known Rory?"

"Hmmph! That scoundrel?" Mawsy scowled again. "More years than I care to recall. He was reckless when he first started working for the committee, and he's still reckless. We even thought he got caught on his first mission. Poor Ben went searching for him, risked his own life for that no good... And do you know where he found him? Playing poker with the plantation owner who he later snatched the package from."

"I believe it," Rebecca said. "He cares for no one but himself."

"A gambler through and through." Mawsy looked toward the doorway, waited a minute, and turned back toward her. "He likes to run with those painted women," she whispered.

Biting back her smile, Rebecca nodded. "I know. He took me to one of their establishments."

Mawsy laid a hand over her heart. "That man needs salvation from himself," she declared. "And only the love of a good hearted woman will turn a man like Rory into a redemptive soul. And the merciful Lord above to get him into Heaven."

"I'm afraid he hasn't yet met the woman who can

do that," she said sadly.

Mawsy took Rebecca's hands between hers. "Then we should pray he meets her, and soon, before he loses his life and spends eternity paying for his sins."

They bowed their heads and silently prayed for Rory's soul.

"Amen!" Mawsy handed her the plates as Ben and Jared came back into the kitchen.

"Rebecca," Ben said. "I believe you've found yourself a good man. I'll perform the ceremony."

She sat the plates on the table and rushed to hug him. "Thank you. I couldn't think of anyone else I'd want performing my marriage. May we do it now?"

"Yes. I have the necessary documents for you both to sign. Do you have the rings?"

Jared nodded, reached into his pocket and pulled out a small box. He took the rings out and handed them to the parson.

"Not so fast, Ben." Mawsy stepped forward and spoke to Rebecca. "You go into my room and freshen up. Don't come back until I call for you."

Rebecca nodded and turned to leave the room, but Mawsy grabbed her arm and led her into the hall. She leaned close to Rebecca and whispered, "Don't worry, child. Tonight will not be that horrible, though young women have the right to be fearful going to a man's bed for the first time."

Heat flooded Rebecca's cheeks and she hurried from the room grateful the pitcher in the bedroom was still full. She poured water into the washbowl, splashed her face, and blotted it dry with a clean towel. Staring at her reflection, she took a long slow breath to steady her wildly thumping heart. "There's nothing for you to be nervous about. You're marrying Jared."

"You certainly are," he said from the doorway and she jumped, turning toward him. "But if getting married tonight feels rushed, we don't have to do it. We can wait until we return to Jackson, plan a small wedding, and invite our friends."

She shook her head. "No. I want to do it now. I-I think I'm excited about it to the point of distraction. It's hard to believe and yet it's happening. A girl waits for this day all her life. When I woke this morning I had no idea I'd be going to bed as your wife tonight."

He came forward to take her hands. "If you're sure?"

She smiled up at the man with whom she intended to spend the rest of her life. "I am."

"Then Ben is ready when you are." They slowly walked back to the parlor, and Mawsy began playing the small upright piano in the corner.

Ben stood in front of the mantel and waited for the music to stop. "On this special occasion I have the honor to unite you in marriage. It's a sacred bond. Neither of you should enter into lightly."

Rebecca looked at Jared, carefully watching his expression. Ben's words filtered through her ears and into her heart where she felt them with much joy. When they exchanged vows, she repeated the words as instructed and slipped the gold band on Jared's finger. It was a piece of metal that had no meaning before she put it on, and now it meant he was hers. She watched as he put a similar band on her finger where he'd placed the emerald that afternoon.

"By the power vested in me by the State of Tennessee, I pronounce you husband and wife," Ben concluded.

Jared didn't wait for the traditional command, "you may now kiss the bride." Instead, he pulled her into his arms and gave her their first kiss as husband and wife. She wrapped her arms around his neck and eagerly returned it. From this day forward they'd face the trials of life together.

****

When they entered the Exeter Hotel later that evening Rebecca went up to her room to collect her things while Jared stopped at the front desk. He spoke with the clerk and settled the bill on Rebecca's room.

"Congratulations, Mr. Hollingsworth," the clerk said. "I heard about the excitement in the dining room earlier today. We didn't realize you'd be making it official so soon. If you'll kindly reregister as husband and wife there will be no problem."

"Thank you." Jared took the pen and signed the book again. When he finished, he looked at the clerk. "There is one other service you can do. I've learned another guest is asking questions about me. His name is Stuart Delaney. I'd appreciate our privacy until we check out."

"O-of course," the clerk stuttered. "I-I beg your pardon, sir. It was a simple mistake. He said he knew you, but couldn't remember where you were from."

"Neither my wife nor I want anything to do with the man," Jared said firmly. "Is that clear?"

"Y-yes, sir. Bu-but you won't have to worry about Mr. Delaney bothering you. He checked out this afternoon."

"He did?"

The clerk nodded.

"Did he say where he was going?"

"No sir, but he did say something about going to collect on a debt owed him."

Any sense of relief knowing Delaney wouldn't bother them further vanished, and Jared swallowed the bile rising in his throat. Good God, if Delaney was headed to Oak Hill, he had to get there before the man arrived. He didn't trust him to do the honorable thing anymore than he trusted Rory not to gamble the money away before he paid his debt.

"Is there anything else I can do for you, sir?" the clerk asked.

Jared grabbed the pen and drew a line through his signature. "Change of plans. I need to settle my bill. Do you know when the next train to Mississippi leaves?"

"Sir, did I say something wrong?" The clerk asked. "I never meant to make you want to leave the Exeter."

"No. I thank you for telling me that Delaney left." Jared tried to put the clerk's mind at ease. "It's where he's headed that concerns me. I need to get there before he does. Now, about the train schedule? When is the last train leaving Memphis today?"

The clerk opened a drawer and fumbled with its contents before holding up a railroad timetable. After glancing over it, he said, "It left at four-thirty this afternoon. There isn't another one until noon tomorrow."

Damn. If Delaney was on that train then he'd have high tailed it out of town after he learned Rory was at Oak Hill with the money. Jared never should have told him that. "Is there a stage?"

"There is, but it won't leave until morning. But if you must leave tonight, you can hire a coach to take you as far as Grenada where you can catch the connecting train to Jackson. That should get you there before Mister Delaney if that is your intent."

"Where can I hire such a coach?" Jared asked.

"Let the Exeter arrange it for you while you pack your bags. It's the least I can do, sir."

"All right. I'll be ready to depart in half an hour. Will that be sufficient?"

"Yes."

He paid his bill and headed upstairs to pack. He arrived at his door at the same time as Rebecca. "Perfect timing, Mrs. Hollingsworth."

She smiled. "I like hearing you call me that."

"I like saying it." He took her bag from her, opened the door, and sat the bag inside the room. Turning back to her, he grinned because she hadn't moved an inch. Before she could protest, he swept her up into his arms and carried her into the room.

"Jared!"

He kicked the door closed with his foot and leaned against it. She kissed him and he wanted to carry her over to the bed and make love to her, but that wasn't going to happen. He put her down, breaking their kiss. "We have to go back to Jackson tonight."

Alarm widened her eyes. "Why? What's happened?"

"The clerk told me Delaney checked out this afternoon to go collect a debt," Jared said grimly. "That means—"

"That means he's headed to Oak Hill," she finished for him.

"But how did the clerk know all of this?"

"Delaney boasted about it." Jared went to the closet

and got his bag from the top shelf. Putting it on the bed, he quickly packed, and shut it. "I'm afraid our wedding night will have to wait."

Her cheeks pinked, and he went back where she stood at the door. He pulled her close and kissed her until she sighed.

Closing his eyes, he slowly breathed to regain his composure. "I promise to make it up to you."

"I'll hold you to that, Mr. Hollingsworth."

Chapter Eighteen

In the early morning light, Josephine rocked Lucas and thought about when she'd held Mariah like this many years ago. It had been difficult at the time having given up the child as her own at birth, but she'd been grateful to her brother and sister-in-law for taking her to Europe during the pregnancy so no one at home knew of the transgression. She leaned her head against the back of the rocker, closed her eyes and sighed. She hadn't allowed herself to even think about that time, even after Mariah's death. She'd stayed away from Lucas as much as possible even though she wanted to hold him, to heal her wounded heart.

With Rebecca gone these last few days, she'd finally allowed herself to feel something for the child, her rightful grandchild. She'd never imagined the love she could feel for him in so little time, but now that she did, she didn't know if she could give him up so easily when Rebecca returned. Would it be selfish to want to take him as her own?

Yes. She feared it would. Rebecca loved him, and she couldn't hurt her niece by taking him from her.

"Goodness, Miss Josephine." Charlotte stumbled into the dimly lit room. "I was worried when I didn't find the babe in his bed. Have you been here with him all night?"

"Only since about two. I woke and heard him stirring. I believe it's his teeth again."

"Would you like me to take him now so you can go back to bed?" she asked.

"I'm fine, and he's no trouble at all." Josephine smiled.

Charlotte slowly nodded. "I-if you're sure?"

"I am."

"I'll go order up breakfast."

"No need. I'm not hungry. Only coffee."

"As you wish." She curtsied and left.

Josephine rocked back and forth and hummed softly as her mind drifted to the London townhouse where she'd given birth to Mariah. It had been a cold overcast day. The doctor had arrived shortly before midnight and didn't leave her side until nearly seven the following night. It had been a long and difficult birth, but Mariah had been perfect.

Two weeks later once she was back on her feet, they left London and traveled to France for four months before going to Italy. By then Mariah was getting all fat and sassy.

"That's when you sent me away, Samuel. You and Emily sent me away so your little family didn't have to deal with me."

"Did you say something, miss?" Charlotte asked, coming back into the suite with the coffee service. She closed the door behind her and carried a tray over to the small table.

Josephine didn't respond. She rocked in silence as warm tears rolled down her face, remembering how she'd sailed back to the United States alone.

"Would you like your coffee black?"

Josephine closed her eyes and continued to rock. She'd lost her first love and her child and what did she have to show for it? Nothing. She was well past her prime. In all rights she was on the shelf and had no prospects.

"Miss Josephine?" Charlotte's call jarred her back to reality.

"Black. I'll take it black."

"Yes ma'am." The girl fixed the coffee and brought it to her, but there was nowhere to set it. "Perhaps I should put the child to bed now? And you can have your coffee in peace?"

"Forget the coffee." Josephine shifted the sleeping child in her arms so she could easily get out of the rocker. "I'll put him down."

"Bu-but-"

"Don't stammer, Charlotte. I am capable of doing some things for myself."

"Certainly. Have you been cryin', ma'am?"

She swiped away the moisture with the back of her hand. "Nothing to fret about. Is that clear? I think I will lie down for a while."

With a worried look, Charlotte set the coffee cup back on the tray and curtsied. She collected it and scurried out of sight.

Josephine carried Lucas into her room, put him on the bed and lay down beside him. She hummed a soft tune, watched him sleep until her own eyes grew heavy, and she too drifted off to sleep.

Tiny hands, patting her cheeks and wet, slobbery drool dripping on her face woke her a few hours later.

"Ma-ma."

She opened her eyes and smiled. "Mama isn't here

now. She'll be back soon." She sat up and he crawled to her.

"Ma-ma."

He'd been calling her that off and on since Rebecca left and each time it made her heart ache. Mariah had never called her that, nor had she ever wanted it back then, but now, if she could only have had that memory.

"Ma-ma." He reached his hands up to her.

"Mama isn't here, Lucas. She's on a trip, but hopefully she'll be back today or tomorrow."

"Ma-ma." He smacked his lips together this time and she picked him up. He laid his head on her shoulder and patted her.

"I bet you're hungry. Let's go get you something to eat." She carried him into the sitting room, but stopped suddenly in the doorway. Ancil sat at the small table where they ate their meals, having coffee while listening to an animated Charlotte. The maid hushed and looked at her with a worried expression.

What had the girl been telling him?

"Let me take him from you, Miss Josephine." Charlotte rushed to her side and took Lucas. "I'm sure he needs changing. Like you need to change and fix your hair or you'll be late for Mass."

Josephine's spine stiffened at the mention of church, but she and Ancil always went to the daily Mass. Why should today be any different? "Ancil, I didn't realize you were here. You should have had Charlotte wake me."

"I hadn't been here long. She was telling me how you were up most of the night with him," he explained. "If he's having trouble sleeping I can give you something to rub on his gums that might help."

She smiled. "I must look frightful. Let me go change."

"Is everything all right with you, Josephine?" He stood and walked to her. "Charlotte said you were crying earlier."

"Can't a woman cry?" she asked.

"A woman yes, but Josephine Davis? It isn't like you and it frightened the poor girl."

She took a deep breath. "Let me go change. I don't want to keep you from Mass. Perhaps we can get some lunch later? I'd like to talk to you if you have the time."

He nodded.

Once inside her room, she closed the door and hurried through her toiletry, splashing water on her face and fixing her hair before putting on a fresh dress.

When she returned Charlotte sat at the table holding Lucas while he drank his bottle.

"Doctor Gordon and I are leaving now."

"Will you be gone long, miss?" Charlotte didn't look up when she spoke.

Josephine glanced at Ancil. "An hour or so?"

He nodded. "Maybe longer."

They walked through the hotel in silence, but once they were outside Ancil asked, "Are you sure you feel up to going to Mass today? You look troubled. Maybe it would do you more good to talk than hear a sermon."

"I am troubled."

"Perhaps we should get something to eat? If you care to come to my place, I can fix us something. It won't be fancy, just some bacon and eggs, but at least you can speak in private."

She nodded. "I don't know if I can tell you. You may not want to speak to me again once I do."

Ancil took her arm in his and patted her hand. "I doubt there is anything you can say that would make me feel that way."

She took a jagged breath and prayed he was right. They walked the distance in companionable silence. She drank in the fresh air and tried to relax, but her mind wouldn't let her.

When they finally reached his place, they went into the kitchen and he began preparing the food while she waited. "Are you certain I can't help?"

"Yes." He cracked some eggs in a bowl and whisked them while the bacon fried. "So what has you so melancholy?"

"I'm a hypocrite."

He stared at her for a moment. "Can you explain?"

"I use my work with the church as a disguise to keep others from suspecting the truth about me. I'm a wretched sinner."

"We all are, Josephine, but what makes you feel you are so bad?" He opened the cabinet and took down two cups. "Do you want coffee or tea?"

"Coffee." She placed her hands on the table in front of her and stared at them. "I disgraced my family when I was a young girl. I had a child out of marriage. And that child died giving birth to Lucas."

He sat the cups down on the counter and stared at her. "L-Lucas isn't Rebecca's?"

She shook her head. "My brother and his wife took me to Europe to hide my pregnancy and to save me from ruin. They took Mariah as their own, raised her, but left her in my care when they died."

"Does Rebecca know?"

"No. She was too young to remember all that went

on back then. As far as she knows, Mariah was her sister, not her cousin."

He reached for the coffee pot and poured them both a cup, bringing hers to the table. "Mariah is your daughter, but she died after giving birth to Lucas?"

"Y—yes. She asked Rebecca to take him as her own before she died. At least that is what Rebecca told me. I-I wasn't in the room for the birth. I-I was in the parlor praying for forgiveness and mercy. I gave up my child and when she was in my care, I allowed her to be seduced by a gambler who took her innocence. I wasn't fit to be a mother when I had her, and I wasn't fit when she needed me most."

The smell of burning bacon drew Ancil's attention back to the stove. He turned and removed the frying pan from the stovetop and transferred the bacon to plates. "You've carried this burden so long, what has changed to make you reveal it now?"

She smiled and tucked an errant strand of hair behind her ear. "Lucas. I avoided touching him from the time he was born, but with Rebecca gone these last few days, I've been taking care of him. He calls me Mama."

Tears began to flow from her eyes. "Mama. The sweetest word ever spoken. I know he doesn't realize what he's saying. He's only learning to talk, but hearing him say it... it... it worked its magic on me. It made me feel things I never allowed myself to feel when I gave birth to Mariah. I was scared and too worried about society's convention back then, but I loved her father so. We would have been married if he hadn't taken ill and died. I know Charles would have loved her and been proud of her."

She brushed away the tears, but new ones fell. "I was grateful to my brother and his wife for loving me enough to save my reputation, but I wasn't as kind to Mariah. She was not even seventeen, Ancil. She was so young and naïve."

He dipped a portion of the grease from the pan and placed it back on the stovetop to heat. "We all were at that age."

Josephine nodded and took a sip of her coffee. "I blamed her for her naiveté, but maybe if I hadn't taken her to New Orleans that winter this wouldn't have happened. I blamed her for believing that gambler married her during the party she'd slipped off to attend with him. I was livid when I found her on that riverboat in his bed the next morning. Of course, he wasn't there. He'd left moments before I arrived to get them breakfast."

He poured the eggs in the pan and stirred them. "I'm listening. Go on."

Josephine swallowed and remembered the pleased look on Mariah's face that morning. "She proudly showed me the piece of paper proclaiming her Mrs. Stuart Delaney, but I had my doubts. I hadn't trusted the man from the moment we met. I forbade her to see him again, but she had a will of her own, and she'd slipped away in the middle of the night to be with him. In my anger, I forced her to get dressed and I dragged her from the boat despite her protests. When we got back to the hotel, I had our things packed quickly and we left on the next train."

She sobbed, covering her face with her hands. He placed the eggs on their plates and carried them over to the table. When he set them down, she looked at him again and he handed her his handkerchief. She dried her eyes and took another jagged breath.

"Mariah cried for days. It didn't matter what I said, nothing consoled her. She wrote letter after letter to New Orleans in search of her supposed husband but they were all returned to her unopened. In an attempt to put our minds at ease, I even made inquiry through a friend into the priest who signed the marriage certificate. As I had feared, he did not exist. There was, however, a man by that name known as a gambler and a close friend of Stuart Delaney's. Mariah took the news badly. She stayed in her room for days. I hadn't wanted to tell her, but I couldn't allow her to spend the rest of her life searching for a man who never loved her." Josephine sighed and shook her head. "Everything had finally settled down when we discovered she was with child. Thankfully Rebecca had finished her schooling and was home at that point."

He reached for her hand and brought it to his lips, brushing a kiss across her knuckles. "I'm sorry you had to carry this burden for so long, but you cannot blame yourself for Mariah's death. There are many dangerous complications in childbirth. How did the doctor say she died?"

"She hemorrhaged. The doctor was unable to stop the bleeding."

He nodded. "Yes. I've had deliveries end that way. They are never pleasant, but we do the best we can."

Josephine pulled her hand away and picked up her fork. She moved the eggs around on her plate, but her stomach rebelled. "I suppose I'll have to tell Rebecca now."

"Not unless you absolutely want. Does she need to

know the truth? Will it make a difference?"

"Yes. She does. I don't want to deny Lucas anymore. He's my grandchild, Ancil. He's my Mariah's baby."

The tears formed in her eyes again and her vision blurred. She blinked and the tears spilled forth onto her cheeks. Ancil pulled her into his arms and held her while she cried.

When her tears finally subsided and the last sign of them had been wiped away, he kissed her and pulled her into his arms again. After the kiss ended, he held her tenderly for a moment more.

"Ancil?"

"You are a very important woman to me, Josephine. I don't want you to worry about the past. I want you to think about the future. Nothing you have said changes the way I feel about you. Is that clear?"

"Feel about me?" Her heart skipped a beat and she swallowed.

"Yes. I feel deeply for you."

She smiled and her eyes began to water again, but she blinked the unshed tears away. "Oh Ancil."

"A doctor's life is lonely and tiresome. I can be called away for days at a time to care for the sick and even during the night. I couldn't think of asking someone to join this life with me unless I was sure they understood what they were agreeing to share."

She nodded.

"You've made a difference in my life since we met. Because of my profession I never allowed myself to believe I could have a family. But I believe you understand the required dedication because of your work with the church. You say it was a disguise, but I believe you do it with your heart. I've watched you. Your dedication is real. It may have started out as a way to redeem yourself, but I believe it is more now."

In spite of her resolve not to cry, the tears came again, but this time they weren't of pain, but of joy. She dried them away as fast as she could with his already damp handkerchief. "I-I don't know what to say, Ancil. I never dreamed anyone would want me in their life after what I've done."

He smiled. "I'm not asking for an answer right now. I want you to think about it. I want you to be sure. But if you think you could build a life with a doctor I will be ready to hear your answer."

"Not just any doctor, but you, Ancil Gordon. That is who I'd be agreeing to build a life with." She hugged him and kissed him on the cheek. Perhaps she did have something to show for her life after all.

Chapter Nineteen

A noise as loud as the cracking of a whip woke Jared. The hot sun streamed through the carriage window, and he moved a hand to shield his face from the sun until his eyes fully adjusted to the light. Beside him, Rebecca stirred.

"Are we in Grenada yet?" she murmured, sitting up.

"I don't think so. Stay here." He moved to the door, opened it, and climbed out of the hired carriage, which was parked, by the side of the road. The driver was nowhere in sight. The horses were still hitched, but the reins were tethered around a nearby tree. He walked around the carriage and noticed the right front wheel was cracked.

"Damnation." He stepped back to the open door. "Don't be alarmed, but it looks like we've been deserted. I'm hoping the driver has only gone for help. There's a broken wheel."

"What are we going to do?" Rebecca moved to the door to climb down, and he helped her out of the carriage.

"We wait a little while to see if the driver returns, if not, we take our bags and ride the horses to the nearest town. You can ride can't you?"

"Yes." She smiled.

"I'm surprised we slept through the incident, but the ride was bumpy. A jolt of the carriage when the wheel broke wouldn't have seemed unusual as we slept."

Rebecca nodded. "Surely he'll be back. He was so nice and helpful last night when we left Memphis."

Almost a little too helpful, Jared recalled. Maybe he shouldn't have accepted the hotel clerk's offer of a hired carriage to take them to Grenada. With the broken wheel, they wouldn't be arriving at Oak Hill before Delaney.

"Let's stand in the shade," he suggested. "The humidity is already high, and we don't have any water or food. I don't want you getting ill. This isn't the way I'd have imagined us starting our marriage."

"Nor I." Her cheeks pinked and he felt a jolt when she took his hand. The look she gave him made his trousers tighten. He pulled her into his arms and kissed her, making love to her with his mouth and tongue.

She sighed when he reluctantly pulled away. "Forgive me for not doing this earlier, Mrs. Hollingsworth. I mean to kiss you first thing every morning for the rest of our lives."

The flush of her cheeks deepened and she leaned into him. "I'll have to remember that, Mr. Hollingsworth."

Smiling, they walked to the tree line and the shade. Jared stopped abruptly when he spotted their driver lying in the tall grass about ten feet away from the trees. He couldn't tell if the man was knocked unconscious, or if he was dead. A new carriage wheel lay near him.

Rebecca gasped and clutched his hand tighter. "Is he dead?"

"I don't know." He scanned the area, but didn't notice anyone about. Their bags had still been secure to the back of the carriage, so he knew they hadn't been robbed, yet. But if their driver was injured returning with the wheel he didn't believe they were safe.

"Let's walk back to the carriage slowly," he whispered. They turned but came face to face with two masked gunmen.

"So we meet again, Hollingsworth," one of the masked men said. "When did you start traveling with a lady? It's so unlike you."

Not again, Jared silently groaned. How many times was he going to be mistaken for Rory on this trip?

"Jared?" Rebecca turned to him, worry evident in her green eyes.

"He must think I'm Rory."

"Quiet!" the man barked and jabbed the nose of his pistol into Jared's rib cage. "I want my money back, you thievin' horse's ass."

"I don't have your money," he gritted through clenched teeth.

"Sure you do or you wouldn't have skedaddled out of town after I cut you."

"I tell you I'm not the man you're looking for. My name is Jared Hollingsworth, not Rory Hollingsworth. Rory is my cousin. We were unfortunately graced with the same looks."

"Shut up." The man shook his gun at them. "I don't want to hear none of your lyin'. I heard enough of that swallow in Bixby where you swindled me out my winnings. Now hand it over."

Jared glared at the man. *Was that where Rory got the money to pay back Delaney?* He took a deep breath to still his temper. He had to stay calm. Perhaps if he were rational this man would see the error he was making. "I tell you I'm not Rory Hollingsworth."

The other gunman snorted and lifted his bandana up high enough to expose his mouth and spit tobacco juice. He wiped the excess away with the back of his hand. "Sure looks like 'im." He spat again, repeating the process. "Same eyes, same hair." He walked toward Jared and sniffed. "Don't smell like 'im though. He smells too pretty, like his lady friend here, all lemony."

"It's verbena." The man's sweaty stench surrounded them and Rebecca's nose twitched. "Do you want some?"

He laughed. "Rufus, you hear her? She wants to know if I want to smell all pretty like her."

"Shut up you idiot. Now they know my name," his partner roared.

The other man snickered. "If he's Hollingsworth he should already know it. Come to think of it, why are we wearing these bandanas?"

"Get over here."

The man loped back as ordered to stand beside Rufus, and he smacked him in the back of the head. "Now shut up."

"I know where Rory is." Jared silently prayed the man would take the bait. "I can take you to him."

Rufus shook his gun at Jared. "I know where he is too and I'm lookin' at him, ain't I? We're not going nowheres until I get my money. So stop your blatherin'."

Talking to the man wasn't working. Jared thought for a few seconds and recalled something Rufus had just said. "You say you cut Rory the last time you met.

Where?"

"Your side."

"I can prove to you I'm not Rory. Let me remove my shirt."

Rufus shrugged and lowered the gun, but he didn't holster it. "It won't prove nothin'. You could be healed up by now."

"Not if you cut Rory deep enough." Jared took off his coat and handed it to Rebecca. He unbuttoned his waistcoat and shrugged out of it before pulling his shirt over his head and held out his arms for the man to see. He even slowly turned in a circle so Rufus could get a good look at him from all sides.

"That don't prove nothin'. Like I said you musta healed up."

Jared shook his head as he slipped his shirt back over his head. "A deep cut would leave a scar. As you saw, there isn't one."

The other man snickered. "He's got you there, Rufus."

"Shut up, you fool." He glared at his cohort for a minute before he turned his attention back to them. "No more antics. I want my money, and I want it now."

"I can't give you what I never had." Jared tucked his shirt back into the waist of his trousers and slipped on his waistcoat.

"Shut up." The man gritted his teeth. He swore under his breath and pointed the pistol at Jared again.

"Sir, I'd appreciate it if you'd stop pointing that gun at my husband." Rebecca shifted her weight and planted her hands on her hips. Jared smiled at her spunk, but feared she'd get herself shot.

"Your husband?" Rufus laughed and turned his full

attention on her. "I never thought I'd hear the day that the likes of Rory Hollingsworth would get himself hitched, especially to a fine lookin' lady like you. Maybe if you can't pay me, Rory, I can get satisfaction in another way."

Rebecca gasped, and Jared moved to stand in front of her. "Sounds like you know Rory well? If that's true, then surely you have to be having some doubts that I'm him."

Rufus raised the gun to Jared's head and cocked it. "I said to shut your trap."

Beads of sweat prickled across Jared's brow. There was no reasoning with this man, no matter what he said or did. All he could think about was Rebecca. They hadn't been married a day and she might end up a widow because of Rory and his gambling.

"Please, put down the gun." Rebecca's voice was steady, and despite Jared's attempt to shield her from Rufus, she stepped from behind him. However, Jared saw the fear in her eyes. "I can assure you that this man is Jared Hollingsworth, and he's my husband. We have documentation to prove it. We were married in Memphis before we left. If you will allow me to get my bag from the carriage, I can show you."

"She has documentation," the smelly man jeered. "Rufus, are you going to let her show us? Can I take her to the carriage and get her bag? I'd like to see inside their fancy carriage. Maybe get all comfy with her in there."

Rufus moved the gun away from Jared to point at his friend. "Stop using my name, Amos, or I'll shoot you instead."

Amos' eyes bulged and his nostrils flared as he

stared into the barrel of the pistol. He raised his gun and pointed it at Rufus, slowly cocking it. "A-all right. Just you put down your gun, or I'll be shooting you."

"Not if I shoot you first."

"Do it, Rufus."

"You first."

Jared could see the two gunmen were at a standoff, pointing their weapons at each other, and not paying attention to them. He grabbed Rebecca's hand and urged her to step back. They slowly eased away from the duo until they could safely turn and run back to the carriage.

"Hey. They're getting away," Amos called.

"No, they're not," Rufus shouted, and he fired a shot from his gun.

It hit the side of the carriage, ricocheting off before they reached it.

Rebecca screamed and ducked low. Jared did the same, but he urged her to keep running.

"We're going to get killed," she cried.

"Not if I can help it." Jared picked her up and shoved her inside the open carriage door. "Get down on the floor and stay there." He slammed the door shut and safely slipped behind the carriage for cover, dodging another bullet.

He unfastened their bags from the back and took them with him as he rounded the other side and opened that door. He crouched down as a bullet hit the top of the carriage.

"Here, give me your hand," he ordered as more shots were fired at them. She inched her way toward him and placed her hand in his. He helped her out, and they ran as fast as they could into the woods.

Besides firing random shots from their guns, Rufus and Amos hollered profanities at them as they ran from tree to tree. Finally, the gunshots stopped. But Jared and Rebecca didn't stop running until the only sound they heard was that of their own feet hitting the ground.

Gasping for breath, they finally slowed near a stream. Jared laughed, dropping their bags and sat down on a large rock. He wiped sweat from his brow with his forearm and patted his leg for her to sit. Rebecca collapsed against him, he pulled her into his arms, and kissed her.

"I've never been more scared in all my life," she murmured when he released her. "And I thought I was frightened on the train when I was taking Ruth to Memphis, but that was nothing compared to this."

Jared held her close and kissed her temple. "Sh-h-h. Don't fret. If we're lucky they've ran out of bullets. I'd be pleased to find they foolishly shot one another."

"I pray they've given up on finding us."

He nodded, cupping her face with his hand. He kissed her again, parting her lips with his tongue, deepening the kiss. She sighed and melded her body to his, running her hand up and down his back. Her feathery touch sent tingles running along his spine, and he set her away from him before he lost control.

"What are we going to do?" she asked. "We have no idea where we are. We don't even know in which direction to go."

"We can circle back to the carriage. If Rufus and Amos aren't there, we can change the wheel, check on the driver and if he's alive, take him to the next town for help."

"But what if they're waiting for us to come back?"

"Then we're back to where we were before we ran, trying to convince them I'm not Rory. Not that they believed me."

She shook her head. "How have you put up with him all your life?"

Jared laughed. "When we were growing up he wasn't so bad. It all started after his father died. Rory started drinking, gambling and whoring. And now that his mother has passed, well, there's no stopping him."

"Mawsy said Rory uses his gambling winnings to help the Vigilante Committee so at least he's putting it to good use, even if it's tainted money."

"I still can't wrap my mind around him working for an organization of that nature. He was never one to give a damn about how others felt; at least that is how I perceived him."

"Maybe that's what he wants others to believe. It's a good disguise for what he really does." Rebecca smiled.

"Come on. Let's head back and see if we can get moving toward Grenada again. We might still be able to catch our train to Jackson."

They walked until they came to where they could see the carriage. Jared left her and their bags to wait on a fallen tree and slowly inched closer, checking the area for signs of the duo. When he was certain they were gone, he turned back.

"I'm going to check on the driver and see if I can change the wheel. You stay here."

"Okay." Rebecca watched him leave, but being left alone, apprehension crawled up her spine as if she were being watched. She heard a twig snap and she jumped, turning around as the smell of Amos assaulted her nose.

Everything went dark as he pulled a sack over her head. She tried to scream, but a hand was slapped over her mouth. She fought against her captor, but he had a strong hold on her.

"Got her."

"Good."

Rebecca tried to stomp Amos' foot, but before she made contact she felt herself being lifted in the air and swung onto the back of a horse. Her bottom landed snug against one of her captures legs, the horn of the saddle jamming into her thigh. She squirmed trying to break free of his vice-grip hold as her hands were bound together.

"Now that should hold her," Amos said, spitting.

"Let's go," Rufus ordered, his hot breath penetrating through the sack against her ear.

Rufus had her. At least he smelled better than Amos, but that didn't make matters better. It was difficult to breathe with the sack over her head. Tears threatened her eyes and she blinked several times to keep them away. It wouldn't do to give into her fear. Jared would save her.

The only problem was she had no idea in which direction they were taking her. She only hoped he heard the horses retreating and followed them.

"Let's see if your husband cares about you enough to come after you."

Chapter Twenty

Jared carried the wheel to the carriage and set it down. The thunder of horses' hooves drew his attention away from his task and he turned to see two riders pass, wildly shooting their pistols in the air. For a second, he thought he saw the flash of blue in contrast to the riders' brown clothing.

Rebecca's dress was blue.

Rebecca!

He rushed around the carriage and back through the woods to the fallen tree where he'd left her hidden out of sight. She wasn't there.

"Re-b-b-ecca!" Heart slamming against his ribs, Jared scanned the area, praying for the possibility of her coming through the trees. He choked back the bile rising in his throat at the thought of those vermin having his wife.

My wife. Rebecca is my wife.

They must have kidnapped her thinking he'd give up the money in exchange for her return. The only problem was he didn't have the money to give them. And this far from home, there was no way for him to get his hands on that kind of money. Why couldn't that idiot Rufus believe him about not being Rory? Did they really look that much alike?

He grabbed their luggage and ran back to the

carriage to unhitch the horses. He didn't want to think of what they might do to her. He recalled both Amos and Rufus' taunts about having their way with her. The thought of either man touching her made his blood boil.

At his approach, the horses jerked back, shying away from him, eyes wide with their own fear. "Sh-h-h. No need to be frightened, fellas. I'm not going to hurt you," he soothed, taking the reins and patting them.

"You need any help sir?" a wobbly voice asked.

Astonished, Jared looked up to see the driver staggering toward him. He ran to help him to the carriage.

"More importantly is how you are? You took a nasty hit on the head. Do you recall what happened?"

The driver sank to the nearby stump with his help. "The wheel broke just before dawn. I checked on you and your missus, but you were sleeping so I went for help. Luckily the town isn't too far up the road and the smithy was already up by the time I got there. He had a wheel handy and I returned to change it, but that's all I remember."

"You were ambushed," Jared explained. "The men who knocked you out took my wife. I'm going after them. Do you think you can ride back to town?"

"I'll try." The driver moved to stand, but had difficulty getting up. Jared helped him to his feet and onto the back of one of the horses. He climbed up behind him and led the other horse behind them.

The ride to the next town was short, but seemed an eternity. If he'd run in that direction with Rebecca instead of the other perhaps he wouldn't be chasing after Rufus and Amos to get her back now. They had a good twenty minutes or more lead on him and by the time he found a doctor for the driver, notified the local sheriff and hired a good horse it would be even more.

The town of Grenada looked like most in Mississippi and was populated with people and businesses brought by the establishment of the train line. Buildings stood on either side of the street and he scanned the area for the one he sought. He nudged the horse to go further before stopping near a water troth and hitching post.

"Don't worry about me, sir," the driver said. "I can get along all right. You go after your wife. The smithy I saw this morning has horses for hire. You should get yourself a better horse there."

"Thank you." Jared tethered the horses to the post outside the building that displayed a doctor's shingle. The sign on the building next door said Sheriff's office, which made him happy. He could take care of his business in both easily.

The door opened and he heard laughter. Buford Hayes, an old West Point classmate, stepped out onto the boardwalk wearing a badge.

"Jared Hollingsworth. What brings you to my neck of the state?" He eyed the driver and his brow arched. "What's going on here?"

"No time for pleasantries, Buford." Jared helped the driver around the horses. "Two men abducted my wife because they mistook me for my cousin Rory. I have to get a horse and go after them."

"Rufus and Amos?" a familiar voice asked, and the driver nearly slid from Jared's grasp.

"Let's get you to Doc's, mister," Buford interjected, sliding his arm around the driver and leading him to the office next door.

"What in the hell are you doing here, Rory?" Jared demanded. "Delaney's on his way to Oak Hill to collect his money. I told him you were waiting for him."

Rory grinned. "Nice to see you again too, Jared."

"Why are you here?"

"I heard two men were looking for me and they were headed toward Memphis. After a day of cajoling, Mary finally told me you had followed Rebecca so I knew you were somewhere in the vicinity of where Rufus and Amos were last seen. Being the loveable bloke I am, I thought perhaps you could use my help. But if you'd prefer I deal with Delaney instead…I'll just catch the afternoon train and go back to Jackson, leaving you to handle them."

"Those two are more trouble than they're worth," Buford added as he rejoined them. "I'm going to lock them up for good this time." He disappeared back into his office.

"You know Rufus and Amos are both harmless as long as they haven't been drinking," Rory called over his shoulder before looking back at Jared. "Had they been, Jared?"

"Harmless? If knocking our driver unconscious, holding us at gunpoint, and shooting at us when we tried to escape is what you call harmless I'd hate to see them dangerous. They abducted my wife, threatened to do her bodily harm in exchange for the money they want back, but you call them harmless. I don't have time to chit chat about this. I have to find Rebecca."

He turned to leave, but Rory grabbed his arm to stop him.

"Your wife?" He looked stunned. "Congratulations. When did this happen?"

"Last evening, before we left Memphis." Jared took a jagged breath. "We have to find her, Rory. We have to find her and get back to Jackson before Delaney arrives. He can have the place if he wants it. I only want Rebecca back unharmed."

"Lucky for you that won't have to happen. I left the money with Mary to pay him when he calls." Rory patted him on the back. "We'll get Rebecca back. Don't you worry."

Buford returned with three shotguns. He handed one to each of them. "I think we'd best be going to find those rascals."

"Is the driver going to be all right?" Jared asked.

Buford nodded. "He was talking to Doc when I left, so I wouldn't worry. Good thing for Rufus and Amos. Kidnapping is bad enough without adding murder to their charge." He turned to Rory. "How much did Rufus lose to you at the table?"

"Less than a hundred dollars, but he'd been winning up until I joined the game. I think this is more about a bruised ego than the money. The game was all fair and square. Judge Templeton can vouch for me. He was playing with us and lost three times that, but he wasn't sore. He invited me to dinner the following night."

Jared stared at Rory. His cousin had been playing cards with a circuit judge, was now spending time with a sheriff and according to Mawsy had worked for the Vigilante Committee for years. Rory had even come all this way to try to help Jared when he'd learned there could be trouble for him. This wasn't the Rory he thought he knew. In fact, he was beginning to suspect he didn't know his cousin at all.

"Are you coming, Jared?" Rory called as they headed down the boardwalk.

"Yeah." He forced his feet to move again and hurried down the street behind them. They walked toward the livery and the smithy.

"How long has it been since they abducted Mrs. Hollingsworth?" Buford asked.

"I guess about an hour or more. Our carriage wheel had broken and our driver had returned with a new one when Rufus and Amos happened upon us and took Rebecca with them. In our haste to get moving, the driver and I rode bareback, not easy for horses only used to pulling a carriage."

"Why were you and Rebecca traveling by carriage and not by train?" Rory asked. "If you had been none of this would have happened."

Jared grimaced. "We wanted to get back to Oak Hill before Delaney, but we had missed the train and didn't want to wait until today."

"That means you had no wedding night."

Jared glared at Rory. "No."

Rory turned to Buford. "They had no wedding night. We have to find her."

Buford's lips twitched, threatening to turn into a full-blown grin. "You boys go get horses and I'll check the train station in case they decide to hitch a ride."

Jared's heart sank. "Would they stow away?" he asked. "Even having Rebecca with them?"

Buford's grin vanished. "Especially then. It would be the quickest way out of town. They tend to hop a ride whenever they can."

He stepped off the boardwalk to head toward the train station, but sudden gunfire mingled with thunderous horses' hooves stopped him. The three men turned toward the approaching noise.

In the distance a flash of blue sent a wave of relief blasting through Jared and his hands choked the shotgun. *Rebecca. Thank God.*

"It's them," he shouted. He ran into the street with Buford and Rory on his heels.

The commotion brought people pouring out of the shops lining the street. The horses raced by, but the riders slowed them and came back, stopping in front of the men. Rebecca sat in front of Rufus with a burlap sack over her head, her hands bound by a rope.

Jared gripped the gun tighter and found it difficult to breath.

"Are you going to give me the money now, Rory?" Rufus sneered. He yanked the sack off of Rebecca's head and cupped her face with his hand. "Or do I get the pleasure of her company."

Jared's heart lurched. The sight of his beloved's hair unkempt from the sack and her face pale with fright, started a rage pounding behind his eyes. Only the thought of them not having a future together kept him from shooting the bastards who held her from their horses and damn the consequences.

"Let her go," he demanded, raising the shotgun to his shoulder, grateful for His West Point training. It was all he could do to restrain himself from shooting Rufus off the horse.

Rory and Buford raised their weapons as well.

"Do what he says, Rufus," Buford advised. "Judge Templeton will take your cooperation in this matter under advisement when he charges you both."

"Uh, Rufus," Amos said, his horse dancing in

place.

"What is it now?" Rufus growled.

"There's two of 'em." Amos motioned with his head toward the grim faced Rory and the sheriff.

"What?" Rufus turned his head and seemed to see the other men for the first time. "This some kind of tom foolery?"

"Hello again, Rufus," Rory said. "Now put the lady down off the horse, gentle like, and no one will get hurt."

Rufus grunted. "Not until I get my money."

"You want your money then you'll have to let Rebecca go first."

Rufus sat on the horse without moving for a long moment. "Fine," he spat. "But if you try anything, I'll shoot her in the back." He shoved Rebecca off the horse, and she fell, landing on her hands and knees in the dirt.

The crowd gasped, and Jared tossed his gun to Rory. "Cover me," he ordered as he closed the short distance to Rebecca.

He gently picked her up and led her away from her captors, tossing a direct order to his cousin over his shoulders. "Shoot them."

Rory laughed.

Once they were safely across the street he took out his pocket knife and cut the rope away from her bound hands. "Did they hurt you?" he whispered against her hair, crushing her to him.

She shook her head and flung her arms around him. "No. But I'm so glad to be away from them. I want to go home. Please take me home, Jared. Take me to Oak Hill, now."

He nodded and brushed kisses along her cheek and her neck, stopping at her ear. "Of course, darling. I'll take you home as soon as the next train will get us there."

Chapter Twenty-One

It was early evening and the sun dipped low in the hot summer sky when the train from Grenada pulled to a stop in Jackson. Jared still found the new knowledge about Rory remarkable as he helped Rebecca off the train. His beautiful and strong Rebecca, he thanked his good fortune that Mitchell had asked him to be her escort or they might not have met. She'd withstood so much since then. Some of the danger was her own making while the other was unnecessary because of Rory.

Rory. It would be a long time before he could forgive Rory. Not just for putting Rebecca in danger, but for all the trouble he had caused.

"Should I hire a horse and ride on to Oak Hill?" Rory asked walking a few steps behind them, carrying their bags. "I can send Higgins back with the carriage and Mary can have a proper wedding supper prepared by the time you arrive."

Rebecca stopped and tucked a stray tendril behind her ear. "After today's events, I'd prefer a hot bath and to retire early tonight. Perhaps we can have a celebration tomorrow and invite a few friends?" She looked to Jared for his approval.

He nodded. "Anything you like, my love."

Rory stepped between them. "I'll still send Higgins

to fetch you."

"Have him call on us at the Bakersfield Hotel." Jared instructed.

A sly smile formed at Rory's mouth. "Can't wait until you arrive home, Cousin?"

Rebecca's cheeks flamed at his words, but she continued to smile.

"We're going to see her aunt and tell her the news," Jared explained. He fought the urge to grab Rory by the collar and throttle him for his crudeness.

"Beg your pardon," he said with a grin.

"No harm done," Rebecca assured him, touching his arm. "Thank you again for your aid today. You didn't have to come in search of us, but you did, and for that I'm truly thankful."

Rory half-bowed and flashed a smile. "It was the least I could do. You did marry my cousin and for that *I'm* eternally grateful. Perhaps now he'll be less cross with me."

Jared grimaced at his cousin's attempt at charm. "Get going."

Rory sauntered a few steps ahead, but turned back. "I'll get rid of Delaney if he should be waiting around Oak Hill. After all, I instructed Mary to be cordial and offer him a room if he wished to wait for my return."

"How very hospitable of you," Jared grumbled.

Rory shrugged. "He does believe the place mine, so why shouldn't I be generous?"

Rebecca remained quiet until he'd left them. When he was out of hearing, she turned to Jared. "You don't think Delaney is waiting for Rory at Oak Hill, do you? Surely if Mary paid him the debt, he'd take the money and leave."

Jared sighed and offered her his arm. She placed her hand on it and they began walking toward the main street. "It's hard to predict what a gambler will do, and after meeting Delaney, I could see him wearing out his welcome."

"I can't take Lucas to Oak Hill until I know Delaney is gone." Her brow creased with concern. "Maybe I should…stay in town…tonight while you make sure he has?"

"No." Jared's stomach tightened in frustration at the thought of another night apart from her. Damn Rory and his interference.

"We both should stay in town?"

"Yes. We are married now. Don't you think we should stay together?"

A wicked grin lit up her face. "And as your cousin has reminded us, we haven't had our wedding night yet. Besides, you did promise to kiss me soundly each morning when I wake."

"Yes. Yes I did. And I can't very well do that if you are in town and I am at Oak Hill. It just isn't a way to start a marriage."

He slowed their pace and turned to face her. "However, as much as I detest the idea of being apart from you, I can wait for our wedding night, if we must. And I can stay at Oak Hill alone tonight if you desire. But if we stay apart I promise to arrive early to keep my word and to bring you home to Oak Hill."

She smiled. "Darling, there is no need for us to stay apart. I want to be with you tonight and I can bear to be away from Lucas another night to ensure he's safe from Delaney. I will ask Aunt Josephine to bring him out tomorrow. Besides, we will need time to prepare him a room before he arrives."

Jared cupped her cheek in his hand. "The nursery is already furnished. It only needs to be cleaned, and I'll set Mary on it first thing tomorrow, but I think you will find it sufficient for his needs."

Rebecca blinked and her green eyes glistened. "Oh Jared. The room that was meant for your son? Are you sure you want my Lucas to have it?"

"Our Lucas," he corrected.

Her eyelids fluttered and a lone tear rolled down her cheeks. "Our Lucas," she whispered. "I like the sound of that."

"For now and for always."

She nodded and he brushed his lips against hers, not caring who might see them. They were married now.

They began walking again. "It's such a beautiful evening. I wonder what your aunt will say about our news."

Rebecca laughed softly. "She'll be pleased. She thought we were eloping and that was the reason behind my going to Memphis so suddenly anyway. I assured her it wasn't, but you changed that."

"I'm glad I did."

It wasn't long before the Bakersfield Hotel came into view. From behind the doors, gay music could be heard. "They must be having another extravaganza in the dining room," Rebecca said. "I wonder what the theme is tonight. Aunt Josephine and Doctor Gordon went to Italian night together."

Jared smiled, recalling the morning after Mrs. Paxton gave birth and the good doctor and Miss Davis drinking coffee at his table. Rebecca had confided in him that the pair had been flirting. "Do they spend much time together?"

Rebecca nodded. "They meet at the corner every day and walk to noon Mass together. They're both devout Catholics."

He slowed again, considering her words. "And being such a devout Catholic do you suppose she will mind that we were not married by a priest?"

"We were married by Parson Ben. She will not mind one bit about that."

As they drew closer to the music, laughter and voices could be heard. Rebecca squeezed his arm. "It definitely sounds like a party."

Jared pointed at the carriage. "That's Mitchell's. Do you suppose he and Elizabeth have returned from their honeymoon tour and have come to call on you?"

"Now *she'll* be the one cross with us for eloping." Rebecca picked up the skirts of her dress and hurried up the steps into the hotel lobby. Jared followed.

"Ah, Miss Davis. It's so good to have you return. You have been missed."

"Thank you." The clerk's greeting surprised her. "Is my aunt in?"

"I believe she is in the dining room with a few other guests."

"Thank you." Rebecca turned to Jared and held out her hand. "Shall we go in?"

He took it and felt her hand tremble. He squeezed it to reassure her, but her cheeks paled and she bit her lower lip. Where had the strong woman he knew gone to so quickly? Was she suddenly afraid of her aunt or Elizabeth's reaction?

As they walked into the room, he spotted Mitchell

and Elizabeth seated at a large table with her family and Doctor Gordon, Miss Davis and Charlotte holding Lucas.

"Miss Rebecca!" Charlotte exclaimed. The music stopped and the chatter ended as the people turned to look at them.

Josephine rushed to hug Rebecca. "I'm so glad you are here," she exclaimed. "I have so much to tell you."

Rebecca returned her embrace. "I'm glad to be home. I have something to tell you as well."

Josephine stepped back and looked at Jared. "Mr. Hollingsworth? What brings you here tonight?"

He bowed. "Miss Davis."

"What do you have to tell me?" Josephine asked, glancing back to her niece.

Rebecca took Jared's hand again. "We're married."

Josephine clapped her hands together, smiling as tears ran down her cheeks. "How wonderful. Simply wonderful news." She turned toward the group of people. "Ancil darling, did you hear? My Rebecca and Mr. Hollingsworth have eloped."

Elizabeth squealed and rushed across the room pulling Mitchell behind her. "Eloped? But I had hoped to plan your wedding."

"Don't be too upset. We didn't want to wait," Rebecca explained. "I'm so glad you've returned.

Mitchell shook Jared's hand. "Congratulations. I heard in town that you found Rory."

Jared nodded. "Yes and he's taken care of that matter I spoke to you about."

"Excellent news. So there was no need to..." Mitchell glanced at Rebecca and smiled. "Yet you did anyway?"

"Did what anyway, darling?" she asked, slipping her arm around his waist.

Jared lovingly glanced down at her and caressed her cheek. "Marry again."

A chill ran down her spine. Had Mitchell wanted him to marry for the dowry a new wife could bring? She swallowed hard and tilted her head, recalling the carriage ride when he'd first asked her to marry him. He'd told her about how Oak Hill was in ruin and how he had no right to ask her to marry him until he could save the plantation. Thankfully that hadn't been needed. He'd wanted her regardless of the security her dowry could bring him, even if she had offered to cover Rory's markers if necessary.

"Yes, Rory is paying his debt to Delaney and Oak Hill will be safe once again," she said.

Josephine's happy expression vanished. "Did you say Delaney?"

"Yes, but don't worry. Jared and I married to give our son protection."

"Your son?" Josephine's eyes widened and pulled Rebecca further away from the others. "So you told him? He knows about Mariah?"

Rebecca nodded. "I had no other choice after Delaney mistook me for her. I never thought we looked much alike as sisters. Nothing like Jared and Rory do as cousins, but Delaney saw it."

Doctor Gordon left the table and joined them. "Congratulations, Rebecca. I know you and Jared will be most happy together."

"Thank you, Doctor." Rebecca looked past him to where Charlotte stood bouncing Lucas. "How's my boy been while I've been gone?"

"Perfect. He's been absolutely perfect." Josephine looked over at him too. "There's something I need to tell you Rebecca. Can Ancil and I steal you away from the party for a few moments?"

Her aunt had called the doctor by his Christian name twice that evening without blinking an eye. The doctor had also looked at her aunt fondly. Both looked utterly happy together and Rebecca began to wonder what had transpired in her absence. "Certainly. Let me tell Jared…"

"Perhaps he should come too," Doctor Gordon suggested, slipping his arm around Josephine's waist.

Rebecca noticed his action and she bit back a smile, wondering what they wanted to speak to her about.

Josephine nodded. "Yes, please ask him to join us upstairs in our suite."

"If you like. We'll be right up." Rebecca waited until the pair left and went to speak to Jared. They made their apologies to Elizabeth and Mitchell before leaving the dining room.

Upstairs Rebecca found her aunt pacing while Doctor Gordon begged her to sit down beside him. "What's wrong?" she asked.

Doctor Gordon stood and went to stand beside Josephine. "First off, your aunt and I have news of our own to share, Rebecca. I've asked her to marry me and she has agreed."

"Married?" Rebecca gasped. "You're getting married? Oh Aunt Josephine I couldn't have hoped for better news. But what is wrong? Why are you so nervous?"

"Congratulations to you both," Jared said.

"Thank you," Doctor Gordon replied, leading Josephine to the sofa. "Sit, dearest," he said gently. "You're going to wear yourself out."

She sat, but fidgeted, bunching the material of her skirt with her hand. She shook her head before she finally spoke. "I beg you to forgive me, Rebecca. I beg you to forgive me for what I'm about to tell you."

Rebecca went to the fainting couch and sat on the edge. Jared moved to stand behind her. "What could you have possibly done that you should beg my forgiveness?"

Tears running down her face, Josephine took a deep breath. "There is something you need to know about Mariah. There is no easy way to say it other than to be blunt. She wasn't really your sister. Your parents weren't her parents. She…she was my…daughter. Your parents agreed to take her as their own since I was unwed and alone. They raised her and only gave her back to my care when they died. Yet I failed her again. I wasn't able to protect her from the likes of Stuart Delaney. I blamed myself. I blamed her, but mostly I blamed me for my weakness."

"No." Rebecca shook her head. "This can't be true. I remember when—"

"It is true, dear." Josephine cut her off and took another jagged breath. "We were in Europe and you were very young."

"I remember." Rebecca stood. "But you blamed Mariah for Delaney. You were so cruel to her. If she were your daughter how could you—"

"Yes. Yes I did. I blamed her for being so foolish that she found herself pregnant and alone just like I did. My Charles took ill and died, but I was still alone and unwed. I sinned and I was punished for my transgression. And in the end I lost my Mariah just like I lost my Charles."

A heavy silence fell over the room and no one moved or spoke for several long minutes. Finally, Josephine smoothed the wrinkles from her dress. "I can't change the past. I tried so many years to atone for my transgression. I threw myself into work for the church. But it didn't cover the sin I had committed. I still carried the guilt inside me until I allowed myself to love again."

Rebecca slowly sat down again.

"And the hardest part of confessing my past to you is now I find myself wanting Lucas. I want to raise him as my own, but I know I can't. I have no right to him. He's yours. You've cared and loved him from the day he was born."

Rebecca swallowed, unable to take her eyes off Josephine. It was several long moments before she was able to respond. "This explains so much. I can understand why you said the things you did about Mariah dying for the sin committed. You weren't talking about hers, but yours. Don't you think you've punished yourself enough? You were young and in love."

Josephine broke down crying. "You don't hate me?"

"How could I hate you?" Rebecca went to Josephine and knelt before her. She hugged her.

"Not even for my wanting Lucas?"

"Not even Lucas." Rebecca took the handkerchief Doctor Gordon offered and dried Josephine's face. "He's your grandson and I understand you wanting him with you now. Just because he will be living with me and Jared at Oak Hill doesn't mean you can't visit him or he visit you when he's older. He needs grandparents as much as parents."

Josephine gave her a wan smile. "I didn't think you'd give him up and I didn't want to ask you to either. I never expected to feel anything for him like I do."

The suite door opened and Charlotte came in with Lucas. Seeing Josephine, he held out his arms to her. "Ma-ma. Ma-ma," he called.

"I'm sorry, miss, but he wouldn't stop asking for you." Charlotte carried him over to Josephine and she took him. He patted her face. "Ma-ma. Ma-ma."

Tears ran down Josephine's cheeks again and she sniffed. "No, darling one, I'm not Mama."

"When did he start calling you that?" Rebecca asked.

"After you left." She sniffed again. "I told him I wasn't, but he wouldn't stop saying it."

Rebecca reached for him and he went to her, laying his head on her shoulder. "Ma-ma," he cooed. "Ma-ma."

She kissed his head. "I've missed you so much," she whispered.

"I suppose you will be taking him with you tonight?" Josephine asked.

"Actually no," Rebecca said. "I can't take him tonight because we don't know if Delaney is at Oak Hill. I thought you could bring him and his things out tomorrow?"

"Of course I will," she said with her old spirit. "After all, he's my grandson."

"And not just him, Miss Davis," Jared said. "I want you and Charlotte to come to Oak Hill until you and Doctor Gordon are married."

She beamed at him. "Thank you, but I think I'll stay here. Charlotte can go with you to help with Lucas. You don't need me hovering around your new family."

"Nonsense. You are our family." Rebecca got to her feet and walked Lucas to get him to sleep.

"Oak Hill is large enough that we won't be falling over one another," Jared added. "You can have my mother's suite with your own private balcony that overlooks the flower garden."

"At least think about it before you turn the offer down," Rebecca suggested, heading for the bedrooms to put the baby down. "Charlotte, I'll need you to pack our things and be ready when the carriage comes for you tomorrow."

"Yes, miss." She followed Rebecca into the room. "Can I pack you a fresh bag for the night?"

Rebecca nodded. "Yes please."

When Rebecca returned she found the trio chatting quietly. Jared smiled when she entered the room.

"Higgins has arrived. Are you ready to go?"

"Yes. This has been a most eventful day."

"Yes it has," Doctor Gordon said, standing. "We'd best rejoin our dinner party. The Calhouns will be wondering where we've run off to. Though I doubt the Coopers will have observed our absence for more than a minute. They are still so engrossed with one another."

"As all newlyweds should," Josephine cooed, slipping her hand into his.

Rebecca noticed her aunt had repaired her face and you couldn't tell she'd been crying. She hugged her one last time before she left. "Thank you for telling me about Mariah. I'm sorry you've had to bear that burden alone for so long. Papa and Mama never said a word."

"They wouldn't, dear. They vowed to never speak of it for all our sakes. And don't worry about Lucas. I know you'll be the best one for him to be with, and it's what Mariah wanted. It was a foolish notion and I shouldn't have said anything."

"No. No. It wasn't foolish. I'm glad you told me how you feel. Even if we aren't living in the same house we can share him."

Josephine kissed her on the cheek and nodded. "He'll have the best of both of us."

Chapter Twenty-Two

Once settled in the carriage, Rebecca laid her head on Jared's shoulder and closed her eyes, still hearing Josephine's words echo in her head. "I can't believe Aunt Josephine was Mariah's mother."

"Neither can I. That was the last thing I expected to hear when we joined them upstairs."

"I know. I feel sorry for her. She has had to carry this secret for so long and to lose Mariah without getting to tell her she was her mother is simply unfair." Rebecca sat up and looked at him. "When I think of some of the things I personally said to her. How I teased her for her strong beliefs about premarital relations. I am ashamed of myself."

"Darling, you had no idea. Exactly what did you say?"

"It doesn't matter now."

"Come on, Rebecca. Tell me."

"I said I'd have no problem taking a lover before marriage if he was someone I loved."

"Is that so?" Jared tilted her chin up with his finger. "Did you have anyone in particular in mind?"

"Oh Jared, don't read more into it than what it was."

"Exactly what was it?"

"Words. Simply words. I was teasing her. Still I

had no right... When I think of how hard it must have been for her to keep this secret, especially after Mama and Papa died. She could have easily told Mariah the truth, and yet she kept silent. I couldn't have done it."

He smiled. "I think your aunt is a very lucky woman."

"Why do you say that?"

"Well, take Doctor Gordon for instance. He didn't seem to mind her past. It goes to show how much he must love her to overlook what she did in her youth. Don't you agree?"

Rebecca nodded. "Yes. You're right. It does prove he loves her dearly and I'm so thankful for that. Aunt Josephine deserves a man who will love her unconditionally. No matter what scandal the truth might have brought if it fell into the wrong hands."

Rebecca sighed and settled back in his arms, resting her head against his chest. "I'm worried about Delaney being at Oak Hill when we arrive. Did you by chance ask Higgins if he'd been there?"

"Yes. He's been there and Mary was feeding him supper when Rory arrived. Higgins left so he doesn't know if Rory was successful in getting him to leave or not."

"So we may have a house guest?"

"We'd better not," Jared growled, squeezing her shoulder.

Rebecca laughed softly. "I quite agree."

She became silent and soon he realized she'd fallen asleep. He closed his eyes as well and longed for a night spent in her arms, enjoying the splendor of her body. He pulled Rebecca closer and rested his chin on the top of her head. Breathing in her faint verbena scent he chuckled, recalling her offering Amos the use of her perfume, as the movement of the carriage lulled him to sleep.

"We're home, sir," Higgins shook his arm to wake him. "Mr. Hollingsworth, we're here."

Jared opened his eyes and blinked a few times. "Very good, Higgins. Thank you."

"Can I help you and the missus to the house?"

"I'll carry her if you can get her small bag."

"Very well, sir."

Jared gently rubbed her cheek with his hand. "Rebecca, we're home, darling."

"What is it?" she murmured unsteadily swaying on the seat.

"We're at Oak Hill."

"That's nice."

Jared climbed down and reached for her. "Come here."

She moved to the door and he helped her down. Once she was steady on her feet he swept her up in his arms. "May I officially carry you over the threshold, Mrs. Hollingsworth?"

She giggled. "I'm too worn out to stop you."

"Good, because I am too tired to argue." He carried her to the verandah where Mary met them with a lantern.

"Welcome home!" she cheerfully called.

"Thank you, Mary. Has our visitor left?"

"Afraid not, sir. The gentleman was most insistent on apologizing again to you personally for mistaking you for Mr. Rory. But Rory said you weren't to be disturbed this evening so he's entertaining the gentleman in town at Monique's. I never heard of the place before, have you?"

"So we have the house to ourselves?" Jared asked, glancing at Rebecca. "Rory's at Monique's."

She giggled. "May he stay there all night."

"Except for me, sir." Mary's smile broadened. "It's good to have you with us, Mrs. Hollingsworth. This place needs a woman to cheer it. I hope you find yourself at home here."

"Thank you, Mary."

"Rory said you'd want a light supper and a hot bath when you arrived. I've seen to both. They're waiting for you in your room and I set up a second tub in your study, Mr. Hollingsworth."

"Then we'll see you in the morning," Jared told her, eager for her to be gone.

"I'll prepare a hot breakfast for you in the morning when you want it."

Jared carried Rebecca into the house and up the stairs. "I'll give you a better tour tomorrow," he said, "but I think you recall where the library is if you should need a book for reading tonight."

"I—I don't think I'll need one," she whispered, running her fingers through the hair at the back of his neck. "I have other things in mind to preoccupy me tonight if I'm not sleeping."

"Perhaps you can share those ideas with me?" he teased, opening his bedroom door. He carried her inside and sat her down gently.

As Mary had promised, a table was laid out with their meal; soft candlelight glowed from the candelabra on the table and steam rose from the tub partially concealed behind a folding screen.

"Would you like to bathe first or eat?"

"Bathe before the water gets cold."

"Then I'll leave you to take care of it and I'll return shortly." He kissed her lightly on the lips. "Welcome home, Mrs. Hollingsworth."

"Don't go far," she said. "I won't linger in the water long."

He slipped out the door and hurried down the hall to his study. True to her word, Mary had another tub brought in, a clean towel and his robe waiting on him.

Stripping out of his clothes, he sank into the hot water and washed away the sweat and dirt from their travels. He wasted little time lingering, even though the hot water soothed the aches of riding all day. He stood, reached for the bucket of rinse water and poured it over his head. Setting the empty bucket down, he grabbed the clean towel and dried himself, before stepping out of the tub to don fresh clothes.

When he returned to his bedroom, he knocked before he entered. Rebecca was already dressed in her gown and robe, and was drying her hair with a towel.

She smiled when she saw him. "You bathed?"

"Yes. Shall we eat?"

She shook her head and hung the towel over the screen. When she turned around, she untied her robe and let it drop to the floor. "I'm not hungry."

She stood before him in her thin gown, the material almost translucent in the candlelight.

His body hardened at the sight of her. "You're not?"

She shook her head again and walked to him, wrapping her arms around his neck. "No, I'm not. All I want is you, Mr. Hollingsworth."

His breath caught in his throat and he lowered his

head until their lips met. She feasted on his kiss until she heard him groan. He pulled her closer against him, cupping her bottom and lifting her until she was pressed against his arousal.

The feel of him startled her and she found her body reacting in a very strange way. Heat spread over her and pooled between her legs as he kissed her neck while his free hand fondled her breast. Slowly, he traced her nipples with his forefinger, and they puckered at his touch.

"Jared," she gasped, tilting her head back. He trailed kisses up her neck, across her jaw, until he came to her mouth again. His kiss was no longer gentle, but hungered and his tongue parted her lips to dart frantically within exploring the depths of her mouth.

She clung to him, kissing him ardently in return while marveling at his strength and the hard contours of his torso. This was the man she loved, the man she'd married and he was all hers from now until eternity.

He scooped her up and carried her to the bed. He let her slide down his body to stand before him, letting her feel his arousal. She untied his robe and slipped it off his shoulders, running her hand down the hard plane of his chest and over his hips. She glanced down between them and then back up to his face.

"I love you, Rebecca," he said, slipping the straps of her gown off her shoulders. He pushed the thin material down to her waist exposing her breasts. Bending down, he captured one nipple in his mouth and suckled.

"Jared," she gasped as her legs almost buckled from under her and the heat exploded between them again.

"Shhh. It's all right, darling. I'll take care of your need." His voice was husky and he shoved the material the rest of the way down to her feet. He slowly lowered her onto the bed, staring at her for a long time before he moved to lie beside her.

Rebecca swallowed hard and tried not to stare at his fully aroused body.

"Is something wrong?" he asked, pulling her into his arms.

"Nothing." She smiled and felt her face warm. "It's just… I've never seen…been with a man before."

He cupped her face with his hand and kissed her softly. "I know and there isn't any reason for you to be afraid. We'll go slowly. I promise to be gentle. It may hurt at first, but I assure you the bliss you'll feel will make up for the pain."

He moved until his body covered hers, entwined his fingers with hers, and kissed her again until she moaned. Releasing her hand, he trailed kisses from the valley between her breasts to the flat plane of her stomach. He gently placed his hand on her mound and parted her folds with his finger. He found a wet haven and his finger slipped to her core easily enough.

"Oh my," she gasped, her muscles tightening around him. Slowly he withdrew and moved his finger back and forth until she writhed against him and the bed.

She reached for him and he moved back to cover her. He kissed her as he parted her legs and positioned himself to enter her. He thrust slow and withdrew. He thrust again and felt the tightness of her barrier. He withdrew and thrust with a little more force, pushing past it.

"Jared," she cried, clinging to him. Her body quivered and he stilled. He kissed her gently and squeezed her breast and he felt her wetness increase.

"It's all right, darling. The worst is over," he assured, withdrawing. "I didn't hurt you, did I?"

She shook her head. "No."

"Good." He kissed her eyes, the tip of her nose and her parted lips. This time when he entered her, she arched her hips up to meet him as he thrust again and again. She wrapped her legs around him and he thrust deeper.

"Jared. Jared." Her calling out his name was bliss to his ears and he withdrew and thrust again and again until she cried out in release. He thrust one last time and joined her in the ecstasy of their making.

He collapsed beside her, and pulled her back against him, holding her close. Neither spoke until their breathing stabilized. "Are you all right?"

"Hmmm," she murmured, taking his hand in hers. "That was like nothing I ever imagined was possible."

He kissed the back of her neck. "We can do it again whenever you like."

She turned to face him. "I like."

He smiled and brought her palm up to his mouth to kiss it. "I'm glad to know you find love making enjoyable."

"I do." She kissed him, running her fingers through his blond hair and he rolled her onto her back.

He playfully bit at her lip. "What would you like to do now?"

"This." She kissed him and ran her hands over his back, enjoying the feel of him. She pushed against him and they rolled until he was lying on his back. His hardened arousal against her leg drew her attention lower than she ever imagined she'd explore. She trailed kisses down his chest, stopping at his stomach.

Touching his arousal seemed almost taboo, but she took a deep breath and traced a circle around the tip. He jerked and he sucked in his breath. She pulled her hand away. "Did I hurt you?"

"No." He threw back his head and a deep rumble of laughter erupted.

"Then why—?"

"Because I want you."

"Oh." She crawled back to his arms and they kissed, making love again and again before finally curling up together. Yawning, Jared reached and pulled the sheet up around them before they slept.

Chapter Twenty-Three

Rebecca woke smiling the next morning. She stretched, feeling sore in a few places, especially her backside from being jostled by Rufus' horse on that mad chase ride. Sighing, she rolled over and saw Jared's housekeeper on the opposite side of the room.

"I hope I didn't wake you, Mrs. Hollingsworth," Mary said, sitting down a pitcher of water at the washstand. "Mr. Hollingsworth asked me to bring this up to you first thing."

"He's not here?" Rebecca sat up, the sheet slipping from her. She quickly grabbed it and pulled it up to her neck.

"I'm afraid there was an emergency that called him out to the Paxton's, but he said he'd be back as fast as he could and for you to stay in bed until he returned."

"He did?" Rebecca's cheeks heated. She propped a few pillows behind her and pulled her knees up to chest. "Has something happened to Isabella or the baby?"

"No ma'am. They've been right as rain since the birth," Mary offered. "It actually had to do with Rory and that Mr. Delaney fellow. I'm not sure what transpired, but it must have been urgent if Mr. Hollingsworth left you before you woke. Can I bring you a tray while you wait?" Her eyes twinkled as she spoke. "I noticed the food wasn't touched last night. You must be starving."

Rebecca's stomach rumbled in protest and her cheeks further heated. "A bite to eat would be nice, but are you sure I can't dress and come downstairs?"

"No ma'am. Mr. Hollingsworth was adamant that you stay put until he returned. He was mumbling something about keeping his promise to you if it was the last thing he did as he went out the door." Mary winked.

"Oh." Rebecca smiled. "He promised to kiss me awake each morning. Isn't that sweet of him?"

"Yes ma'am, it is." Mary returned her smile and loaded the tray with last night's dishes. When she finished, she gave Rebecca a thoughtful look. "He's a changed man since meeting you. I thank the good Lord for it too. I'll be back with some biscuits and preserves and a little coffee."

When she was alone, Rebecca got out of bed and put on her robe from the foot of the bed. She wondered if Mary had picked it up off the floor or if Jared had before he left.

Walking behind the screen, she poured water from the pitcher into the bowl and washed her hands and her face. After a quick sponge bath she put on her robe and began to brush the tangles from her hair.

The door opened again and she looked up to see Jared.

"I thought I left instructions for you to stay in bed?" He smiled at her.

"You did."

"And yet you chose to disobey me?" He frowned but there was no mistaking the twinkle in his eyes.

She smiled. "I wanted to be presentable when you returned. If you had tarried a little longer I would have been back in bed waiting for you."

He crooked his finger at her and she went to him. "I made you a promise that I intend to keep, Mrs. Hollingsworth."

"And I intend to hold you to it."

He wrapped his arm around her waist and pulled her snug against him. "I missed your kisses."

"Is that all you missed?" She ran her hand up his arm to his shoulder. "Or did you perhaps miss all of me?"

"What do you think?" He captured her mouth with his and hungrily kissed her, his tongue slipping into her mouth and matching the kisses from the night before. As they kissed, his hands roamed over her body renewing the feel of his caresses. Her robe fell to the floor around her feet and he ran his hand down her stomach and touched her mound, letting one finger trace a path until it sank into her wetness. He rubbed circles around her clit and she moaned. Sweeping her up into his arms, he prepared to carry her to the bed when a knock sounded at the bedroom door.

Without waiting for a response, Mary pushed open the door and entered with a breakfast tray. Her eyes widened when she saw them and she looked away quickly. "I didn't hear you come into the house, sir. I had no idea you'd returned."

"Obviously." His tone reflected his annoyance. "Leave the tray and go, Mary."

"Yes, sir." She hurried across the room, put it on the table, and retreated with the same speed. "I'm sorry to have disturbed."

As soon as the door closed Rebecca giggled. Jared laughed as well. He carried her to the bed and laid her down.

Unbuttoning his shirt, he pulled it from his trousers and tossed it onto the floor. Sitting down he pulled off his boots and socks before he unfastened his pants. Discarding them he joined her on the bed. "Now where were we?"

"I'll never be able to face her again." Rebecca hid her face against his shoulder.

"Don't give it another thought. She'll try to forget it as well. In a few days no one will remember it."

"That is easy for you to say, darling. You weren't the one naked."

"I don't think there is a more beautiful sight than you naked." He picked up her hand and began to nibble kisses at her fingertips, her palm and her wrist. "In fact, I think I'd like to keep you in this room…in my bed…just as you are."

"You would, would you?"

"Yes." He looked up at her. "And do you know where I'd be?"

She shook her head and made her eyes go big with mock innocence.

"I'd be right here with you. Feasting on your beauty. Making love to you night and day."

"I'm sure you'd lose interest eventually when I became all sluggish and fat with child."

"Never." He pulled her to him and kissed her again, rolling her until he was lying on top of her.

She wrapped her arms around him, shifting to adjust to his weight. "I love you, Jared Hollingsworth."

He nibbled kisses at her mouth. "I love you and I

need you more than I ever thought I could need anyone ever again."

"I know what you mean, darling. The feeling is overwhelming."

He smiled, slipping a hand under her bottom and brought her leg up over his hip. His entry was effortless as he sank into her wet depths, but he took it slow and enjoyed the way she tightened around him. He watched her lips part and her eyes close as he moved in and out. Her back arched and she moaned.

"Oh Jared. Jared."

"Yes, darling." He squeezed her breast and she bucked against him. He kissed her as she climaxed. She wrapped her legs around his waist and she climaxed a second time as he came. He collapsed on her, rolling them over until she was lying on top.

She sighed, trailing kisses up his chest. "If we were to start every day like this I may not want to get out of bed either."

A rumble of laughter escaped him. He held her secure against him and turned them onto their sides until they were facing. He brushed a tendril of hair away from her face and ran his finger down her jawline. "What shall we do today?"

"We have to prepare for Lucas," she reminded him.

He nodded. "I haven't forgotten, but I was hoping to postpone that a little while. Delaney is coming back and I'd rather he be gone before we send the carriage into town to fetch him, Charlotte, and your aunt—if she decides to come live here."

Recalling his departure from their marriage bed, Rebecca frowned and asked, "Why is Delaney returning? And what was going on at the Paxton's that called you away this morning?"

He propped himself up on his elbow. "Rory got the man drunk last night and they were thrown out of Madame Monique's. They walked back to Oak Hill, but got themselves turned around in their drunken stupor and ended up down at the field hand quarters. My men were not happy when they were disturbed from their sleep at four this morning. Paxton was roused from his bed and so was I."

"Where are Rory and Mr. Delaney now?" Rebecca asked.

"Passed out in the stables where Paxton and I dumped them. Hopefully they will sleep it off until noon giving us more time together."

"And will Delaney leave then?"

Jared shook his head. "He told me he wanted to talk to me."

Rebecca sat and pulled her knees up to her chest, hiding her face in the sheet. "Why can't that man move on? Don't you know what it does to me to have to see him? Knowing what he did to sweet Mariah? If he were to find out about Lucas—"

"Shhh. I'm sorry, darling." Jared sat up also and rubbed her back. He kissed her shoulder and she looked back at him, kissing him. He pulled her into his arms and lay back with her, holding her close.

A knock at the door disturbed their solitude. "Who is it?" Jared called, getting out of bed. He reached for his pants and put them on.

"Rory," a voice called from the other side of the door.

"Go away," he called. "I'm not ready to see you again today."

"Come on, Jared. How many times do I have to say I'm sorry for disturbing the Paxton household or your field hands?" A solid knock sounded on the door. "I'm not going away until you open this door.

Jared turned to Rebecca. "I'm sorry. It looks like we're going to have to…"

"I understand." She moved from the bed and picked up her robe off the floor, putting it on.

He opened the door and braced one arm on it. He placed the other on the doorframe, blocking any attempt by Rory to enter. Glaring, he demanded, "What's so damn important that you couldn't wait for me to come downstairs?"

Rory shrugged. "Sorry, but Delaney is insisting that he speak with you and Rebecca before he leaves. He doesn't care that it was your wedding night last night since he thinks he bedded her first."

"He what?" Jared's question rang down the hallway. "Where the hell is he now?"

"In the dining room having breakfast."

"Tell him to be patient. We'll be down momentarily and I'll speak with him."

Rory nodded and tried to see past Jared into the room. "Sorry, Rebecca."

Jared slammed the door. Rebecca came from behind the screen wearing a cream colored frock with a pale green sash that tied at the back. Fury or embarrassment stained her cheeks bright pink, and her hand seemed determined to choke her hairbrush.

"I hope you know I never slept with that man. Of all the nerve…"

"Has anyone told you how beautiful you are when you're angry?"

She blinked and shook her head. "No, and I have no intentions of starting my married life being angry." She smiled and added, "But you may tell me how beautiful I am as often as you like."

"I'll tell you every day if you wish but mine is a biased opinion."

"One I'll gladly accept," she said with a laugh then her smile vanished and she cast a glance at the untouched tray. "I don't want to hurt Mary's feelings, but I don't think I can eat until we finish this business with Delaney and send him packing."

"Just coffee, then." He poured from the carafe into the lone cup and drank before refilling it and handing it to her. She drained it and set it on the table. "That will do for now."

Jared took her hand. "Let's go face Delaney and see him off. Then we'll have a proper breakfast."

Chapter Twenty-Four

"I thought you said they'd be right down?" Delaney held his cup out for Mary to refill.

"They will. You need to be patient. It isn't like you have anywhere you must be within the hour, do you?" Rory said.

"Would you like more eggs or sausage, sir?" Mary asked.

"No, Mary. The meal was delicious."

"I'm glad you are enjoying our hospitality, Mr. Delaney," Jared said as he and Rebecca entered the dining room hand in hand.

Delaney stood and bowed to him. "Good morning, Mr. Hollingsworth. Mrs. Hollingsworth. Your cousin has been a most gracious host. He told me about your run in with those ruffians yesterday. It was a good thing he was there to stop them and return Mrs. Hollingsworth to you safely."

Jared looked at Rory, who shrugged. Leave it to his cousin to retell the story with a colorful twist.

"I pray you have concluded your business?" Jared said.

"Yes. I have agreed to take the money he owed me in exchange for the plantation. After touring the grounds upon my arrival, I realized managing property this size would require more effort and energy than I have the patience for. I'm a gambler. I enjoy my freedom."

Jared nodded and led Rebecca to the far end of the table. He pulled out her chair and she sat. "I'm glad to hear that."

Delaney took his seat again.

Jared pulled out a chair and sat next to Rebecca. "This land has been in our family for generations and I long to see it stay for many more." He waited until Mary filled his coffee cup before adding, "To getting what we all want."

Delaney held up a hand. "However, there is one matter that is unsettled."

A knot formed in Jared's stomach at Delaney's words and he prepared himself for what the man would say next. "What's that?"

"I finally figured out where I know your wife." Delaney smiled and winked at Rebecca. "By the way, congratulations on your nuptials."

"Thank you, Mr. Delaney," Rebecca said and reached for the coffee cup Mary sat before her

"Cut the pleasantries," Rory ordered. "I already told Jared that you believe you bedded Rebecca in New Orleans."

"Good Heavens," Mary gasped. "Rory, watch your language."

Rebecca sipped her coffee and looked up at the housekeeper. "He did not."

"I think I did." Delaney smirked. "Why else did you faint when I first saw you at the Exeter Hotel?"

"This is absurd." Jared laid his hand over Rebecca's.

"Furthermore, I married her myself in New

Orleans. We spent one hell of a night together. It's hard to forget a woman like that."

Rory laughed. "Isn't that the funniest thing you've ever heard? Rebecca and Mr. Delaney?"

"No. It's not," Jared barked, moving to stand behind Rebecca's chair. He held her hand tight and squeezed her shoulder with his other hand to reassure her. "And it couldn't be farther from the truth. I insist you stop with this idiotic nonsense at once and apologize to my wife."

"Of course the wedding wasn't real." Delaney confessed studying his fingernails. He glanced up at Jared and Rebecca. "I tricked her by having a friend pose as a priest and I believe that is why she pretends not to know me. I upset her by my ruse."

"I'm not pretending anything, sir. I never met you before our meeting at the Exeter hotel. And I fainted because…because I knew you…you held the markers to Oak Hill."

Delaney shook his head. "I find it hard to believe you, my dear Mrs. Hollingsworth. I wonder why that is?"

"Are you calling my wife a liar?" Jared demanded, stepping toward the man.

Rebecca held his hand firmly, preventing him from harming Delaney. "Don't let him upset you, darling. He isn't worth your energy. He's nothing more than a riverboat gambler who takes advantage of innocent young girls."

Rory looked at Jared. "Am I missing something here? Is any of this true?"

Jared shook his head. "I think you've outstayed your welcome, Mr. Delaney. If you'll gather your belongings I'll have my driver take you into town."

"Not just yet. I'm never wrong about the women I bed."

"You're wrong about this one," Rebecca said. "I can assure you, Mr. Delaney, I never visited New Orleans, nor did you trick me with a false wedding at a Mardi Gras party just so you could bed me."

Delaney jumped to his feet, knocking over his chair. "What did you say?"

"Good Lord." Rory pushed back from the table.

"I said I never married you."

"You said Mardi Gras. How did you know about Mardi Gras?"

Rebecca stared at their unwelcome guest. "How else would you have tricked a girl into believing a priest performed the marriage ceremony except at a Mardi Gras party?"

Jared stepped to stand behind her again. "I think you should leave, Mr. Delaney."

"No. I'm not going anywhere until she tells me what she knows about Mardi Gras."

Rebecca ran a hand over her face and shook her head. She'd done it now. That slip of her tongue told Delaney she knew more than she was willing to say. She pushed her chair back and stood.

"All right, Mr. Delaney. I know about Mardi Gras because the woman you mistook me for at the Exeter hotel was my younger sister. When you first asked me about New Orleans I didn't think it was possible that you had met her, but then you said your name. And that is the reason I fainted because I knew then that you were the man who broke Mariah's heart."

Delaney clapped his hands together. "I knew it. I

knew there was a reason I felt I had met you before. So Mariah is your sister?"

"This isn't something to celebrate. In fact, I can't see how you can stand before me and be so happy. You tricked Mariah into believing you married her just so you could take her innocence and then you left her to face the wrath of my aunt."

"I went to get us breakfast, but when I returned she was gone. If anyone did the leaving, she did." Delaney snapped his fingers. "Your aunt…I remember her. Scary woman, always carried that damn rosary. She didn't want Mariah having anything to do with me. But I found a way around that. Do you know where I can find Mariah?"

A silence fell over the room for a moment.

"You can't." Rebecca closed her eyes and took a jagged breath. She opened them and glared at him. "She's dead. She died last Christmas."

Mary gasped and covered her mouth with her handkerchief. "Poor child."

"Well *that* changes things," Delaney said. He picked up his overturned chair and sat back down at the table.

"How?" Jared asked.

The man shrugged. "I thought I might try to find her. She was a sweet girl. Thought we might make a go of it, maybe even get married for real, but if she's dead…can't rightly do it now, can we."

"Thank God for that," Rebecca cried and ran from the room.

"Now I think *you* had better leave, Mr. Delaney. You've upset my wife and I do not wish to lay eyes on you again. Rory, see him out."

Delaney laughed. "He acts like he owns the place instead of you."

"He does." Rory stood and held out his arm toward the front door. "After you."

Delaney nodded and walked past Rory. "You're a dishonest man, Rory Hollingsworth."

"It takes one to know one." Rory followed him to the front door. But before they reached the foyer, Higgins opened the door and helped a pretty blond woman with a baby inside.

"Higgins?" Rory looked from the driver to the woman. "Who's this?"

"Excuse me, Mr. Rory, but this is Charlotte, Miss Davis'...I mean...Mrs. Hollingsworth's maid. And this young fella is Master Lucas."

"Well. Well. Rebecca has a son?" Rory turned around. "Jared! Jared!"

Jared was half-way up the stairs to check on Rebecca when he heard Higgins in the foyer and then Rory calling for him. He returned to find Rebecca's fear coming to light. Delaney had laid eyes on Lucas, but the man was more interested in collecting his belongings to more than glance at the boy. At least that was in their favor.

"Charlotte? What are you and Lucas doing here so early? I was going to send Higgins into town to fetch you both this afternoon."

"Mrs. Hollingsworth said to be ready this morning and we were. And your driver did come to fetch us."

Jared looked at Higgins. "You did?"

"Yes, sir. I thought after the incident this morning with Mr. Rory and Mr. Delaney, the last thing you needed to worry about was getting Master Lucas here.

So I went on into town."

Jared nodded. "Thank you, Higgins."

"D-d-d-da," Lucas said and reached for Jared.

Charlotte laughed. "He knows you, Mr. Hollingsworth. He knows his papa."

"So he does," Jared said.

"I hate to spoil this little family reunion, but I believe I was being thrown out?" Delaney sneered.

"Right." Rory said and ushered the man out of the house.

"Charlotte, Mrs. Hollingsworth is upstairs," Jared said, getting the girl's attention.

"Yes sir, Mr. Hollingsworth. Should I take Lucas up with me?"

"No. He can stay with me for now. We should get better acquainted."

"Very well, sir." Charlotte turned to the driver. "Mr. Higgins, can you bring our luggage upstairs?"

"Higgins. Just plain Higgins, Miss Charlotte."

"Higgins," she repeated and turned to hurry across the foyer to the stairs.

Jared turned around and found Mary standing in the doorway of the dining room with her hands on her hips, staring at him. "What is it, Mary?"

His housekeeper wiped her eyes with her handkerchief and shook her head. "You look right at home with the boy in your arms. That's all, Mr. Hollingsworth. It does my heart good to see this day. And I hope there'll be a day when this house is full of little ones."

He grinned. "Whoa now, Mary. Let's not get ahead of ourselves. Rebecca and I only married. Give us a little time to settle into married life. We have Lucas to raise for now and in time we might…"

"What happened with Charisse won't necessarily happen with Rebecca, sir. Even when Mrs. Paxton delivered it didn't happen. We have to trust that things happen when they do for a reason. Trials come and they make us stronger, preparing us for what comes next."

Jared nodded. "The nursery needs cleaning today in preparation for Lucas. Rebecca and I will help do whatever you need. Just let us know."

Mary nodded. "I'll get on it as soon as I finish with the breakfast dishes. I've already been preparing for tonight's meal. Will there be any additional guests?"

"I expect Rory to return."

Mary smiled. "Thank you for coming to peace with him, sir. It was a pleasant surprise to find he's matured while he's been away."

Matured. Jared rolled that word around in his head and tried to think of Rory in that manner, but it didn't rightly fit. He was still having difficulty seeing his cousin as anything but a troublemaker.

"Will there be anyone else?" Mary prodded.

"Possibly Doctor Gordon and Rebecca's aunt, Miss Davis. You've met her before."

"Yes. I remember her. If you decide on others, please let me know and I will add another course to my menu. If you'll excuse me now, I have work to tend to in the kitchen."

When she was gone Jared looked at Lucas and the baby was chewing on his fingers. He pulled his hand from his mouth and Lucas gave a toothy grin.

"D-d-d-da," he gurgled and blew slobber.

"Da-da-da. Let's go find ma-ma-ma," he told him walking toward the foyer again. They had reached the stairs when Rebecca appeared at the top. She lifted the hem of her skirt and descended quickly to join them. Lucas saw her and clapped his hands.

"Ma-ma-ma," he squealed.

"How is my precious boy?" She cooed, touching his face and kissing him on the cheek. She stepped back and looked at Jared. "I couldn't believe it when Charlotte found me upstairs. Please say Delaney didn't see him."

"I wish I could, but he did. However, the man paid little attention to him. He was more concerned with leaving than with Lucas being here."

"That's good then." She nodded.

"Plus Charlotte did call me his papa." Jared wrapped his arm around her shoulders and they walked upstairs. "Let me show you the nursery."

Rebecca smiled. "How close is it to your room?"

"It's next door to *our* room and there is a hidden door that connects the rooms so you can check on him any hour of the night."

"And where will Charlotte sleep?" she asked as they reached the top step.

"If you prefer her to be near Lucas, we can set up a bed in the nursery for now. Otherwise, there is a room on the main floor next to Mary's for her."

"Downstairs is fine. That will give us more privacy right now." Rebecca walked ahead of him and called to her maid, "Charlotte?"

The girl appeared in the hallway with her arms full of soiled sheets. "Yes, ma'am?"

"When you finish tidying up in here, Mr. Hollingsworth will show you to your new quarters downstairs."

"Yes ma'am." The girl turned to go back inside.

"And Charlotte," Rebecca said. "Did my aunt happen to mention whether she was going to come live at Oak Hill?"

"No, ma'am. She didn't. Though she said to tell you she and Doctor Gordon would be by this afternoon after they attend Mass."

"Thank you, Charlotte." Rebecca turned back to Jared, frowning.

"Maybe we can convince her then," Jared suggested. Lucas patted his face.

"Perhaps."

Chapter Twenty-Five

Josephine walked to the corner where she always met Ancil before going to Mass. He was late, or was she early? It was hard to tell. The hotel suite had felt so alone since Charlotte and Lucas left earlier to go to Oak Hill.

Rebecca had married Mr. Hollingsworth without even letting her know. But then, why should her niece have consulted her? Rebecca was a grown woman and could do as she pleased. Still, Josephine would have liked to have been included in this decision.

"Why are you frowning, my dear?" Ancil asked joining her at the corner. He carried his doctor's bag.

"I was thinking about Rebecca. She married so quickly. Shouldn't she have consulted me?"

Ancil smiled. "One rarely consults family members when they elope, my dear."

She sighed. "I suppose you are right. It isn't like I oppose her choice in a husband. And I voiced my approval before she made her sudden trip to Memphis, so perhaps she thought she already had my blessing."

"See there. You are fretting over nothing. Come, let's walk to St. Anna's." He offered his arm and she took it.

"I see you carry your bag. Have you been to see a patient already this morning?"

He nodded. "Only a routine visit on an elderly couple. I try to check in on them every week or so. They have no children."

Josephine sighed again. "I hope we are blessed with children, Ancil. You don't think I'm too old to conceive do you?"

He stopped walking and looked at her, a grin forming at his mouth. "You simply amaze me, Josephine Davis. Where is the rigid, too tightly laced-up woman I was called to examine when we first met? She is gone and like the caterpillar that sheds its cocoon. You've turned into an amazing butterfly that I have the good fortune to spend the rest of my life with. I never thought I'd marry and now to hear you say you want us to have a child…I can't even begin to express my happiness."

"Oh, hush." She swatted his arm.

"And to answer your question about whether you can have a child or not we'll have to wait until we're married to find out."

Josephine blushed and he added hastily. "Medically speaking, you've had one child so there shouldn't be a reason you couldn't have another, but if it doesn't happen within time I know a specialist we could see."

Her blush faded and she gave him a shy smile. "So you don't think I'm too old?"

"No. I've seen women older than you conceive and deliver. Of course they had been birthing babies for years, but that doesn't mean it can't happen for you."

Josephine slipped her arm around his, and they began walking again. "I'd like to try."

"When should we speak to Father Bohannon about

the wedding? Rebecca's home now and we've told them of our plans."

"I'd like to have the wedding as soon as possible, Ancil. There is no need for me to move all the way out to Oak Hill only to move back to town. I don't want to stay at the hotel alone for long either. Would you be opposed to having a small ceremony three weeks from this coming Saturday if Father Bohannon is agreeable? That should be sufficient for the reading of the banns."

The grin quirked at the corner of his mouth again. "I think three weeks from this Saturday is fine. Are you certain you'll be ready by then?"

"Y-yes." Josephine frowned. "I already have my dress picked out."

"What is it?" he asked.

She pointed down the street at two men walking in their direction. "Isn't that Mr. Hollingsworth with that gambler?"

Ancil turned and looked at the two men. "That isn't Jared."

"It looks like him."

"Yes it does, but Jared has a cousin that could be his identical twin if you didn't know the difference."

"You don't say. What is this cousin's name?"

"Rory Hollingsworth. He's a free-spirit, but I didn't realize he was back in town. I think the last time I saw him was when his mother passed away. Once her will was read and he received his inheritance he left, bidding Jackson and Jared good-bye. I wonder what brings him back now."

"Interesting. You know, that man he's with looks vaguely familiar for some reason."

Ancil laughed. "You think you know that

gambler?"

"Good Lord." Josephine stopped and clutched at his arm as the men came closer. "That's Stuart Delaney. The man who...the man who...seduced Mariah."

Ancil dropped his bag and caught Josephine as she fainted, collapsing against him. "Josephine. Josephine."

"Doctor Gordon, do you need help?" Rory asked, running toward him.

"Yes." He glanced at Rory. "In my bag there are smelling salts."

Rory knelt and opened the bag. He rummaged around until he found what he was looking for. "Got them."

Ancil took the vial and removed the lid, waiving it underneath Josephine's nose. She jerked and sputtered, blinking madly.

"Wh-what happened?"

"You fainted, darling," he explained, recapping the vial and handing it to Rory. Ancil helped her stand on her own, but kept a supportive arm around her waist in case she had another spell.

"I thought I saw..." her words stopped and her eyes enlarged as she saw the man standing beside Rory.

"Hello, Miss Davis," Delaney said. "I almost didn't recognize you without your rosary."

"I still have it," she retorted. "What are you doing here?"

"Last time I checked it was still a free country for white men. That means I have the right to go and do whatever I like."

"Let's go, Ancil. We'll be late for Mass."

"Yes, run away to your precious church. You were always good about that. Did you know Mariah despised you for it?"

She gasped.

"Come on, Delaney." Rory advised. "You've upset Rebecca already. You don't have to upset her aunt as well today. Besides if we don't go now, you'll miss your train."

Delaney checked his pocket watch. "Quarter till twelve. Another few minutes and that whistle will blow as the train pulls out. I guess I could stay in town another day."

"I think not." Rory grabbed his arm and urged him forward. "I don't relish the idea of going back to Oak Hill and informing Jared you are still in town. If he didn't do you bodily harm, Rebecca might scratch your eyes out. I've never seen her so upset."

Delaney chuckled and nodded toward Josephine. "Good day, Miss Davis."

When they were gone Josephine turned to Ancil. "He's been to Oak Hill. What if he's seen Lucas?"

"There's only one way to find out. We must go to Oak Hill immediately."

*****

Jared and Rebecca were coming from the back of the house to the verandah when a carriage pulled to a stop. Ancil jumped down and helped Josephine out.

"Your aunt doesn't look happy," Jared said.

"No. She doesn't. I'd better go see what's wrong." Rebecca rushed over to them. "I'm so glad you came. Charlotte said you'd be out after Mass."

"We didn't go. I had to come see you and Lucas were safe." Josephine paused to take a breath. "I saw Stuart Delaney in town."

"Oh. You did?" Rebecca planted her hands on her

hips.

"Yes. That man is still unpleasant to be around."

Rebecca nodded. "He was supposed to be catching a train."

"He did, or at least Rory was trying to make sure he did," Doctor Gordon offered.

"What happened, Rebecca? Rory said Delaney upset you. Please tell me that man didn't see Lucas," Josephine said.

"Everything is fine. Delaney did upset me, he was still here when Lucas arrived, but he paid little attention to him. The good thing is Delaney's gone now. Hopefully we will not see him again. Come inside. We'll have some sandwiches and lemonade and I will tell you all about it."

Josephine nodded, wiping moisture from her eyes. "A part of me wishes the man knew so we didn't have to keep the secret. I'm tired of secrets."

Rebecca swallowed and wrapped an arm around her shoulders. "Then let this be my secret to bear the burden."

After they ate, Rebecca took Josephine upstairs to see the nursery. Lucas was sitting on a blanket in the middle of the large carpet with Charlotte, playing with his blocks.

"It's a nice room. I know he will be happy here." Josephine went over and picked him up. She kissed him and he squealed in protest. "He's got a temper."

"I think that goes with his hair coloring," Rebecca said. "Don't you agree?"

"Yes." Josephine smiled, putting her grandson back on the floor. "Are you liking your new home, Charlotte?"

The maid looked up. "Yes ma'am. So far it is heavenly here."

"I'm glad." Josephine walked to the doorway and looked back at Lucas. "He'll do just fine here."

Rebecca closed the door and they returned downstairs to the parlor. "I never imagined when we came to Jackson for Elizabeth's wedding that our lives would change."

Her aunt laughed, settling on the settee. "And to think I protested about us making this trip. I shudder now to think how alone I would have spent the rest of my life if we hadn't come."

"Would you like more lemonade?" Rebecca asked. "I'll be happy to get you a glass from the kitchen."

"No, dear. I'm fine. I wonder where Ancil and Jared have gone?" Josephine asked.

"Having cookies in the kitchen," Mary said, coming into the parlor. "Would you like to join them?"

"Thank you, Mary. We'll be right out."

They walked arm in arm out to the kitchen where their men sat at the wooden table eating cookies and drinking coffee.

Josephine took the chair beside Doctor Gordon, but Rebecca went over and sat on Jared's knee. She kissed him on the cheek. "Life couldn't get any sweeter than this."

He wrapped his arms around her and pulled her close. "But we can spend the rest of our life trying."

A word about the author...

Award-winning author Leanne Tyler lives in the South and her writing reflects her heritage. She writes Sweet and somewhat Sensual Southern romances, whether historical or contemporary. Leanne's debut release *Victory's Gate* was the 2007 American Rose winner of the Through the Garden Gate contest and was released electronically by The Wild Rose Press in December 2007. Finally in December 2009 the Through the Garden Gate Anthology became available in print and includes the four winning entries.

Stepping into the Contemporary circle, she debuted with her Class of '85 Reunion story *It's Always Been You* in August 2011. And her first full-length historical novel *Season of Love* (Nov. 2011) is a time-travel set in 1850 Charleston, SC. A recent release from Books to Go Now, *A Country Kitchen Christmas* (Feb. 2012) is a light inspirational romance. In May and August 2012 the first two books of The Good Luck Series were released from Amazon: *The Good Luck Charm* and *The Good Luck Spell*. *Ava*, a short story in the Love Letters Series, was released in November 2012.

Leanne invites readers to step into her world and enjoy the passion.